SALTWATER SORROWS

EDITED BY

RHONDA PARRISH

SALTWATER SORROWS

EDITED BY

RHONDA PARRISH

TYCHE BOOKS LTD.

Published by Tyche Books Ltd.
Calgary, Alberta, Canada
www.TycheBooks.com

Cover Art by Kayla Kowalyk
Cover Design by Indigo Chick Designs
Interior Layout by M.L.D. Curelas

First Tyche Books Ltd Edition 2023
Print ISBN: 978-1-989407-51-6
Ebook ISBN: 978-1-989407-52-3

This book was funded in part by a grant from the Alberta Media Fund.

Alberta
Government

Dedicated to Jo

TABLE OF CONTENTS

INTRODUCTION

RHONDA PARRISH

This is the fourth water-themed anthology I have edited but, as I recently said on Twitter, I could spend the whole rest of my career editing water-themed anthologies and not get tired of it. Water is my favourite element. It always has been, it always will be.

The idea for this particular anthology came to me while I was watching a play. I can't remember the name of the play or even its plot, but it featured the ocean—a significant portion of the stage was dedicated to it. I spent most of the play rolling connections around in my brain, anxiously waiting for a chance to slip into the lobby and email myself some notes. Very early on in the play something was said about a woman who was drawn to the sea, and when I heard those words, I had the same feeling as when you place the final piece in a jigsaw puzzle. Everything fit and a whole picture came together. The funny thing was, though, I hadn't realized there even *was* a jigsaw puzzle until it had all come together.

When that actor spoke about the one woman being drawn to the sea, I started thinking about all the ways women and the sea are connected, are depicted similarly, are associated. I thought about sirens and mermaids and about widow's walks and waiting. I thought about the moon and how it is so strongly associated with cycles—women's, the tide's. I recalled imagery, descriptions, clichés, and poetry about both women and the ocean—deep, unknowable, changeable. So many things. And I thought, "I really want to do an anthology about this. About women and the sea . . ."

In the call for submissions, I asked for:

The tranquility of sunlight dancing upon placid waters and the deep moon energy of rising tides and waves slamming against rocks. I want lonely lighthouses on rocky outcroppings, wind-whipped hair and melancholia, transformation and exaltation. Salt and sorrow.

And that is what I got. All of that.

These stories are everything I'd asked for and I couldn't bring myself to contain them in an anthology with a title as mundane as that which I'd originally pitched: *Women and the Sea*. When I approached the publisher about changing the title, she was open to it but we couldn't quite figure out what to change it to until her daughter suggested *Saltwater Sorrows*. Perfect.

All of these stories are sorrowful in their own way. That is not to say that they don't have happy endings because several of them do, but rarely unambiguously. Their sorrows come from a great many places, from loss, longing, loneliness. Some stories include difficult subjects such as death by suicide and death of loved ones (including young loved ones). If reading about these subjects will be traumatic for you, I suggest reading the content warnings we've included at the end of the book or only proceeding "with your shields up".

I also recommend reading this collection a bit at a time rather than by immersing yourself fully all at once. Much as with the ocean, with sorrowful stories, it can be easy to get in over your head.

If that seems discouraging or weird, I apologise. I truly hope you will enjoy these stories in all their poetic, mournful beauty, as much as I do. I hope you feel them pull at you, like the waves and the tide, wearing away the ground beneath your feet until you are swept away as I was.

Rhonda
Edmonton
2/3/23

A Witch's Christmas

E.E. King

It was a grand old place, all curving mahogany staircases and domed glass ceilings. I'd come at Christmas, come for peace—peace and time to breathe, think, and finish the damn thesis dangling over my head like some literary sword of Damocles.

It was "perfectly normal," they'd said. "Many of our most brilliant students suffer issues of completion." But I could hear the whispers, or rather I could feel them, creeping out of night corners like phantom rats gnawing at my fragile sense of purpose and belief.

My mother had been haunted by similar demons, as had my aunts, grandmother, and her sisters before her. My lineage reached backward into a pedigree of despair. They were all gone now. All dead by their own hand before age thirty, and all around Christmas.

My mother received her medical degree from Harvard. She only practiced for a year, before going to Oxford to study history, where she'd met my father, who was finishing his doctorate in Physics. They had fallen madly in love, married, and had me.

Two years later, on a Christmas trip to the Cornish coast, she had waded into the cold North Sea, never to return.

I thought I'd escaped. I'd been a quiet, calm, studious child, reaching for nothing more emotionally challenging than stones and bones. I had few friends. I was taunted for my thick, black eyebrows and unruly dark hair, though now I realize it was not so much my appearance, but my bookish introspection that made me an outcast.

At nineteen, I entered the Earth Sciences department at Oxford, and a year later, I waded into the pond at Island Wood, my pockets weighed down with fossils purloined from the lab.

3

My father, now a Physics professor at Oxford, was called. Rest and medication were prescribed. And so, I'd been sent to recuperate at Trelawny Manor, the oldest Estate in Cornwall.

I packed a sketch pad, charcoal, and a panoply of medicines. Antidepressants that kept me from feeling joy. Mood stabilizers that fogged my brain, and pain killers to soothe my ankle, which I'd broken in my wade toward eternity. The grey cloud that had enveloped my world had lifted slightly, but only because I was too numb to feel anything as strong as despair.

During the summer, Trelawny Manor was a stop for scholars and tourists. In winter, it was mostly deserted.

I'd taken a train to Cornwall and a cab to the manor. The driver was a red-faced man with inquisitive blue eyes. My small bag, which he tossed in the trunk, was dwarfed by his huge, meaty hands. Would he speed away with my belongings, leaving me alone and without clothes, shoes, or medication?

He slapped me on the shoulder, genially, but with such force as to propel me into the polished leather back seat. He was just being affable, but my spirit shrunk from the contact.

"Welcome to Cornwall." His breath smelled of winter nights by ageing pub fires. "And Merry Christmas. You've come to the best little county in Great Britain, not that I'm prejudice.

"Me name's Charlie. Lived here all me life I have, and I can tell you just about anything you want to know." He started the cab and peered at me, keen eyes curious.

"Well now, I haven't even asked where you're headed? Me missus always said I talk more than I think."

"I'm going to Trelawny Manor," I whispered.

He made no sound. I looked up, fearful that a glance might unleash another torrent of unwanted chatter. All colour had drained from his ruddy cheeks, leaving him pale as a peeled potato.

"Do you know it?" I asked.

"'Course I do," he said. "And a mighty fine place it is . . . in the summer . . . but at Christmas . . ." His voice drifted away like a fading wind.

I thought of asking what was wrong with the Manor at Christmas, but I dreaded conversation more than mystery.

Trelawny's roots reached back to the 1600s. Four stories of stone that coiled above the land like an enormous ammonite. The coast was miles away, but to my left it curved sharply inland and looked to be an easy walk from the Manor.

Charlie pulled up to a grand circular entrance and handed me my bag.

"If you don't like it here, Miss," he said, pressing a card into my hand, "just give a call. There's many another place that'd be happy for lodgers."

I twisted my mouth into what I hoped was a smile; my face felt stiff, the muscles unused from staring into the void.

The large wooden doors opened surprisingly easily considering their mass. Behind a walnut desk sat a tight-lipped, doughy woman with an unruly halo of blueish-grey curls. It was the only free, even slightly wild, aspect of her person.

The corners of the woman's mouth turned upward as she handed me a key, but the smile didn't reach her cold blue eyes.

"I'm Mrs. Molchany," she said. "You're the only one here, and I'll be the one seeing to your needs.

"I serve breakfast at eight, elevenses at 11:30, luncheon at one, tea at four, and dinner at six, but I never stay overnight.

"There are many paths through the moorland, but don't use the track on the left. It leads most direct to the sea, but it's dangerous. Many a sheep and more than one child has been lost there. Once the black mud gets a hold of you, you'll never escape." She said this with an odd satisfaction.

"You'll be wanting to look at this," she said, pushing a faded, red-leather book toward me. "It's been our guest book, since 1602, signed by each and every one of our guests." She said this smugly, as if she had personally supervised the inking of each and every signature. "And which part of our rich history will you be investigating while you're with us?"

"Ancient," I said. "Precambrian Serpentine."

She didn't reply, just stared at me out of those probing cool eyes, as if I were a not very interesting relic, which she needed to keep safe even if she doubted its value. Or perhaps it was me, floundering in a sea of suspicion, and finding it, even where there was none. I took the key and turned away.

My room had a large bay window that looked out over Cornwall's shaggy moorland and cold, raging sea. It smelled faintly, not unpleasantly, of lavender and slightly fermented kelp.

Despite my fatigue, I couldn't sleep. I took the one sleeping pill I was allowed and waited. Perhaps a tiny exploration would exhaust me?

The hall was like the inside of a giant, chambered nautilus, a creature whose relatives date back to the Early Pleistocene. Swirling mahogany balusters hung with Yuletide holly swept upward to a stained-glass crystal cupola. Beneath the dome stood a huge Christmas tree, hung with tinsel. What day was it? Boxing Day? Christmas Eve?

I smelled the library before I saw it. A fragrance of vanilla and almonds. Father said that the smell was caused by the breakdown of chemicals in the paper. Odd that decay should smell so sweet. Perhaps there is a heaven for books that people never dream of, where ideas live on.

The thought made me uncomfortable. I liked facts, fossils, the hard clarity of science. Not these fanciful notions drifting through my mind obscuring the hard, unwavering light of reality. If I cut down on the mood stabilizers, would I be clearer?

A powdering of stars twinkled through the bay windows. Bookshelves lined the walls, but they were disappointingly bare. I turned to leave, finally wearied, when a slim leather volume caught my eye. It had no legible title, only the indentations of worn script and a flash of gold embedded in the vanished text.

Tragedy at Trelawny was inscribed in curling letters on the frontispiece. I took the book to bed, where I fell into a dark dream.

Something wakened me.

Moonlight poured through my window. Every blade of grass seemed etched into the land. For the first time in months, my mind was equally clear.

To the left, where the coast bent closest toward Trelawny, I could make out dark huddled figures around a small fire. Odd that anyone should venture there, where Mrs. Molchany had said the cliffs were the weakest, but perhaps my bearings were confused by the wandering clouds and flat light. Perhaps it was some local Christmas custom?

One of the figures straightened up and began walking toward my window. It was a woman, as small as I, but so slender and well-formed, she gave the impression of great height. There was something ominous about the intensity of her focus. She seemed so fixated on me, or at least on my lighted window, as to be ignoring her surroundings, though she walked along the very edge of the roaring waves.

⟋⟍

I woke late, not leaving my room till 6:00 pm. Mrs. Molchany awaited me in a preposterously large dining room with overcooked greens, a desiccated turkey, Yorkshire pudding, and a small mince pie. Was I feasting on the remains of some other, more festive Christmas?

"You must have needed your sleep?" She smiled, but there was a sharpness in those cold blue eyes.

"I-I've been ill," I stammered.

"So I've heard."

The blood rushed to my face. I tried not to think about what she'd heard.

"*Depression was nothing to be ashamed of,*" they'd said.

"And—and the moon was so bright," I added.

"Moon?" she said. "You must'a been dreaming. T'was a new moon, black as a Newgate knocker."

⟋⟍

I spent my days, resting by the window, studying *Tragedy at Trelawny* and the venerated guest book. Both books were extraordinary. One for what it said, the other for what it implied.

Tragedy at Trelawny was an account of the trial of Truth Device, the first guest of the manor. Accused of witchcraft by her ten-year-old daughter Grace, Truth had been burned at the cliff's edge, on Christmas 1659. It was a list of dates, prosecution, and death, brutal and horrible.

The guest book was different. Its swirls of signature were open to interpretation. I liked tracing my fingers over the slightly indented curves, the pages filled before typewriters had destroyed the art of calligraphy. There was personality evident in each, essence in ink, a mirror of the soul.

I had never much been interested in souls, or philosophy either. Those things less real than science and mathematics. If you learned a formula or the properties of a stone, you had data that would never change. A plant that was edible was always edible, but a theory about the soul, or God was as malleable as wet tissue. And history looked very different depending upon which version you read. Now though, sitting on the window seat, looking over the moors and the frothing sea below, I ran my finger over the old signatures, imagining the people who had written them. It may have been a lonely way to spend Christmas, but it was what my soul craved, as well as what the doctor ordered.

☙

True to her word, Mrs. Molchany had a huge, largely indigestible breakfast on the sideboard at eight, which gave way to stale granola bars at 11:30, followed by tea, and dinner. Tea was the only meal I enjoyed, not the dry, hard scones, but the rich, slightly grainy, clotted cream with strawberry jam that filled all the corners in my hungry heart.

I began to cut the dose of the antidepressants and mood stabilizers, trying to find the perfect balance. The painkillers didn't dull my perceptions but made them sharper, like bottled clarity.

I awoke early, avoiding the shale and serpentine cliffs that held both the fossil past and my own unfinished thesis. Instead, I tramped the narrow paths of mud and moss till I was tired, then returned to my window seat, running my hand over the rough penmanship of Truth Device. I couldn't say why her signature had such power over me, just that it drew me to wonder about its origin as before I had only wondered about fossils and bones.

Then the sky opened and poured for two days. I should have worked on my paper. I could have written letters detailing my progress and health, instead I sat in my window, inhaling the fragrance of vanilla and almonds that drifted up from the guest book, until a signature caught my eye. Nicole Turner, December, 1998. It was my mother's; made the same year she had marched into the sea never to return.

I closed my eyes, seeing in that inner darkness her leaving me, without a backward glance. What had driven her into the cold, unfeeling waters? What had driven me? Nothing solid, nothing specific, just an unbearable sadness, a dark, suffocating curtain I could not see beyond. It was written into my genes, engraved by maternal hands so deeply, there was no escape.

I began to leaf back through the pages. Each name a dark house, concealing lives behind ink walls. And there—fifteen years before my mother's visit, I found another familiar name: Alice Turner, my grandmother, which was as far back as I could trace. With a family like mine, you don't look for ancestors. You're afraid of what you might find.

The next day gave way to a sudden, unexpected burst of sun. The moors glittered. Steam rose from the grassland like departing spirits. There was something almost transcendent in their vast loneliness.

I packed a small bag with water, a few purloined granola bars, my sketch pad, my painkillers, a small spade and set out toward the cliff, where I had seen night fires burning.

I dared not take the most direct route. It looked an easy walk, but I remembered Mrs. Molchany's warning. Without trees as signposts, land and sea flattened into an endless perspectiveless swath of green and grey. It took me more than an hour, mud sucking at my shoes as if to pull me down beneath the emerald carpet. At the bluff's edge, the ground gave way.

The sun was bright, but winter brisk. I shivered. Still, having come this far and found this . . . whatever it was . . . I pulled out spade and began to dig. Beneath the grass was a hole, almost a metre deep and about half again as wide.

The bottom of the hole was covered in black clay and lined with white feathers. It might have been a bird-plucking hollow, such pits were common at the turn of the nineteenth century. But no—what I had thought was dark clay was really a charred body. As my eyes grew accustomed to the dimness, I could just make out small, outstretched limbs, a long sinuous neck and a tiny, delicate head that was mostly orbital lobes. It was a carbonized swan, lacking only its beak.

There is a legend that swans were introduced to Britain in the twelfth century by Richard I, but the bird is native. Ownership was recorded by marks nicked into the beak. Any swan that didn't bear one was the property of the crown. The penalty for ignoring swan marks, or for killing birds, was a year's imprisonment.

On top of the swan nestled fifty-five eggs, seven of which contained chicks close to hatching. The shells of the eggs had mostly dissolved, but moisture had preserved the membranes. There was something unutterably sad about the dried, yellow embryos, curled in on themselves like pictures of despair. As little as I liked to admit it, this seemed like a witch pit.

Uncover a nest or discover a den, and there will be a reason for everything, every twig or dropping or bone. But witch pits were the product of delusion, the human drama I'd been trying to avoid my whole life.

The killing of swans has been illegal since the eleventh century, and the witchcraft laws were only scrapped in 1951. A shiver snaked up my spine as I imagined someone digging a hole and carefully laying in these offerings. What had made them desperate enough to risk death if caught?

As I turned the bones over in my hands, I realized they were bound together with faded orange cord—a synthetic twine not manufactured till the 1960s. Stuck to the twine was a scrap of newsprint. I could just make out a faint headline. "Dr. Nicole Stevens, to join History department at Oxford."

I imagined generations of women coming here to ask favours of their gods, devotees reaching back into the 1600s in an unbroken chain, but surely my doctor mother had not been among them? I leaned back, hoping for support, but as sweater touched the wet mud the anguish of the body superseded the torments of the heart.

I snipped the string on either side of the paper, not an approved collection practice, but I needed to get back, and I wanted—no needed—this paper. It was proof that I was not mad.

The sun had begun to sink into the waves. Gray clouds blew in like an advancing army, blotting out sea and shore, encasing me in pervasive twilight. My pocket flashlight was dead.

An ice-cold raindrop slapped my face. I didn't know how far I had gone, or even if I was headed in the right direction. I might be walking straight toward the cliff and the sea below. For the first time in forever I didn't want that. No, I wanted to live, at least long enough to discover why my mother's name had been buried in a witch pit on the Cornish coast, and why my mother and grandmother had visited Trelawny Manor. But neither the yearning to live, nor the desire to die are enough to make it happen. I stumbled and lay on the wet grass. The rain driving me into the earth. I imagined my body dissolving in the bog, my bones turning to fossils for some later archaeologist to discover.

When I awakened, Father was sitting by my bed. His pale grey eyes peered at me over wire reading glasses.

"You were found on the moors." His voice was as detached as

if he were explaining a simple equation to a slow undergraduate.

I looked down at my hands. They were empty.

"Did you see the paper?"

He shook his head, "All they found on you was your pack, a dead flashlight, and an empty bottle of pain pills. Your fist was closed, but nothing was in your hand."

My evidence, dissolved in the rain.

"Did you know Mother was here?" I asked. "I found her signature in the guest book."

He shook his head. "I didn't, but she was studying the history of Cornwall. It's logical she might have visited."

His face was proof against necromancy. I would not tell him that my grandmother had also been here. I would not tell him of the witch pit with my mother's name bound up in twine. He would have an explanation. As for the newspaper, he might believe it to be a delusion of my fevered mind. It sounded more reasonable than anything I could conjure.

Father had brought me a few sad Christmas presents; a tin of biscuits and a book on Crowell's fossils. It was worse than being forgotten.

When I was well, or at least well enough to lie in bed and read, he left. He had classes to teach, and papers to write, a life outside of Trelawny and his crazy daughter.

"Be healthy," his slightly chapped lips brushing against my cheek. "Finish your paper, but don't pressure yourself."

My father had made certain I followed the doctor's dosage. It made me foggy. I needed to think. I needed to work. I halved my dose of anti-depressants and quit the mood stabilizers altogether. But instead of studying the Precambrian shale, I delved into the witches of Cornwall.

The witch trials of Western Europe lasted three hundred years and killed more than eighty thousand witches. Orthodox wisdom attributed the hysteria to a slate of almost supernaturally bad weather, freak frosts, plagues of mice, even a couple of rains of frogs. But it wasn't just the ice age that caused the witch hunt. Protestantism had recently emerged. And what better way to make coverts than to combat satanism? The hysteria began in Germany, with "The Hammer of Witches," a guide on how to identify and interrogate necromancers. It was ugly stuff. The reason I'd studied rocks and stones was to avoid these dramas. I had enough trouble with the demons in my DNA.

⌒⌒

A man bends over me, head shrouded by a black hood. Piercing blue eyes stare out of the darkness.

"Is it not true, Grace Device, that your mother, Truth, is a witch? Is it not true that her spirit can enter the likeness of a brown dog?"

He bends my small, pliable fingers backward.

⌒⌒

"Wake up, Miss, wake up."

Someone was shaking me. Mrs. Molchany's chill blue eyes examined me.

"You were having a nightmare, Miss."

I wanted to ask Mrs. Molchany if she'd seen *Tragedy at Trelawny,* but the words stuck in my throat.

"A history of Trelawney? I'm sure I don't know what you are referring to."

Had I spoken aloud?

"I don't know of any such history, Miss."

Why was she lying?

⌒⌒

It was almost two weeks before I felt well enough to leave Trelawny. Then, almost against my volition, I found myself wandering toward town and The Boswell Museum of Witchcraft.

As I reached up, the door opened. An old woman stood inside.

"I'm Mrs. Gypsy Evansleaver." She smiled, her skin crackling into a million welcoming folds.

"Welcome to The Museum. Centuries have passed, yet in this wee, quiet corner of England, we are unchanged, perched right on the edge of the beyond."

She took my hand. A pulse of electricity raced up my arm.

"My mother was here once." It felt like a confession. "Not here-here, I mean," I stammered. "But in Cornwall."

"What was her name, dear?" She leafed backward through a guest book.

Nicole Turner, December, 1998

"Did-did you know her?" I whispered.

She shook her head. "I fear there's things ye need ken to that only the dead may tell. Come to my house this Wednesnight. We will ask the coven. Mayhap it will put your soul at peace."

I shook my head, but even as I did, I knew I would go. I had never been to a séance. While my school mates clustered together in darkened rooms over Ouija boards, I read about rock substrates. My dead were already too close, woven into my genes like a warning.

⸺

I called Charlie to take me. He arrived in his old black cab, shiny as a hearse.

"How good it is to see ya, Miss." His round, red face broke into a smile. "Where are you going?"

"To Mrs. Evansleaver's."

His lips tightened. He said not a word but sped through the night, stopping so suddenly I slammed into the rear of his seat. My door opened into darkness.

"It's thata way. Just follow your nose. When you see a slate path, take it."

He disappeared before I could ask how to reach him.

I stepped down, twisting my weak left ankle, and washed down a pain pill with a swig of the whiskey I'd begun carrying with me since the witch pit fiasco.

I found the turnoff, not by sight, but by the scent of moist earth and some odd sense of having turned this way before. It wasn't until I got close that I could see the house, a slender stream of smoke rising from the thatch like departing spirits.

The door opened before I could knock. Gypsy Evansleaver was bordered on each side by two old women, three plump, one thin, and all sharp eyed. Wrinkled by years, yet somehow unfettered to time. Behind them, six wooden chairs formed a half circle. The fire in the large brick hearth cast their faces in an orange glow.

"Come in, me dear, come in," said Gypsy. She took me by the elbow. Again, I felt that strange flow of current.

The crones bent around me like an undiscovered country. They were made timeless by their obvious belonging. I coveted that sense of rightness. I was a stranger, born out of season, haunted by an idea called home.

Gypsy propelled me toward a chair. I wondered at the

fortitude of such women who denied even the comfort of cushions to their old bones

"Take a sip of this, dear." She poured me a shot of some golden liquid. It softened the edges yet made the room somehow clearer.

⟳

Only the glinting of eyes beneath his hood shows me that this is a man and not death himself.

"Confess," he says. "Confess and be saved."

A crowd surrounds me. Them I have known since I was but a wee tacker. Yet they gaze on me as if I am a stranger.

In the centre my mother is chained to a pole, clothes torn, breasts bare for all to see. I point a small trembling white finger toward my mother. "I have heard her talking to a brown dog," I whisper.

"Louder," cries the man.

"She smears the fat of murdered babes on her broom-end!" I scream.

"Witch," says the man.

"Witch," echoes the crowd.

I hear her voice. The same that used to sing me lullabies, but it is harsh and raw.

"If my flesh and bone accuse me, so it be. And this same curse now be in the blood through the generations. Not one woman of my flesh shall live past my years of twenty-nine Christmas tides. As you have cursed me, I curse you."

⟳

"Are you all right, me dear?" Old faces bent over me. The same faces as were in the crowd.

"I must go!" Hands grabbed at me. I staggered into night. In the road Charlie's cab was waiting. I was saved! I dove into the back seat.

In the mirror his eyes met mine. They were the cool blue of my inquisitor.

I rolled out into the damp grass. He would not trap me again. I had been given another chance. This time I would not betray my mother. I could save her. I will save her. I head left, taking the shortest path toward the coast.

⟳

"Interesting reading material," my father nodded toward a pile on the bed. He leafed through *The Cornwall Witches*.

"The main witness against Truth Device was her daughter, Grace, who was but nine years old," he read, then picked up a newspaper.

"And the tale continues."

Witches of Cornwall, 2010

"An Archaeologist has unearthed three witch pits in Cornwall. One contained twenty-two eggs, all with chicks close to hatching. Another held a burned swan. The egg pit dated to the eighteenth century, the swan pit to the 1980s.

"And it seems you haven't been taking your meds," my father's voice was as dry as Mrs. Molchany's scones.

"We pulled you out of the bog on the edge of the cliff. It's a wonder you aren't dead. You will stay here for a while, where you can be . . . monitored. And no more reading about witchcraft. I know it's a sad place to spend Christmas, but next year will be better." He scooped up the books, kissed me on the forehead, and left.

Christmas? It was not yet Christmas?

The door opened and a tight-lipped, doughy woman, face framed by an almost unruly halo of blueish-grey curls entered.

"I'm Nurse Molchany," she said. "I'll be the one seeing to your needs."

Portrait of a Mermaid as a Young Woman

NATALIE CANNON

The day my father's heart stops beating, Mami kicks us kids out of his hospital room. "You must remember him better than this," Mami says, as she pulls the forget-me-not blue ICU curtain closed. My teeth weld together. She is the wife and she is strong enough for the final second; we are the children and barely strong enough for the final half hour.

My jaw aches so much I can't ground out any protest. I grip my sisters' hands tighter. "But where's Daddy going?" Alma asks.

"He's not coming back," I say. That's the important part.

"But where's he going?" Dee repeats.

"Let's go to the beach," I say. My learner's permit is in my wallet. I can't drive without an adult in the car yet, but the sun is setting. The cops won't see my face.

"Is Daddy at the beach?"

"No, not yet." The ashes won't be strewn for . . . days? Weeks?

"When will he be there?"

"Not today."

I walk my sisters out of the chilled hospital hallways on the unbearably white tiles. My hands obey me perfectly. My nail polish doesn't even chip on the plastic buckles of the twins' car seats. I place the keys in the ignition and find the deserted end of the Pacific Coast Highway.

I'm okay.

I'm in control.

It's after seven o'clock, no Park Service is around. I drive past the wooden kiosk and park in the fading spaces. There are no tears coming out of my eyes. That would mess up my makeup, and strong women, women who want to be taken seriously, women who want to be listened to, have perfect makeup.

Daddy was a surfer, and a sailor, once. I am a reader.

My sisters are wavering. Restless. They climb out of their car seats like I'm the moon and they're a trickling tide. That is, reluctant.

On nights when I couldn't stop tossing and turning, Daddy read the *Island of the Blue Dolphins* in his deep voice, the one that turned hoarse and tearful when the dog died, because he had held his dog like that too. He read that book to me cover to cover—Newbury Medal sticky and warped, the main girl, Karana, staring out at me across the sea. There was always an ocean between her and me.

From the parking lot, I tell the ocean its own sophomore-level, Google-it mathematics: that foam forms fractals; that the cresting wave's ideal angle breaks rarely; that 3D models of Greek letters and tiny numbers flow in its wake. "What are all these numbers for?" Alma asks.

I recite Longfellow's "Wreck of the Hesperus" to the sand-dusted concrete steps down: "The breakers were right beneath her bows,/She drifted a dreary wreck,/And a whooping billow swept the crew/Like icicles from her deck."

The ocean's still restless. Dee says, "I don't want to go on that boat."

I remember how Mami bundled us up, layer after layer of warmth against skin, thermal shirt under sweater under windbreaker under mittens before we trundled onto Daddy's sailboat. How I gave up on my hair making any sort of sense and being grateful no one hot lived on Santa Cruz Island.

I sing the Anglo-Saxon poem "The Seafarer" to the driftwood—"but the roaring sea,/the ice cold wave." I remember collecting the new millennium quarters, the freezing minted iron in Daddy's criss-crossed palm. Who knew his lifeline was this short?

Alma whispers, "Why are you singing such sad things?"

Slime and seaweed churn at my ankles; sand crabs slip under my toes while I parse my thoughts on *The Interesting Narrative of the Life of Olaudah Equiano.* Oxygenated ice water froths, and I grow goose bumps up my arms as I unfold the horrors of the Middle Passage. Lights on the horizon watch, shrouded in fog, unblinking, like teeth with eyes bored into them.

"It's too cold to swim!" my sisters scream when I hand them the car keys and my phone.

Kyoshi Takahama's "The water is deep/In the ocean;/Drought in the land" walks me past the shallows. I remember the hot, homey meat of tamales in December, how we all huddled in the dark sand and watched the grey water chop while cliff shrubs dug their roots yet deeper.

"I don't think Mami would like this."

I whisper Byron's "Apostrophe to the Ocean" to the breakers. I hated that I had to pretend to hate the sand, the water, the kelp, and the washed-up dead. A strong woman could encompass that too.

"Where are you going?"

I duck and weave through the vengeance of Jeanne de Clisson, the riches of Grace O'Malley, the armies of Ching Shih, pirates all. I kick out my legs, push my hands against the tide, and think about the fish I saw during my kindergarten trip to the aquarium. Their languid, black tails and sedate eyes—how feeding time would come, and with sudden violence, they'd smash the glassy water ceiling and risk saving themselves from drowning to bite the biggest flakes.

"We're going to stay here!" my sisters assure me from the shore.

I tell the ocean the story of Karana and her island of blue dolphins, and let the human go. I let the green water slide syndactyly through my fingers, let the stark, underwater darkness of my feet converge, let gills and films sprout like they were always there. I dive under to have rivulets and bubbles adorn my hair, have it curl wild in the surf. I want to see Daddy again and there's no other place his soul would go.

I look up.

The ocean is calm. Calm in sunset, calm like lavender glass pressed against the top. Perfect makeup. I flip my fins and shatter the waves.

The ocean's meant to be restless.

Skelf

MORGAN MELHUISH

There is perhaps nothing more cruel than standing at the edge of the sea, drowning my sorrows in the sight of all that water, longing to be swept away.

Yet here I remain, cold grey brine seeping through my sand spattered brogues, drizzling rain forming jewels in my hair, tears on wet cheeks.

The house is my prison. They've conspired to snare me in a well-oiled contraption of routine: woken at half seven by Ellen, my lady's maid, with breakfast on a tray, luncheon at one, tea at five, dinner at eight . . . Although I am mistress of the house, it matters very little to them whether I'm here at all. The silver would still be polished, the gas lamps lit, vegetables grown for the table. I'm simply a figurehead of authority, wooden and lumpen from all these meals.

The staff watch my every move.

It is the imposing Mrs. Keats who really rules the roost, the housekeeper with her keys and lists.

"You know best," are the words she loves to hear from my lips.

I am convinced she writes to father, reports on my confinement, whether I have finally become compliant and biddable.

I like to think I have chosen to acquiesce, but really there is no alternative. My resistance is formality.

They will not give me a horse for fear I might flee the county, but in my own two legs there can be no objection. The grounds of the house are large and should I not appear at mealtimes a search mounted, I'm sure!

So, I find solace in walking. Pacing, like some creature at Regent's Park zoological gardens, I feel the bounds of my cage. Fences and fields on three sides, a copse, and then at the end of a sloping lawn, my own private cove.

"That's right, Miss," Mrs. Keats encourages, "put some colour in your cheeks."

They don't understand it is not sickliness or unnatural predilections which have produced this grim pallor—it is grief.

Not your death, but the circumstances which mean I shall very likely never see you again, whisked off to a new life in which I will not feature.

There seems little point in writing letters that I know will never reach you. I suspect Mrs. Keats would fling my lines into the kitchen's fire should I attempt it, all the while smiling and saying they're with the post boy.

Instead, like some cheap clairvoyance act, I talk to you in my head. I yearn and long and hope you might receive my inept telepathy, messages from the love you left behind.

Today the storm has passed, leaving in its wake a bright mackerel sky, white cloud shredded against the blue. The air is warm and I breathe it in deeply, filling my lungs with salt and freshly mown grass.

A sense of possibility and hope lingers despite my gilded enclosure.

Have I become inured to captivity? Have I forgotten you? Never.

Yet, I am not blind to the simple pleasures in my exile. The freedom of leisure, sunlight, striding down to the coast, the crescent of beach exposed by the low tide.

Here I'm unseen. I hesitate for the tiniest moment before slipping off shoes, removing stockings, feeling those tiny grains seek the cracks between toes, the crevices of my feet. My behaviour hardly befits a lady of my status, but blast it!

I walk to where the water rolls in, the tug of wet sand sucks gently at my feet, the rush of water over toes. I cry out, partially in delight, somewhat shocked by the cool sensation. Then I laugh at my silliness, paddling in the breaking surf.

No higher than the ankles, I tell myself, but a wave shatters my promise, a dark wet breakwater appearing on the frill of petticoats gathered just above my calves.

As children we always ran down to the cove after a storm to see what had been washed up. We hoped for pirate gold or a message in a bottle, but the most exciting was a torn lobster pot and on another occasion some potatoes—we'd no idea how they'd arrived, nestled on the sand like ostrich eggs!

More thrilling were the gifts the sea gave up: rock pools of hermit crabs, the scarlet and pink explosions of sea anemones, burst black mermaid's purses.

I search the shoreline, picking over shells and bladderwrack as a sanderling might do.

And that's when I find her . . .

The fragment of a face, gazing up at me with unseeing eyes. She lies in a pool formed in a scar of dark rock. The water's so still it's a mirror, me looking at her, looking at me, looking at her. Our faces almost merge.

She isn't painted and her carved and varnished beauty is a little weather worn. Natural. Who knows how long this piece of figurehead has been adrift, to come away from her prow, to lose herself, the rest of her form. To wind up here like a siren on a rock waiting for me.

Did her vessel fall foul of a tempest? An attack?

I struggle to think of reports in the papers, battles or piracy that might have been given column inches. Are Prussia and Denmark still at it?

She could be Nordic, I suppose, her hair swept away from her face, full lips, a slight nose as if someone's hand slipped with the chisel. Unseeing eyes. Perhaps they should have been painted on.

The effect makes this figurehead look both comely and demur. I wonder whose sister, whose young wife or daughter this was, to have the honour of travelling the seas, face first in the wind and buffeted by spray—the freedom of movement her living doppelgänger would never have. There's a spiteful irony that isn't lost on me as I stoop to scoop her from the water.

I can't help but think of cradling china dolls I was given as a child. They were always too perfect, not to be played with, only admired. I felt sorry for them, sat on shelves. It reminds me of the women waiting to be asked to dance, debutants sat contritely in a row, eyelashes fluttering, and made up when a man deigned to offer his arm. I never wanted to be like them.

"Now look at me, eh?" My voice is hoarse and wistful. It's been so long since I've shared secrets with a doll, and she is not that, this fragment of face.

"Miss Arabella!" Ellen calls from the lawn.

They're after me.

"Damn," I whisper. "I'm tied to tea times as you're at the whim of the tides. But at least I can rescue you."

The call comes, louder this time, closer.

"Just coming!" I manage to put the brightness of the day into my voice, grit reserved for sandy feet.

"Come," I stride up the beach, talking to the ravaged figurehead. I scan the shoreline for somewhere appropriate. "Let's get you hidden, let's get you safe."

In the British Museum there are galleries of curiosities, little carved figurines from all over the colonies. Do you remember? Easter Island heads and statuettes made by the Rapanui. Canoes from New Zealand complete with decorative clay deities, figureheads from various nations in the South Pacific.

I recall how we walked the rooms, arm in arm, dreaming of places where life is different, rules and expectations topsy-turvy, where we might belong. Do you ever think back to the fertility totems with their engorged and enlarged members that made us giggle? The disapproving looks and sharp glances sent our way only tickled us more. We were a pair of naughty school girls and had to run from the room.

I dream of all those idols bobbing like corks on a tempestuous Regent's Park lake. Our boat had capsized and we desperately clung to busts and effigies like buoys, desperate to weather the squall. Like ships in the night, I lost sight of you, disappearing under rolling waves . . .

Which is when I wake to Ellen drawing the curtains, a flood of brilliant morning light coursing into the room.

I wonder, did you experience the same dream? Is that all we share now? Memories and night tremors.

"It's a beautiful morning, Miss," Ellen says.

"It looks it." I sit up, stare blearily at the sun's glare. As dreams dissipate my first thought is to return to the beach and my buried treasure.

Ellen plumps pillows to support my back and passes me the breakfast tray.

Our fingers brush and she flinches. So much so the tea cup rattles in its bone china saucer, the ornamental jug does a pirouette.

What sort of a monster does she imagine me? I knew they would all know. Confidences are held like water cupped in a palm here. Does she dread waking me? Does she imagine it catching?

"S-s-sorry, Miss."

"Don't worry," I try to be kind, a rattle in my own voice. "No use crying over spilt milk."

She nods gratefully, half curtseys, and backs away.

I sigh. My appetite has deserted me entirely.

Which is when I notice the letter stood in the toast rack. My pulse races until I see the familiar copperplate of my father. In London, letters meant news from friends, invitations to dinner and gay little parties, coded billet-doux from you.

I take a butter knife to the envelope and devour its contents.

I am sick. I am empty.

I slam doors, ball fists, gnash teeth, and cry out. I stomp down to the shore, trying to trample and shut out his words. They mean to tame me as your family did you.

A husband!

I am no pet in need of a Master!

It is the sea which calms me, looking out on the roiling slate, a vastness in which my turmoil is only a drop. I want the escape of waves, wide horizons, and inky depths.

I slump, crestfallen. I already knew I was at Father's mercy, but to have it tested so . . . to disobey would be heresy, and yet . . . I wish . . .

As a child I'd sit here, weaving pink coronets of thrift, staring out to the middle distance and hoping for a glimpse of mermaids.

The only tails I saw were pods of dolphins but they still delighted me.

I was a queer fish even then.

I sigh—the tang of salt brings thoughts of you.

Syrupy plunder.

Lost love.

I remember the figurehead, cross the sands to pull it from a crevice formed by two rocks. I gaze upon its face, hold her as Hamlet grasped Yorick's skull.

"Alas, poor lady, that I knew you not." I smile at her, the roughness of the bashed in back of her head all sharp slivers. "We could have run away together!"

I am foolish and frivolous. It must be the susurrations of the waves on the shore, but it almost feels as if she is whispering back. Sweet nothings. Reassurances.

I plant a kiss on her forehead. Stroke her cheek, gasp in pain! I flinch like Ellen, whipping her hand from mine.

The head tumbles to the ground and I look at the splinter in the middle of my palm. At once I have my lips to it, sucking at the hurt, trying to remove the vicious barb embedded in my softness.

The figurehead's blind eyes are turned from me, snubbed.

The moon makes a pathway of light across the surface of the sea. From my bedroom window it looks as though I might walk upon the water and into the heavens. The thought is tempting but we both know my soul would not ascend, I am anchored to the depths.

Arabella!

I look sharply for the source of the words, but I am alone. They seem to come from within.

Here.

I look down to my palm and the irritation I've worried at all day.

I am part of you.

Here.

The near fullness of the moon illuminates the dewy lawn and on it stands a figure. The bedraggled woman wears a soaking shift. Her eyes are closed but her head is tilted right up at me, as if she knows exactly where I am. There is defiance in her chin.

Her arms rest at her side. Stock still. She is a silver and silent spectre.

You hold me.

Let me help you?

I draw my hand away from my mouth, where it has been in astonishment, gather up my night dress, and slip from my bedroom. I race downstairs, padding on the polished wood, out the French windows of the sitting room, past the ornamental fountain, hopping from flagstone to flagstone.

When I reach the lawn there is no one there. I pant white clouds in the stillness of the night, the chorus of the waves below. Though it felt like a bargain had been made, they are empty promises I clutch at.

℃◡◌

I might have thought it a dream, were it not for the footprints. On the stairs and the landing, they had vanished by the time I rose, scrubbed from sight, but from the threshold to the bed are eight dirty prints, dried dew, laced with earth, a smudge on clean sheets.

℃◡◌

The wound grows in my palm like *Treasure Island*'s fatal black spot.

My father's letters are a sort of death warrant too; they remind me of the charred slip of parchment Billy Bones unfolds.

I dread reading his missives, those terse instructions. His cruelty phrased as kindness.

I used to thrill with the idea of running away to sea, stowing away in a barrel of apples.

I still do.

Father writes he will be here with my intended within the fortnight. He exhorts me to go to church and confess. To open my heart to a happy future. To put you behind me.

Between the lines are unwritten warnings. Chilling blank spaces.

I wonder which of us is more afraid of what might happen, if we ignore the other.

℃◡◌

On the beach my washed-up friend fares better. I visit her and while neither of us speak, there is an understanding in her blind eyes.

Like sodden driftwood she seems to swell. No longer can I hide her in the crevice in the rocks.

I swear her hair is growing longer, the beginnings of a neck appearing. One cheek looks almost rosy.

We both know the transformation of a kiss.

꿈

On Sunday there is church.

The chapel stands on a rocky outcrop, a lighthouse of faith. Inside, it is whitewashed and cool, flecks of coloured light from stained glass stipple the walls.

I sit at a darkly varnished pew, trying to pray. All I can think of is the wedding that will take place here, the vows you have taken, the waves dashing themselves on the rocks below.

Our Lord hangs, a crown of thorns, waiting for his liberation. I feel for him.

In my palm a stigmata festers, weeps tears of clear pus when I squeeze at it. The sensation in my skin deadened to pain, the joints in my fingers tightening. As I fail to pray, my knees creak like a vessel flexing.

꿈

I take to wearing gloves. Even to bed. Long black lace affairs for mourning. There are a few raised eyebrows amongst the staff, but nothing is said in my hearing.

Every day I go to bathe my hand in the salt water, each day I visit her.

Impossibly, she grows.

Her rough body with its now rounded shoulders reminds me of the peg dolls of the county fair, simple creatures roughly hewn and brought to life by pencilled eyes and scraps of fabric. I was never allowed them, when peddlers tried their luck to entice with bright ribbons, corn dollies, or lucky heather.

"We don't want those in the house!" Mother would hiss. "Filth and superstition."

It didn't stop my longing.

When I hold this broken girl, this slip of a wooden lass, those elicit feelings rush back up, surging like the waves on the beach.

Her bashed in skull feels fuller while mine spins with dizziness. My glands are stiff with stress and anxiety as the days pass.

I cling to the facsimile like a spar.

❧

"You've a fever, you're staying put." Mrs. Keats is sharp, her hand cool against my forehead. "No wonder, traipsing about the grounds at all times."

Her words make me wince. Behind the housekeeper, Ellen looks concerned.

I start to object but I am mute, my tongue thick in my mouth. Every limb aches, my body a leaden weight.

I take root in bed. I feel like one of those weather-beaten trees, bent into shape by the elements and held there even when the storm has died down.

They are making me like you, no matter how I resist.

My dreams are of weathered ships withstanding storms, my figurehead making shore, dragging herself from the sand, finding land legs, stumbling, crawling, clawing her way to me.

The switch cannot be stopped now.

❧

"But Miss, you're not well, you can't . . ." Ellen implores me.

I've managed to lumber down the stairs, rocking from side to side.

"Don't tell me what I can or cannot do," I bark at her, the words, like everything else, take effort, driven by emotion.

"The master will be here in the morning, why don't you wait?"

This is exactly why I must go now. Father will arrive, ready to give me away, to seal my fate.

I feel the heavy ache in my limbs, the stiff hurt in my palm. My forehead prickles with sweat and fever.

And yet the coast beckons—I know I must see her.

❧

She stands on the beach, fully formed, the grain of wood only just visible in the contours of her pale skin. She is a blind ghoul made flesh and blood while I am naught but bark and splinter.

"What have you done?" I want to scream but no words emerge. Somehow, she hears.

"Helped," her lips part with the snap of dry twigs, her voice brittle.

Then I realise, just like you she will make a blushing bride. She will stand, woodenly, say "I do." Her sea faring days are over, she longs the security of place, the mundane.

I can't be like either of you.

I belong to the sea, to brine.

I try to kiss her but my lips will move no more. Salt water trickles down my cheek.

This curse, this gift, the figurehead has given me. It terrifies me.

We are two totems on the shore.

Then her lids lift, two piercing human eyes stare from her sculpted face. She blinks. Released from the grain she exhales, takes a tentative step towards the house. The figurehead turns, her chiselled smile both triumphant and pitying.

I feel her warm hand on my sharp shoulder. Then she shoves my hardened frame, and I topple, face first, full of sand and wet, sea and sky, over and over. A blur of nausea.

It ends as the surf embraces me, the turning tide won't fail, won't leave me high and dry.

I bob, the initial panic replaced by serenity, as I get used to floating, not drowning.

In the dying embers of the day, I catch one more glimpse of the fleshy figurehead, slender legs striding purposefully up the lawn, shift billowing like a sail.

I wonder, will Father even notice the difference? Will he embrace this facsimile of a daughter and take her to heart?

I try not to think, to ignore these pangs and unmoor myself.

There is a world out there.

With susurrations of excitement, I have ventured out, into the surge of slipstreams. I am off, wherever the wind and currents will deliver me.

I am free.

Salt Breeze

Paul A. Hamilton

Grey light pulls me out of my sleepless void, one nothing fading into another. I drop a colourless shift over my naked body. Not for the sake of modesty; more just out of habit. The coffee tin is empty so I heat some water in the tea pot her mother gave us a few summers ago, even though I know there's no tea, either. A squeeze of lemon at the bottom of a cracked mug will have to do.

The back door opens onto the balcony. I have to step carefully to avoid splinters in the creaking wood, and rest the mug on the railing, trying to find a spot where the paint isn't peeling too badly. Wisps of steam rise up to meet the low-slung fog like an excited puppy bounding toward a grouchy old bitch.

The beach is empty again. Grey sand meeting the slightly darker grey of the water in that reluctant exchange of the tide. The exhausted sea blends with the fog somewhere in the hazy distance. She always loved these mornings, the ones that feel like someone forgot to turn on the colour knob. The ones that make you forget you're not dreaming.

If she were here, though, she'd comment on the lack of a sea breeze. "Salt breeze," she used to say, tilting her head back and closing her eyes as if hoping to absorb some of what the ocean was offering her. She loved the wind, and I loved the way it moved through her soft hair with such playfulness, giving her a sense of dance even when standing still. Without the salt breeze, nothing moves, including—especially—my heart.

I leave the mug on the railing and step into the sandals at the top of the stairs. I can almost hear her chastising me in that airy, unserious way of hers, "Someone will trip on those things one day, tumble down into the sand below. There has to be a better

31

place for them." If there is a better place, I'd love to find it.

At the bottom of the steps the sand is cold, pulling on the sandals, tiny grains ricocheting off my stubbled legs as I wander past the low rises spotted with beachgrass. Maybe I'll shave my legs today. She used to compliment them, and I've always thought they were my best feature. They used to be strong, reliably moving me miles up and down this stretch of shore on my many sunset runs. I don't have the energy to run any more, and I can't remember the last time I saw the sun setting.

I don't know why I'm down here. I haven't been on the sand in weeks and there's nothing compelling me today. The lack of wind means I have to get close to hear the surf, close enough that I can smell the brine coming off the scattered heaps of seaweed.

I haven't been avoiding the beach, exactly, but I imagined the next time I came down it would be later in the year when the sun would push back the fog, push back my memories.

Squinting up into the sky doesn't change the smooth emptiness. There's no discernible cloud edge, no seam at all to suggest the presence of sun or blue behind. It might as well be slate straight up into black where the real nothing begins. I hold my hand up against the sky, wondering if it, too, will be monochrome. Maybe something came along in the night while I wasn't sleeping and stole everything's hues. But, no. There's my skin, brown and featureless against the equally feature-deprived blank expanse masquerading as a sky. At least it's a shade of something.

I leave my sandals behind, two flat boats side-by-side in eternal partnership. Or at least until one of them gets picked up by the receding waves, leaving the other to stare out at the water like a post left after the dock it once supported has long since been washed away.

As soon as my toes touch the wet edge of the water line, I stop and let out a small but audible yelp. The saturated sand here is so cold it pulls my breath and betrays the painful iciness of the swash below. I know it wouldn't have stopped her, though. Nothing ever could, especially if it was a chance to feel the backwash tugging against her like a lover trying to coax her back to bed. I think about all the times she'd turn to me, blue-lipped and chatter-teethed but smiling, beckoning me to join her a few feet in. Salt breeze and lover's waves were the wells that she'd draw, drinking in the mystique of the surf-buried toes and the rushing pulse of being deaf to everything but atmosphere hurrying off the sea.

Now I remember why I haven't been out here yet. She is still here, this close to the ocean. I'm not ready to be this close to her again.

Or, I thought I wasn't. I pause on my retreat back to my sandals. All I want is more, now. More remembering, more imagery, more insight into the things that made her everything she was. More her.

But no. I can't let the tears start. Not here, not at her sanctuary. Not now when it's so far from dark, when it's not night and I'm not several glasses of wine deep.

The thing that hurts most about her absence is that the hole I'm left with would be so much easier to deal with if she were here. She always knew how to soothe me, always found ways with her words and her presence to reassure and drive back the edges of darkness and doubt. For the thousandth time I squeeze my eyes tight and silently ask her to come back, just for a moment, just long enough to explain to me how I'm supposed to handle everything alone.

It feels like sacrilege to be down here by the water getting drowned by the grief. She was never unhappy at the edge of land and sea. "It's the most beautiful transition we have," she said. "The line between earth and sky is invisible, indistinct, yet hard and unsatisfying. The border of flatland and mountain is obstinate, those sweeping hills and secret canyons never being sure what they want. Only the sea takes the time to make arrangements, negotiating and softening deliberately with the shore."

"Where was our soft arrangement?" I ask the water. I wasn't offered a negotiation. The transition has been hard and unsatisfying, obstinate and full of secrets. She liked to speak in poems, but she never told me what they meant.

In the first month, I used to climb up onto the railing back at the balcony. I'd dangle my legs over, chug wine from the bottle, and stare at the moonlit waves. I thought then with a manic certainty that I'd see her striding up out of them. I anticipated a slick black swimsuit reflecting the moon or maybe a pale slash of nude skin against the roll of dark water, a skinny-dipping vision of freedom and self-assurance. I risked toppling drunkenly off the railing into the jagged decorative stones below just to be there to see her emerge. Just to have the chance to sprint down the steps and collapse her into my arms, drying her with my relief.

Once I stopped watching for her, I stopped coming outside as much. Stopped wanting to feel the sand between my toes. Began avoiding making eye contact with the shore. I kept the curtains drawn and my back to the balcony. None of it was a conscious choice; I didn't think about it. Things just shift and change beneath us without noticing, like the tide pulling the sand we're standing on back, slowly burying us.

A well-meaning friend, Venu, keeps asking why I don't sell the house. He's not in real estate, so it's not really self-serving, but I think he'd like to buy it if he could. His place is nearby, but he doesn't have direct access to the beach. He doesn't frame it in selfish terms though, he asks things like, "Why stay here with the view blocked and the balcony falling apart?" One time he quietly added, "With all the ghosts you have haunting you?"

"I'll think about it," I always say. It's not a lie, exactly. I have thought about it. In some ways it may be all I do think about. The question of whether to sell the house, pack up, move away, move on, start over, is the basis of every musing. Every recollection my belongings and surroundings dredge up each morning asks it. It's carried in every replayed conversation and disagreement echoing through the shiplap-covered rooms while I try to wait five minutes longer before I start opening bottles. Every tear that falls and lands on a spot of the hardwood floor where her bare feet once danced evaporates into it.

I haven't come up with an answer for a year and a half. Not one that has form enough to carve into words, at least. Would it hurt less to cry on carpet she never walked across? Maybe I'd not drink so much in unfamiliar spaces. If only I could be sure that leaving the coast would leave her behind as well. Circular reasoning strips away logic like turpentine on a balcony railing, so I take no action, make no moves to improve my circumstances. I exist in endless sameness shuffling back and forth like the surf, barely dampening my shores.

Without noticing, I've drifted farther toward the foam bubbling up the sand. Tiny gurgling holes on either side of me mark the nestled clams under the sea-soaked beach. Strange that

I've not focused on the cold since I first abandoned my sandals. Instead, it's her that has caught my attention. And not in the way that she always holds my mind, cupping it in her thin fingers the way she used to cradle my face. Her usual grip is firm, uncomfortable, inescapable. This is more of a presence. She feels more real here than I've grown accustomed to. Funny that I never noticed when she transformed from an ache into an apparition.

Hello? I'm not sure if I whisper it out loud or just in my head.

There's one heartbeat where she doesn't answer. The same heartbeat I've been feeling since the day I don't let myself think about. The question then was the same, only the greeting held her name instead of something universal, something open for anyone to respond. I can hear my keys hitting the small table inside the door, the one that collected junk mail and half-finished lattes. I can feel the wet hair slipping inside my collar. It was raining, which isn't unusual in a seaside town, but later I would tell myself, "The rain should have been a warning."

I called her name, a question, and my heart beat once thinking I'd hear a reply. My expectations in that single pump of blood promised her voice, light with an audible smile. Or a rustle as she pulled off the smock she'd been painting in. Or a scrape of the chair away from the table where she'd leave a hardcover book spread open to the page she was reading, a mug of neglected cocoa leaving a ring because she never remembered a coaster.

The next heartbeat never came because she didn't answer.

Nothing after that is worth remembering. It was phone calls and deep-voiced uniforms and dry throats and black veils and spilled wine and balcony railings and closed curtains and grey mornings. What it wasn't is the answer. An answer. Any answer. Welcome home. Oh honey, you're soaked. How was your day? You're late. Here, let's get you into something dry. How I've missed you. I'm so glad you're back. Do you want to hear a funny story? Come here, I want to show you what I've been working on. Look, we need to talk. Hi, you. I've got something to tell you.

Maybe no question comes with an answer. Everything is just questions wrapped in questions, each one more difficult than the last. I wonder, how much of my time have I spent waiting for answers that never come? I wonder if answers of any sort are a lie people tell themselves in order to get out of bed. I called her name and I received no answer. I stretched out my hand and she wasn't there to take it. She slipped away while I cried her name and there was nothing left to do but wait to find what the reason might be.

I didn't get any reasons. I got a lot of sympathy. A lot of hugs and cupped cheeks. A lot of people who told me they knew what it was like, a lot of people who told me they just couldn't imagine. My mother told me to trust in God, because God had their reasons. If that was true, God never shared them with me or with anyone down here who might pass them along.

I got plenty of other questions, too, ones I hadn't even thought to ask. Why was I late? Had we been fighting? Was there anything unusual about her behaviour lately? When was the last time I spoke to her? Wasn't she a strong swimmer? Was I sure? Was I absolutely sure there wasn't anything I was forgetting?

Now I ask the silent question. The simple one, the greeting in query that might be for anyone. The kind of thing you might ask to a dark alley or a silent house: *Hello?*

The wind moves the gauzy fabric around my thighs. Anxious air, eager to get from the sea to the land, giggles past my ears. My hair isn't soft and light for blowing, it's not the kind that dances behind me when I run or tilt my head back from the ocean. But the breeze carries the bright zest of salt and it picks up my dress and my arms. The wave crashes and the water slides grainy past my legs, cold of course but much less so than I expected. My arms spread wide and I let the dress billow up, not caring that my bare skin is visible. The beach has been empty for weeks and even if it wasn't, I'm past modesty.

I wade in deeper, a brown spot ruining the uniform grey. Not ruin in the sense of spoiling. She used to add a single drop of clashing colour to her paintings: a dot of black on a yellow sun; an orange streak in a blue-green lake. She said an imperfection made things perfect. I teased her when her poetic made-up platitudes were self-contradictory. "You can make anything sound deep if it doesn't make sense." I'd grin and bump my shoulder into hers and wait for her stifled smile that let me know I was right but she still knew more than I ever would.

The loose fabric spreads out, an orchid floating on the cresting swells. Seawater reaches my hips and my arms prickle with goosebumps because the roar of the suddenly intensified wind has cocooned me in the exact spot she used to love.

It's right here.

Feet sinking in sand that is almost sea. Body half in water and half in the ocean of air we call home. Colour drained from everything but me. Sound is everything but nothing, smell is simple saline, and all that's left to find her is to close my eyes and tilt my head back.

Something stops me. A thorn of some kind, some caltrop I carried in my sole from the distant bed of my sandals where I left them on the cold, dry sand. It's a loose thread on the salt breeze, a sound that isn't part of the loud womb created by the whooshing air. It's behind me though, and what I want more than anything from the answers that have been so elusive is to tell me how to move ahead. How to leave things behind. How not to turn back over and over again, constantly reaching for what has slipped away. That's where she left me, and I haven't been able to catch up.

So, no, I don't think I'll turn around. I don't think I will concede to curiosity or caution. I won't let the desperation in the splinter they've made in my lovely little cocoon stop me from going forward. For once in a long time, I'm going to see what is ahead.

I didn't realize my eyes were closed. I thought they'd broken her spell. But I did it. After all, I listened to the salt breeze and closed my eyes and raised my chin and became the imperfection in the most beautiful transition. When my eyes open, the grey water is high above my head.

My heart beats again.

And she answers me.

Salt in Our Blood, Salt in Our Tears

Laura VanArendonk Baugh

She was six when the sea took her grandfather. That was the first.

She remembered her mother and grandmother crying, and she remembered the constant shuffle of neighbours and congregants and townspeople through the house, patting arms and repeating the same words that never seemed to make her mother or grandmother less sad. Many of them stopped to speak to her, too.

"The sea takes people, sometimes," said one old woman. Adelia thought she was in her grandmother's knitting circle. "It can take those we love best. It often takes those who love the sea best. Perhaps the sea loves them back and wants them for herself." And then she patted Adelia's cheek and ruffled her hair and said how much like her mother she was growing to look.

She was twelve when the sea took her uncle. Her father—they were on the same ship—said a whale had shoved the boat and he had gone over, cut by the straining harpoon line and then left behind as the boat was dragged on. They went back for him, but they could not find him.

Her father put on a stoic face when he knew she was near, but he was shaken more than he liked anyone to see. When her mother left him once to go check the oven, he began to sob silently, and Adelia had to crawl backward down the hall,

39

avoiding the squeaky floorboard so that he would not know how near she had been.

She was eighteen when the sea took her father. His captain explained soberly that he had taken a cut while flensing their catch, no great danger itself but it had infected, and he had ended with a bad fever. The sickness had not taken him, but the fever had made him unsteady and less thoughtful, and he had gone up the lines and lost his balance and fallen into the endless blue below.

A whaling boat could turn back for a fallen crewman, if slowly; a sailing ship could not. But, the captain had offered, he had been ill, and surely, he did not suffer long.

As her mother wept, Adelia squeezed her nails into her palms, for that was true. The sea did not let its victims suffer long; that torment was for those left behind on land.

She lost her second oldest brother to the sea when she was twenty-four. While her mother cried within the circle of women, widows and brides, always ready to draw about new bereavement which called to their own, Adelia went to the docks to collect his things. His captain had not carried Abel's trunk up the hill to presage his tragic news.

As if his coming alone had not been signal enough.

The collection of benches in front of the dry goods store was full as usual. Men who wanted seafaring positions lingered here, a market of labour as much as the market of soaps and powders inside the store. Adelia wondered darkly how many would die in the next year.

"Good afternoon, ma'am."

The speaker was somewhat out of place in addressing her as she passed; she could not offer him a berth as a captain or owner might, and he was a stranger in town. But he was whittling a peg, so he knew enough to properly advertise his services. And he whittled in the manner that suggested he wanted a boatsteerer's position, so he was no newcomer merely mimicking the others without knowing the code of their negotiations.

She gave him a brief nod and an obligatory tight smile and

went on.

He stood. "If you're going into the store, ma'am, I'd be happy to carry your purchases."

Manners stumbled beneath the weight of her grief. "I am going to the *Dolphin*. To collect my brother's trunk."

His smile faded, and he lowered his peg and knife. "I'm so sorry to hear it. Please let me carry that instead."

She shook her head. "I mean to ask for a handcart."

But there would be few sitting unused on the dock, and the road home was uphill, and her eyes blurred with tears at facing this mundane and terrible task.

When he spoke again, his voice was soft, wary of frightening a songbird away. "I'll go for you, if you like."

She shook her head. "No, I'll go. But—but I would appreciate the aid with the trunk."

He nodded and sheathed his knife, and then he followed her to the *Dolphin* without speaking.

The mate saw her coming and brought the trunk down to meet her. "We all liked him, Miss Kaffrin. He was a good sailor and a good whaleman, and we'll miss him."

She thanked him as the stranger shouldered the trunk. He followed her again past the dry goods store and up Rogers Street and around the bend to her mother's house. He slowed at the white picket gate and spoke for the first time. "May I carry it in for you, or would you prefer I leave it here?"

Social niceties were a lifeline in grief's storm. "Please bring it in and then have some tea."

"Oh, I couldn't trouble you, Miss Kaffrin. Not in your time of sorrow. I'll just set it inside and then leave you to—"

"Please don't," she said before thinking. She could not bear to walk alone into the house full of tears and sympathy and women mouldering in their mingled sorrows. "Please, take the tea."

Surely, he could not understand, not exactly, but he nodded. "I'd be grateful for tea, ma'am."

❦

His name was Dickson. He found that position as a boatsteerer, and his lay of the ship's profits was enough to take a small house on the southeastern edge of town, where the hills grew steep and the shore tumbled down to the ocean too roughly for docks. It was not a stylish part of town, but the house was their own, not to be shared with her mother and her elder brother and his wife, and she delighted in their small, upright house with its white boards and black roof and narrow roof walk for putting out chimney fires which, on their high hill, also looked over the distant waves. She would be able to see ships going and his ship coming home.

Their first months together were joyous. He read aloud to her as she set flowers and herbs in the kitchen garden, or they huddled together in bed as storms battered the shutters. But as each day slipped away, she could not put away the thought that his next voyage must take him from her and back to the ocean.

The sea takes people, sometimes.

But not now. She had already lost four men in her family, and at even increments of six years. Three sixes was evil enough. She would not lose another.

There was a rocky cove below their house, just visible from their roof walk but shielded from the street by thick trees and berry vines, and they liked to go down to sit at the water's edge and talk. Protected as it was, and in a less travelled part of town, they could also kiss and fondle as they planned their future. The incoming waves cooled their bare feet and occasionally splashed them unexpectedly—the sea was unpredictable even in this guarded place. Dickson set a manila rope to help them up and down the slick rocky slope and praised Adelia's agile ascents. "You'd make a fine hand! You're every bit as quick as a greenhorn and a third as fearful."

"I'm not afraid at all," she challenged him, and it was true if they spoke only of the rope on the hill.

She wished that she might tell him when he went that she was expecting their first child, but it did not come to be. She went down with him to the dock and kissed him beside the *Zephyr*, her eyes already streaming tears in the bright sunlight.

He kissed her tears from her cheeks. "Don't cry, my darling. You won't be so lonely, even without me. You'll be glad enough to have my pestering out of your housework, and for once you won't have to scold for new mud being tracked in over your clean floor."

But she could not say that her tears were not for loneliness but for grief in advance, already mourning the terrible news which might come.

He kissed her fiercely, eliciting whistles from crewmates already aboard, and then pressed them apart. "I'll be home soon."

It was not true. He would not return until their ship was full of oil and bone, and that might be four years. It might be shorter, if they were fortunate. But it would not be *soon*.

She went to supper with some friends whose husbands had also gone, on his ship or others, and she listened to their chatter and even joined in occasionally, saying what was necessary and commenting on children's advancements and the flavour of a cake, and then she went home to make a smaller salty sea of her pillow.

ℰ∕ↄ

She did not discover herself pregnant after he had gone, and so she passed the time in the usual ways until the *Zephyr* was sighted one misty morning. She had the breathless news from Mary Rollins, whose husband was a third mate, and together they ran down the ankle-snatching hill to bounce and wave on the dock, glad that the first crisis of waiting was over and praying still that they would crest the second and find their men alive on board.

Even before the *Zephyr* anchored, the crewmen were popping high on the lines to wave toward the town. Mary Rollins cupped her eyes from the sun and squinted out at them. Her eyes were better than Adelia's; had she been a man, she would have been a fine spotter on a whaler. "I see Paul!" she gasped, relief and joy almost tangible in her voice. "I see him! And—and yes, it's Dickson! He's there, too!"

Adelia tried to gasp and sigh at once, choked, and clutched her friend's arm as they both pretended their eyes were dry. Now they had only to wait for the ship to anchor and be settled and the crew to begin boating over to the docks. Adelia's stomach rumbled— she had left her luncheon to cool when Mary had beat upon her door—but she would wait. A whaling wife would always wait.

When Dickson finally came ashore, whole and healthy, their reunion was everything she could have dreamed. They wept and clung and retreated to their small white house for longer reunion.

He caught her hand as they rested and slipped something onto her finger. "It's not expensive. But I thought you might think it pretty, and a promise of riches to come."

It was a ring of abalone and pearl, glimmering in the lamplight. It slid too easily over her knuckle, but that could be fixed with a bit of string when he wasn't looking. "It's beautiful," she breathed. "Thank you."

"Think of me when you wear it," he whispered. "No matter where I might be, think of me, and I'll be with you."

She stilled his words with another kiss.

The next morning, she made breakfast as he distracted her with arms about her waist and kisses upon her neck. Between distractions, he enthusiastically told her about how well the *Zephyr*'s captain had spoken of his work and how he had promised a strong recommendation. "I'll have a better lay, and maybe a chance at mate in the next trip or two!"

She mustered a smile and squeezed the hand on her hip. "That's wonderful," she said, injecting colour into her words. "I'm so proud of you."

But it was too soon to speak of him leaving again, too soon to let him go back onto the ocean. He had come home to her, but this was the sixth year since her brother's death, and she could not think of letting him go again.

But there is little work for a whaleman ashore, and six weeks later, the day inevitably came. It dawned rainy and gusty, unusual for August, and Adelia's heart leapt with hope, but the weather was not too foul to put off the *Marquise*'s departure. She went down with him, kissed him goodbye with the rain in her tears, and watched his boat row away to the ship that would carry him from her.

Sarah, her sister-in-law, stood beside her and held her hand. Samuel had gone away three days before, and her feelings were still tender enough that she could cry along with Adelia. It was tradition to watch the ships sail away, and lore said a voyage's fortune could be told by how the ship departed and how the new crew worked together for the first time.

Dickson was a boatsteerer, not a mate, and so he could not command the crew into a good fortune. His fate was still in the hands of others and of the sea. The *Marquise* wobbled and drifted past the bar and into the open water, sluggish and awkward, as the old hands and owners and armchair captains—fewer in the poor weather—laughed good-naturedly. "Captain McCabe will have her together within a few days," a grey-haired sailor observed. "It will take a bit to settle the greenhands in and they may need longer to fill up with oil, but it'll be sorted in the end."

The spectators drifted away, but Adelia remained, looking out until the *Marquise*'s black speck was indistinguishable in the shifting blue.

She was nearly thirty.

℮⁄◯

It was four days later that the *Amethyst* came into port, bringing news that swept through the town and rushed up to break at Adelia's doorstep.

The *Amethyst* had seen a ship foundering south of port, two days before. They had not been able to reach her in time, and they arrived only to look upon the flotsam left behind. They could not say what the trouble had been, but there had been smoke, and they had seen no surviving boats.

It was possible a boat or several had gotten away from the wreck and headed directly west for land; that would have been the wise thing to do, all the listeners agreed. Maybe in a few days word would come, or someone might even walk out of the woods and tell the wild tale.

But there was only one ship which Adelia knew would have been two days out of port, and whatever sea curse she bore would not have sent its boats to the coast. The town might not be agreed upon which ship was lost or if it might even be a town ship, but Adelia knew it had been six years.

It rained again that night, adding lightning and thunder to the downpour, and Adelia could not sleep for the light and noise and worry. She got up and paced the room, and then the house, and finally she put on her oilcoat and went out into the rain. She did not fear the storm, not when she was descending the hill away from the lightning's reach. She went down to their cove, clutching the rope with both hands and testing her footing all the way. It was dark, perilously dark, but she knew the way well.

Here she was nearest to the sea. Here they had shared time by the water. Here she was nearest to him.

She perched upon one of their rocks, drawing the oiled coat close about her, and pulled her hat down to protect her eyes from the downpour. She cried, warm tears mingling with cold rain. She should not have married. Were the days of happiness in her brief marriage worth the grief now?

She twisted the abalone and pearl ring upon her numb finger. This is what she would have left of him; sea widows did not have a grave to visit like the farmers' wives could. This was what he had carried back to her across endless sea-fields of waves and whales and wishes. This was what he left her, instead of himself.

The ring slid around her finger, loose with the rain and the cold, and then slipped from her grasp and disappeared into the water.

She leapt from the rock and reached after it, but her fingers brushed only pebbles. She raked them as the incoming waves splashed up her arm, even in the protected inlet, and found nothing. She plunged both hands to above the elbow, feeling along the hidden base for anything that might be the ring. But her fingers were so cold, and the storm waves tugged at the shore, and she found nothing. The ring was gone, like its giver.

At last, she retreated from the splashing edge and collapsed against a boulder, sobbing. She could not bring herself to climb back to the house. No one waited for her there.

The coat protected her from the worst of the storm and trapped her wet warmth, so that while she shivered, she was not dangerously cold, and she tucked her hands against her body and half-cried, half-slept until the morning.

Dawn found her shivering as she woke, her face stiff with salt. She got to her feet, rubbed at her empty finger, and rose to face the practiced routines of sorrow.

There was a ship on the water, visible in the cove's opening.

She did not trust her vision. She cupped her hands against the sun, squinted, rubbed her fingers in a stony rain puddle for fresh water to clear her salt-tainted eyes. She turned and scrabbled up the slope, fingernails tearing at the rope. She slipped and took a nasty blow to her shin, but she ignored it; bruises were less urgent.

She ran down the hill, not caring that she was incompletely dressed on the street. The oiled coat covered her. She came breathless to the dock, where the veterans and dockhands were already in motion.

"That *Marquise* is back!" one told her, and she might have kissed him if she hadn't been too winded to move. "Looks in fine shape. I suppose it wasn't her the *Amethyst* saw, after all."

Signals came from the ship as she anchored off the bar; she had lost the top gallant mast to a lightning strike and (probably after spirited debate) it had been determined that, being still so close to the home port, she would return for repairs rather than repairing at sea only a day and a half out. No, no injuries.

Adelia, breathless with relief, thanked the man who passed the message to her and went back to her home to dress and make up a meal for Dickson. He was trusted and local; his captain would let him visit home at this opportunity.

He had given her the ring to think of him, but she needed no ring to remind her. She already knew every moment he was gone. The ring had served a greater purpose, a ransom to buy him back from the sea.

The sea takes people, sometimes. It can take those we love best. It often takes those who love the sea best. Perhaps the sea loves them back and wants them for herself.

But the jealous sea could be given another precious thing to placate her.

When at last she walked down with Dickson to rejoin the *Marquise*, she reminded him to bring her another gift from his travels.

⁓

In the two and a half years he was gone, she received four letters, carried back by other ships that met the *Marquise* or picked up her mail from designated points. When the ship returned, she met him at the dock, smothering him with kisses. The next day, she held her breath, chewing her lip to keep from asking, until he remembered to bring out the piece of scrimshaw he had brought her. "I'm no good at it," he confessed, "but Peter Farthers, he's a harpooner, he's got a real talent. This is narwhal ivory, which he traded at a jam near the Horn and carved near the Galapagos. I traded him for it and brought it home to you."

The whale's tooth was carved with a fully-rigged ship, all sails set, with a compass rose hovering over it like a sun. The initials *PF* were half-concealed in the waves at the bow. "It's exquisite," she said. "So detailed. How many hours must it have taken!"

"Oh, there's plenty of time between whales," Dickson said with a rueful smile. "Lets one get to thinking of other things." And he kissed her.

When five weeks later he went out aboard the *Isolde*, she watched until the ship disappeared over the curve of the horizon. That night, she lit a lantern and went down to the cove to kneel beside the water, gentler in the spring night.

She cupped the carved whale's tooth in her hands. "I give you this precious thing," she said in a low voice, half-embarrassed to speak aloud and too afraid to keep silent. "Please return my precious treasure to me."

The tooth made a hollow *plop* as it struck the water. Adelia stared after it, barely able to see the ripples in the night. She felt foolish. But if the saving of the *Marquise* had been a coincidence, then she had lost nothing more than a pretty piece of worked ivory. If it had not been a coincidence, then she had saved much more.

The *Isolde* filled her hold with whale oil and baleen in record time, and she returned in two years. Dickson brought her a *netsuke* from Japan, a tiny figure of a duck which, when she turned it over, was sitting a clutch of eggs. She introduced him to his twin boys, toddling to this delighted stranger in their house but happy enough to befriend him.

As the years passed, she did not wait for intervals of six; she offered her pact to the ocean with each voyage. She always waited until Nathaniel and Lemuel were sleeping; she did not want to explain her secret trips to the cove. Dickson, now a mate, brought her gift after gift, and by the time he returned years later, he did not think to ask where she put them. Pearl brooch, shell coin, jade beads, carved wooden mask, a length of silk, all went into the cove's waters by night.

Each time, Dickson returned home.

$\mathcal{C}\!\sim\!\mathcal{O}$

Mary Rollins lost her Paul. Adelia carried food to the house, took her children with her own to give Mary time to cry, shared funeral tasks with the others who came to help. Like tides, the townswomen flowed about each newly bereaved and then ebbed to wait for the next death.

After two years Mary took another husband. Adelia understood; it was hard to wait alone, and harder still if one did not wait. In any ten townswomen, two would be widows, and a woman who wished to raise her children well needed funds beyond what clerking at a dry good store or sewing could provide.

Nathaniel grew into a sunny boy with a quick grin and an eagerness to help whenever he saw a need. Lemuel was only a few minutes younger, but he kept his own independence, more careful of his words than his quick-spirited brother and more prone to finding a cloud behind a silver lining. They shared a room at the top of the house and filled their days with playing at whaling or, when older, taking odd jobs in town. They looked more like their father each day. She loved them, but like most sons born in this town, they were promised to the sea.

⊙⁄⊚

Adelia was forty-two. Six sixes and six.

Dickson, now a second mate, had a fine lay of a ship's profits and had offered to buy her a house in a more fashionable part of town, but she had told him she was used to the outlying white house and did not need anything more. She did not want to leave the little cove.

He went there less often with her these days, but at least once each visit home they went down together to eat a lunch and sit upon the rocks. They took the boys at first, but Nathaniel and Lemuel outgrew the need for supervision in just a few visits. Adelia leaned upon his shoulder and held him, breathing the warm scent of him, treasuring this time between voyages.

"Do you think you might give it up?" she asked him once, leaning upon a boulder in the cove. "Stay home?"

He laughed, and then he looked down at her. "Were you serious? Why should I stay home, now that I'm a second mate? I'll be first mate in another ship or two, and then it's not so far to captain of my own. I'm speaking with the right men already. It's only a matter of time."

"Time is what is precious," she whispered, unsure if she meant him to hear. Time was what she had too much of, waiting for him, and too little of, when he was here. For a few weeks at a time, he was everything, and then he was gone for three years, four, five. She wouldn't know for years if his ship were still out filling tuns of whale oil or already lost. And every voyage he took was another gamble, another test of her pact with the fickle sea.

He signed on with the *Emerald* for a spring departure.

She had known, deep within her marrow, even on the day she had given birth. No matter how many times she had pushed the thoughts away over the years, the truth of it was her sons were coming up in years, in a world which idolized whalemen, and it was inevitable that they would at last make their own voyages.

Nathaniel found a place first. He had always been quicker to push himself. At thirteen he was young to go, but not too young, and the captain of the *Fitzwilliam* was a trustworthy man who had been a mate with Nathaniel's father.

It was only cruelty of fate which set the *Fitzwilliam* and the *Maiden*, Dickson's ship, to sail out on the same day. Adelia kissed them both again and again, making an embarrassed Nathaniel rub her tears from his face before his new shipmates, and then watched them rowed out to their respective ships, and then clutched Lemuel's shoulder in a vice grip as the ships made their slow way out beyond the bar.

Lemuel did not cry. He had seen his father leave on a half dozen occasions already. While it must have hurt to see his brother go out, he had hidden his disappointment in boasting that he would have their room to himself and would pick over his brother's things.

Adelia watched until there were no ships to see, until the sky began to darken, until Lemuel tired of waiting silently and took her hand. She turned and let him walk her home.

The hours ticked by. She ladled soup into a bowl she gave to Lemuel. She picked up and put down her mending basket thrice. She rose to go into another room and then circled it aimlessly, having forgotten what excuse she'd given herself to come.

At last Lemuel went to his room upstairs, and she drew a coat about her shoulders and went out of the house.

She would need two gifts this time. She had taken a wooden whale from a bookshelf, an early experiment in whittling which Nathaniel had presented to her. It would have to serve.

As she descended the rocky trail, one hand holding her bribes for the sea and the other clutching the manila rope, she felt a few cold drops strike her through the overhanging trees. Rain was not unusual for this time of year. She would not need long to complete her errand, and then she could return before the storm worsened.

She went to the boulder which pushed furthest into the cove and climbed it. She was crying again. "Bring them safely home to me." She had never really formalized the ritual of this pact; the ocean was a thing of actions rather than words.

She drew out the bone necklace Dickson had brought her, carved in a sweeping curve to a sharp point. It plopped into the water like a slightly larger raindrop, indistinguishable in the pocked waves.

Next, she drew out the wooden whale with its crude planes and asymmetrical flukes.

"Wait!"

She turned, pulling the whale to her chest, caught as if guilty of something worse than love.

Lemuel was sliding down the rocky tumble, using the rope as much as the ground. "Mama, wait. Not yet." He leapt and stumbled across the stony cove to join her on the boulder.

They stared at one another for a moment.

"What are you doing out of bed?" she asked at last.

He rolled his eyes. "I'm not a child, Mama. I'm old enough to join a crew, if I wanted."

That was not what she wanted to hear, not tonight. "Why did you follow me?"

He opened his mouth and then did not speak. He was always more careful with his words. Finally, he asked, "Are you a witch? A sea witch?"

She gaped at him. "What?"

He shook his head, but slowly. "We know what you do, Mama."

She did not know how to answer him. She had never thought to explain it even to herself, much less to someone else, much less to someone who—who did not believe, who had not felt the stabbing grief of loss, who did not know what it was like to do anything, *anything* which might prevent the knife from descending again.

She was crying again, and she saw that distressed him. She rubbed at her face, smearing rain and tears. "Oh, Lem," she tried, her voice barely above a whisper. "How long?"

"We watch you from the roof walk when there's enough moon," he said. "That was how we saw you the first time. We didn't know what you were doing, though, not at first."

That made no sense. "What do you mean, not at first?"

His eyes shifted to the side.

"Lem, what do you mean, not at first?"

"The next morning, we went down," he said, his gaze on the waves, "because we'd seen you throw something, and Nate found the jade in the pebbles." His words quickened. "He was the one who took it, not me."

"Took them?" she gasped.

"That's how he had the money for his spyglass," Lem said half-accusingly. "You know the store doesn't pay so much for a delivery boy."

She had not even wondered at it, assuming her diligent son had done well for himself.

"So, then we watched after that, and we saw it was only when Papa left."

But now her secret's discovery was the lesser worry. "You took the jade? From the sea?"

"Nate did." He pressed on, his words a tumble in defence. "He was the one who said we should take the other things, too. I didn't think we should, but he said Papa had brought them home and so they were ours anyway."

Adelia put a hand to her mouth. They had stolen the sea's gifts. They had reneged on the contract. They had made her a liar.

"Don't you understand?" Her voice creaked like brittle wood. "Six sixes and six! The *Maiden* has six letters! Do you know what you've done? This is Nathaniel's first voyage!"

Lemuel did not understand, did not know what they'd done. He gaped at her as if confused by what he saw. Didn't he know that she meant to protect his father and brother? Didn't he understand that this was the only way she could?

"Mama," he pleaded softly, "what are you doing, talking about sixes and ship names?" He held out his hand. "Give me Nate's whale. Don't throw it away. Please."

Now he would sabotage her pact again. He meant well, but he didn't know. His ignorance would cost them, for the sea would have no forgiveness left after his previous thefts. His curiosity and greed would kill his father and brother.

His voice was low but quavering, afraid for her and of her. "Mama, please give me the whale."

She pulled it back from him and fumbled it, and it fell into the water below. She looked down at it, floating and breeching on the little waves.

"Oh, Mama." Lemuel knelt on the boulder and stretched his arm down for the wooden figurine.

It struck her all in that moment, the years of aching loneliness and the anticipated grief nearly as keen as the arrived grief and the sudden piercing knowledge that others had known of her desperation, had *known*, and had done nothing to help her, had instead profited by her terror.

She dropped beside Lemuel, trying to block him from retrieving the bobbing whale. Her arm was longer, and as her fingers teased the whale, she shouldered him aside.

Lemuel toppled into the water.

Adelia's breath caught in her throat in a spray of salt mist and horror. She had not meant to push him—she hadn't, surely. She had only wanted to keep him from the whale. She had not meant to push him into the water for his father and brother, she had not.

The wind pushed waves over him as he righted himself. The cove dropped off steeply, but even so the water here was only waist-deep. But the waves reached for his shoulders and splashed his face, and he hugged himself as he stumbled upright and gaped in outraged shock at her.

"Lemuel!" she gasped, and the word was apology and prayer and plea.

He caught the drifting whale and then heaved himself around the boulder and out upon the rocky shore, slipping as he went. Adelia turned and slid down her side, hurrying to meet him. "Lemuel! Are you hurt?"

He did not look at her. "Did you mean me to be?"

She stopped mid-step, staring.

"Would you shove me off a rock over a carving?" He continued toward the climb out of the cove.

Her heart beat again. He had not suspected that she might have pushed him off on purpose as an offering—but she hadn't. Had she? It had happened so fast, and there had been no thought in that instant, and no, no mother would offer her son, not even to save another son, not even to save another son and his father, no.

"You think throwing things into the sea will—" But then his

voice checked, and she knew he had guessed the possible truth of it, the truth she did not know herself.

"Lemuel," she said, fast and desperate, "I didn't give you to the sea. I wanted the whale."

The rain fell harder, and a larger wave broke over the cove. Adelia refused to look back a second time. There had been no offering, no pact. The sea was not coming for her retracted sacrifice.

Lemuel pushed forward, shivering, and started the climb out of the cove.

Adelia clenched her fists. "Lem!"

But no, it was foolish to shout it out here, in the cold rain and with the waves growing ever larger on the rocks behind her. They would return to the house, and she would build up the fire and make hot drinks for each of them, and then she would explain what she had done and how it had harmed no one in all these years, and how she had broken the curse of sixes.

Lemuel was halfway up the climb when the rope gave way.

"Lem!" she screamed, for the fall was too quick for him to scream for himself. She dashed forward, stumbling among the rocks, striving for the place where he lay.

"Mama!" he called, and her heart swelled with the sound.

She flung herself down beside him. "Don't move, not yet. Let me see you."

He was slouched between two anchor-sized stones, rounded with eons of waves. He stared up at her, caught between a boy in fright and pain wanting his mother and a wary accusation, as if she had done this to him.

Had she?

"Where does it hurt?"

He gestured. "My ankle."

He had fallen feet first onto a boulder, and the steep angle of his landing had both turned his foot and slowed the rest of his fall. Relief poured through her like a riptide. "We can manage an ankle. Anything else?"

He shook his head. He was lying; she knew he'd be covered in bruises all up his side. But bruises mended faster than bones.

He was still looking at her, and as the initial shock of the fall faded, the accusation remained. He pushed back against the stone. "Are—are you a witch?" he repeated, almost embarrassed to ask it but pressed by fear.

She was crying again, with relief at his survival and pain at his suspicion. "That rope was put there by your father when we were first married. It's old."

He swung his eyes to the swaying broken end. "Manila won't last more than ten years," he agreed cautiously. "He should have replaced it." He rubbed water from his face. "Does he know you come here?"

It was an imprecise question, but she knew what he meant. She shook her head.

Lem's face crumpled, and she reached for him. "I'm sorry! Is it the ankle? I'll get—"

"No." He pushed her away. "Would it—would it have made a difference? If I'd gone, too?"

If I had found a berth as soon as Nathaniel?

A wave broke on the shore behind them and kept coming, rushing up the short rocky distance and burying the boulders in foam as it came. Adelia barely had time to recognize the threat— a sleeper wave, sudden and huge and hungry—and seize Lemuel's wet shirt. His hands closed on her arms as the water struck them, and as the force of it rocked them, she kicked off the stones.

The wave swept over them both, fighting to pry into their eyes and nostrils and mouths. She wanted to grab onto something but she could not release Lemuel, and there was no safe anchorage as the wave battered them against the wall of the cove.

The fallen branches which had littered the cove whirled about them, snagging her clothing. She needed air.

Lemuel's hands were gone—gone!—but she still held his shirt, clenched in unyielding fists. She could feel the weight of him. She shoved him in a direction that might have been upward, pushing herself down.

They tumbled, drawn back by the retreating wave. Her heavy skirts filled with pebbles and sand and tugged at her. She kicked, but she could not guess whether she fought toward land or the open sea.

A wall of stone slammed into her, jarring loose her resolve to hold her breath, and she sucked in a mouthful of cold salt. She began to choke.

But the water was draining away, leaving her stranded against the great boulder where she had offered her sacrifices. Her hands were still clenched in Lemuel's shirt, twisted and stretched now. He was coughing too, spitting brine and bile.

"Are—are you—all right?" she wheezed.

He nodded. In his hands was a length of rope, broken away from where he had snatched it as they rolled against the cove's wall.

The sleeper wave had finished; the next waves would be the tamer sort that usually lapped the cove. Adelia pried her stiff fingers free and folded her arms across her belly as she coughed and retched.

Lem got an arm around her, still clinging to the useless rope. "Are you all right?"

She had tried everything to protect her family, and still the sea had come for Lem when it had not been given its due.

"You held on," he whispered.

"I would never let you go," she whispered back fiercely. "Never."

The carved whale was gone, lost forever with the rushing wave which had carried away tree limbs and shifted stones. The bone necklace too would be buried now, or perhaps a quarter mile from shore.

She could bring more gifts. She could try to buy back the ocean's tolerance, repaying the stolen sacrifices with greater offerings. She could bring Lemuel to barter with her. She could keep telling herself that she was doing something, *something* to help them rather than waiting passively in miserable ignorance.

Lem pushed himself to his knees and seemed to finally notice the rope still in his hand. He gave a strained half-chuckle. "I knew this rope was bad. It had thrown me off just a moment before. But it was all I could reach." His fingers uncurled, reluctantly. Then he looked at his mother, a curious light growing in his eyes.

In that moment, she saw he understood. Maybe not entirely, but enough.

She supported Lemuel limping across the newly scoured cove, feeling anew for a path. They climbed out on hands and knees, her filthy skirts drawn high, not trusting the remaining rope. The rain washed the salt and mud from them as they went home.

ᏀHE ᏀHOST OF VIOLET ᏀRAY

ᏟᎧSARAH VAN GOETHEMᎧ

A knot of sparrows

Arthur Hale marched barefoot down the shoreline, his heart
beating frantically, like the flapping of tiny bird wings in
his chest. The aftermath of the storm had left gloom and
grey, and Arthur was the only soul on the small slip of beach. The
clouds were thick overhead, and the waves crashed against the
rocks, enhancing the now-familiar scent of salt and seaweed.

The anxiety had come on the moment he'd heard the first
rumble of thunder, and now, hours later, ominous thoughts of his
wife still circled in his head. The only outlet was to walk. His
senses were more alive than ever—he could feel every grain of wet
sand in his toes, every breath of wind that teased his black curls
across his forehead. The eerie fog from earlier hadn't been
washed away by the rain and wind, and Arthur found himself
liking how it made the bay feel ethereal, like maybe, just maybe,
the divide between alive and dead wasn't as much as one thought.
Maybe he could walk right through it, to the other side . . .

Maybe he could find Ella again.

He'd walked too far already when a flicker of yellow atop a
craggy cliff caught his eye, jolting him out of his illusion. He kept
his eyes trained on the tiny flame as if it were a lighthouse beacon.
Whoever was out here, shouldn't be, but then he shouldn't be out
here either, especially not right now. He quickly checked the time
on his phone. He'd miss his dinner meeting with the council
members if he delayed much longer, and he had a final report to
give before he could leave the island and go home.

Home. Did he even want to go? Perhaps he was only stalling.
He'd been doing research for weeks now on the rising waters,

the erosion, the demise of these once-flourishing seaside homes.

But that wasn't why he was out here now. Sure, it was the razor blades of panic that had pushed him out the door of the small inn where he'd been staying, but it'd been the lovely shade of indigo in the sky, and the way the old pier was still hanging on despite the battering of the viscous waters, that had drawn him further. The pier was putting up a good fight, he decided, same as the old homes. Same as the people. No one wanted to let Graymouth Harbor go.

Arthur could understand that.

He walked on toward the light, picking up speed. He'd only be a few minutes late if he hurried.

The beach narrowed, cutting in against the cliffside. He'd come further than he'd thought. He hadn't investigated this far in his studies; this stretch of leftover beach front had supposedly been evacuated years ago. Derelict cottages jutted out overhead, precariously close to the cliff's edge. The depressing image only reinforced what he'd decided on the other end; it was time for the inhabitants to vacate soon. He hated being the bearer of bad news, but the rising sea water was quickly swallowing land and shrinking property sizes, and despite best efforts, there was no stopping it.

Arthur had the fleeting thought that he was glad he hadn't bought coastal property, but just as quickly he was reminded of how much his wife had loved the water.

Ella.

What if it was Ella out there? What if Ella had been caught in the storm, or had been hurt, and someone could have found her before it was too late? Arthur picked his way along as fast as he could go on the rocks, regretting his decision to forgo shoes. Seagulls had come out again, squabbling overhead. He imagined them as warning, *Turn back, stranger.* But another few yards and yes, there, through the mist, he could see the yellow light for what it was—a single candle lit in an upper window. He drew closer and the shape of the old Victorian home materialized above: Queen Anne style, with gingerbread trim, a turret, and a wrap-around porch. Arthur knew without asking, this must be the doctor's house, the first one built here in the 1860s, the namesake of the entire village in the bay. Someone was in there. Arthur tried to think logically; it was probably just teenagers looking for a party house, or a homeless person.

Either way, he had to find out. He had to make sure it wasn't someone who needed help. What if someone had turned away from Ella?

He searched for a remnant foot path to climb the dangerous cliff when a knot of sparrows, disturbed by his movement, flew up and out of the grasses and toward the water.

Arthur turned to watch their flight and that's when he saw the woman. Her back was to him, but he knew her; the slope of her slender shoulders, the curve of her waist. The sun chose that moment to make a break in the dark clouds, bathing her in a soft halo of light. She wore a long white dress with a shawl over her shoulders, and her hair, a lovely shade of honey, whipped loosely down the length of her back. The sparrows surrounded her in a flurry of grey and brown, like something otherworldly, and Arthur's eyes blurred with tears.

Ella, he thought.

It's you then, who lit the candle

It wasn't Ella, of course.

That was impossible. Ella had been gone for almost a year now. Arthur was a widower at the age of thirty-one. He'd pictured his entire life with Ella, growing old with Ella, and now he was still floundering like a fish out of water, like he'd severed a limb and could still feel it there, a phantom pain.

As he closed the distance between them, he saw the differences: this woman's hair was more strawberries than honey, her waist narrower. She was shorter, too; probably only reaching the height of Arthur's collarbone, whereas Ella had risen to his nose. She didn't turn until he was right behind her.

Then, she sucked in a breath, startled.

"Sorry, didn't mean to scare you," Arthur said, hands help up. The sun was shining on her, illuminating water droplets on her bone-white skin. "You shouldn't be out here," he told her, and his voice sounded gruffer than he'd intended. Softening it, he added, "It isn't safe."

As if in agreement, a particularly large wave crashed against the sea wall nearby, a futile attempt to stave off nature, and water sprayed in an arc over them.

The woman wiped absently at the wetness on her cheek. "I suppose you shouldn't be out here either, then," she returned. With one last glance over her shoulder at the sea, she brushed past Arthur. "We should go inside. Yes, that's exactly what we should do."

It didn't seem like a question. By the time he'd turned to follow her, she was already carving a path up the hillside. Arthur groaned inwardly; there didn't appear to be a rope railing. "Wait," he called, jogging over. She paused, head cocked to the side, looking down on him. "Your dress could catch on the rocks," he explained. "You could trip, fall to your death."

She waved off the notion. "I've navigated this cliff many times."

"It's you then"—Arthur gestured to the light in the window—"who lit the candle."

"Of course." She looked from the candle in the window and back to him, eyes shining. Then, for his benefit, she hitched her skirt up in a mock display and began climbing again. "I guarantee I won't die today."

Despite her words, Arthur was already stumbling along behind her, worry making his stomach turn. "Now, just wait a minute. At least let me help you."

She only called, "Hurry, Mr. Hale. I'll put the tea on."

I lived a lie

Arthur shouldn't be having tea in a house that was supposed to have been abandoned. He shouldn't have gone out in the first place, and yet here he was. Even as he sipped from the fussy china cup, something nagged at him. Something more than just the dinner he was now late for, and that dinner was important! Everyone was awaiting his final verdict on the fate of the seaside homes. But the fevered blue eyes of the woman before him kept him firmly rooted to his chair.

After he'd followed her up the cliffs, she'd disappeared to make tea, leaving him in the parlour. The house was not at all what he'd expected. A fire burned in the grate, casting a cozy orange glow over the room. Everywhere were opulent furnishings and rich colours, tapestries and patterned wallpapers, doilies and embroidered cushions. The effect was like stepping back in time.

When she'd rejoined him, she'd tossed open the heavy drapes and stood at the large windows for a long while, staring out at the darkening night sky over the bay. After that, she'd lit more candles. The room, Arthur thought, was glowing like a Christmas Eve service. The thought reminded him that the last time he'd been to church was for Ella's funeral.

"I seem to be at a disadvantage," Arthur blurted, shaking loose his thoughts of Ella. "You obviously know who I am, but I have no idea who you are."

"Isn't that always the way of it in a small village," she mused. A beat, and then, "Violet Gray," she offered, nudging a plate of cookies toward him like an apology.

Arthur noticed she wasn't wearing a wedding ring, but then she couldn't be more than twenty. "Gray?" He frowned, her name finally settling in his head. "As in a descendant of the Doctor Gray who founded this harbour?"

"The exact one." Did Arthur note a hint of disdain in her voice?

He took another sip of tea, warming himself. "I thought all of the houses out this way were evacuated and no longer inhabitable, Miss Gray."

"Violet," she said. "You must call me Violet. It seems you were misinformed, Mr. Hale."

"Violet, like the flower," he mused. The name seemed appropriate. Her formal speech prompted Arthur to copy her. "Then, you must call me Arthur."

She raised a brow, and Arthur thought to himself how lovely she was, how like Ella had looked when he'd met her, with her delicate features. Yet there was something underlying her calm demeanour; Arthur noted the way her foot quivered ever so slightly beneath her skirt, the way her eyes flicked to the window, always back to the sea.

"Arthur." His name curled sweetly on her lips. "As in the glorious head of the knights of the round table? Very well. A strong name for such a chivalrous man. I suppose you think you rescued me from my imminent death on the rocks this evening." She smiled, but it didn't quite reach her eyes.

Heat crept up Arthur's neck and he tugged at his collared shirt. If anyone had almost fallen on the cliffs, it'd been him. Violet had the assured steps of a ballerina. "Miss Gra—Violet, do you mean to tell me you still live here?"

"Indeed."

"By yourself?" Arthur glanced about the shadowy room, half-expecting to find a maid or butler in the corner.

"I prefer my own company," Violet said smoothly.

Did she resent his presence now? "You do know it's not safe to live here?"

"You seem to have an obsession with safety." Her eyes narrowed, but not unkindly. More like she was trying to see inside of him.

Arthur shifted uncomfortably. "I—well the thing is, my wife died in a horrible accident. A storm, actually." Why was he telling her this? "So, yes, I guess you could say I'm rather cautious."

Arthur waited for the usual sympathetic response that information normally elicited, but it didn't come. Instead, Violet's eyes seemed to flash in recognition. "It seems we have something in common then. It all makes sense now."

"I'm sorry, what makes sense?"

"You, seeing the candle." She said it simply, then stood, making her way back to the window like a moth to a flame. "You do know that accidents can happen just as easily in lovely, fair weather?"

There was a sadness in her voice that Arthur knew all too well. He drained the rest of his cup slowly and set it back on the matching saucer. He tried again. "Why does it make sense that I saw the candle?"

Before she could answer, Arthur's cell phone dinged in his pocket. Distractedly, he retrieved it. The message was from Sheila Childs, one of the persons he was supposed to be having dinner with at this very moment. *Where are you?* the message said. *Is everything okay?*

Arthur could hardly explain. He noted the time: 8:16. He'd been due at dinner over an hour ago. With a sigh, Arthur texted back, *Sorry. On my way.* He slipped the phone back in his pocket, saying, "I have to go." But when he looked up again, Violet was at the fireplace.

She had a worn-looking blue book in her hands. From its pages, she slid out a photograph. It was curled at the edges, as if it'd been handled time and time again. "This picture is of me with Edward Laurier."

Arthur joined her. In the sepia-tinted photo, Violet stood on the pier, wearing a long old-fashioned floor-length gown with puffy sleeves. The man beside her was tall and lean with light hair. He wore a jacket and had a handlebar moustache. Behind them, an old steamboat was docked in the water. The photo reminded Arthur of the one him and Ella had taken at an amusement park, only rather than Victorian era clothing they'd chosen to dress in Wild West attire, with Ella as a saloon girl decked in feathers and Arthur wearing a cowboy hat.

It was the boat in the photo that gave Arthur pause, though. No boats had docked at Graymouth pier for quite some time, as far as he knew. He took the photo from her, gently, and held it up for closer inspection.

Violet said, "We were to be married within two weeks of this photo."

A shiver crept up Arthur's spine. He questioned her with his eyes.

She paced back to the window where her breath fogged the glass as she looked out at the sea. "He drowned in the shallow water of the bay on a beautiful day." She showed no emotion.

Arthur was at a loss for words. When he'd mentioned how his wife had died, Violet hadn't offered him unwanted sympathy, and he'd afford her the same now. Instead, it seemed the two of them would accept their shared grief. Still, Arthur's arms were covered in goosebumps; something about the way Violet's back had stiffened made him think there was more she had to say.

He really should go. Instead, he found himself saying, "My wife—she was walking our dog near the river in the early morning. A storm brewed up and it poured—" his voice cracked before he went on. "The spring floods made the river higher than usual. It was determined she and our dog had been swept away in the current." The moment that had changed Arthur's entire life.

"You loved her." It wasn't a question. Violet was staring directly at him again with those glassy eyes, seeing inside of him. Her eyes were the same colour as the sea in the afternoon light. Beautiful but deadly. "You loved her and everyone knew it. In life, everywhere you went, everyone knew she belonged to you. And even in death, everyone still knew the truth."

Arthur almost forgot to breathe. It was strange the way she put it, but also the truest thing anyone had ever said to him.

"And now you're here," Violet went on. "Now you're the expert who was called in to tell everyone the truth about the harbour, to save us all from the rising waters, to do what you couldn't do for your wife. Yes, yes, it all makes sense." Violet raised her chin, turning her attention back to the window, where voices could now be heard on the breeze.

Though the window was shut tight, Arthur could hear his name being called. He rushed over and pressed his face to the glass. There, below, several people tottered across the thin strip of sand. "Arthur!" they bellowed. "Arthur! Are you out here?"

"Unbelievable," Arthur said, plucking his phone from his pocket once more. He'd sent them a message. Why had they sent out a search party? But no—his message hadn't sent. He saw that now. He also saw the irony; he'd been telling them over and over how unsafe it was out here. Apparently, they'd listened. "I have to go." After a pause, he hedged, "You really won't be able to stay here, you know."

But something shifted in the air and the undercurrent of anxiety he'd sensed in Violet grew stronger. "You can't go, not yet." Suddenly the curtains were drawn shut in one violent swipe, and she paced about in a circle, wringing her hands. "Just a few moments longer. I've waited so long for this moment, for *you*."

"I'm sorry," Arthur said, doing his best to calm her. "I'll come back, truly. I can help you find somewhere more suitable to live."

"No," Violet snapped. "You don't understand!"

Surprised by her outburst, Arthur felt his defences rising. "I have to let them know I'm fine. I'm sure *you* can *understand* that."

"I'm begging you," she breathed, jabbing a finger into the book she still held. "No one understands. I haven't told you all my story yet." She continued to mutter to herself, "Lovely in their lives . . . in death not divided." She laughed then, and it had a wild ring to it. "It wasn't supposed to happen that way!"

Her agitation had Arthur on edge and he backed toward the door. His gut had told him something wasn't right here, and he should have listened.

She flew at him before he reached his escape. "I lived a lie!" Arthur held up his hands to ward her off, but the assault never came. When he opened his eyes again, he couldn't see her, but as he stumbled from the house, he could still hear her voice, softer than before, pleading. It seemed to echo from the depths of the walls. "I'm begging you. Tell them the truth."

She haunts the bay yet

Arthur was finally having dinner at a quarter past ten. When the councillors had decided he was unharmed, most of them had seemed more annoyed than concerned. He'd been told to take a hot shower, get some food in him, and they'd reschedule for the next evening. Sheila, however, had looked at him with a face full of pity and asked, *Are you quite all right, Arthur? Perhaps it was too soon to work again?*

It reminded him of how everyone had looked at him in the months after Ella's funeral, full of sympathy, and . . . doubt? Doubt that he was mentally stable. He'd thought taking the job in Graymouth would remove him from unwanted attention in that regard, but it seemed Sheila had done her background check. The thought made him bristle.

Now, Arthur sat in the dimly lit tavern eating fish and chips and drinking a beer by himself. There were only a few other patrons in the building: a middle-aged couple in the corner, an old man nursing a rye and coke at the counter, and a group of teenagers inhaling nachos in a booth near the door.

Arthur mulled over the strange evening, his thoughts turning to Violet Gray. No one in the search party had noticed the candles in the old house since she'd pulled the curtains, nor had Arthur said a word about her to anyone, and he wondered about that now. Why was he protecting her? Fine, he knew why; he knew what it was like to have everyone think you were unstable. He'd give her the benefit of the doubt for now. He couldn't let her continue to live there, though. That was an entirely different matter.

Tell them the truth, she'd said. Arthur was one hundred percent certain she didn't mean the truth about the rising waters either. If only they hadn't come looking for him, he might have found out what she meant. Still, he was half-glad they *had* come; there was something unnerving about the woman. He'd realized after he'd exited the house that he still had the photo of her in his hand. He looked at it now.

"Another beer?" The waitress, a young Black girl with too

much energy, bobbed in front of him. She'd been serving him on and off for the past few weeks while he'd worked on his research, and he'd learned her name.

"Oh, um no thank you, Sybil." On a whim, Arthur slid the sepia photo to the edge of the table. "Do you happen to know this woman?"

She planted a hand on her hip. "How old do I look to you?" When he didn't laugh, she said, "Jeez, tough crowd. It was a joke. Okay look, see there on the side of the boat? That's the *Lady Jane*. Everyone in these parts knows about the disaster of the *Lady Jane*. It was the blackest day in Graymouth's history. Hey, Hal!" she called to the man at the bar. "What year did the *Lady Jane* capsize? 1885?"

The old man turned slowly on his stool. "1881."

"Right, 1881. I never did pay attention in history class. Hal though, he knows *everything*." Sybil cleared away Arthur's empty plate. "Cool photo, anyway. It's probably from the same day and taken by the same photographer as the one in the museum. Looks familiar." She started to walk away, but then stopped. "Oh, who *is* the woman, by the way?"

Arthur cleared his throat, still reeling from the information. The dates made no sense, though it seemed obvious now the photo was original and not a reproduction as he'd thought. "Violet Gray."

At the mention of Violet's name, the smile slid from Sybil's face. "Oh," she said, sucking air. "Well, now you'll get an earful."

Arthur was lost in his thoughts again before Sybil had sashayed away. Who was Violet Gray, really? She couldn't be the woman in the photo and the woman he'd met. Perhaps the woman he'd met was a descendant? But why on earth would she pretend to be the Violet in this photo? They did seem to share an uncanny resemblance . . .

"Violet Gray, you say." The old man from the bar—Hal—had shuffled his way over. He dropped into the chair across from Arthur without being invited and tapped the photo with a yellowed fingernail. "Yup, that's her. The young'uns think it's a joke about Violet Gray because they don't know the story and they wouldn't know her face unless it was plastered on their silly social media." His voice was gravelly, the smell of rye overpowering. Arthur shrank back. "But I do." The man tapped his temple. "I ain't lost my marbles yet. It's all up here. Generations of information."

Arthur was curious, despite the fact that the man's words slurred. "Go on," he invited.

Hal wasted no time. "T'was June twentieth," he began. "The *Lady Jane* was supposed to make her third trip to the mainland. It was an excursion boat, you see, brought the tourists here for the beaches and the taverns and fish dinners. Cost fifteen cents a ticket, d'ya believe that?" He shook his head. "That day was busier than usual on account of the town's twentieth celebration. The crowds were rowdy on the pier, where a brass brand was set up, and ice cream was being sold. Another of the excursion boats ran aground that day, and by late afternoon there were too many people all clambering aboard the *Lady Jane* to make the trip back. It wasn't like it is now, weren't as many rules back then. The captain knew there were too many people, but he pulled away from the dock anyway."

Arthur squirmed; he could already see where this was headed. Violet had said her fiancée had died on a beautiful day. Arthur pushed the photo across the table. "So, is this man Edward Laurier?" Arthur asked, wondering if she'd told the truth. "Had he come to visit his fiancée, Violet Gray? Was he on the boat?"

Hal scratched his scruffy white beard and leaned in. "They were *both* on the boat."

Arthur's scalp prickled. *Violet.* But no—the Violet he'd met couldn't be the same Violet as in the photo.

"They were going to the mainland for last-minute wedding preparations," Hal went on. "The captain knew it was wrong; the boat was only supposed to carry two-hundred passengers. Still, he set sail with over three hundred, way past the danger point. Turned it into a joke, the passengers did. No one had proper fear, despite the water pouring onto the lower deck. You know what they said, when they were warned?" Hal pointed a gnarled finger at Arthur. "They said, 'If the boat capsizes in the bay, we'll walk to shore!' Story has it, only one passenger had a premonition of death."

"Violet," Arthur murmured. He could see in his mind's eye the woman he'd met, flitting about the old parlour, wringing her hands. Somehow, he could picture her as the Violet who'd been on the boat all those years ago.

Hal nodded.

The teenagers had finished and left, and the room seemed deathly quiet. "What happened next?" Arthur asked.

"Dominoes. That's what. Too many people. The boat wasn't far out when the brass band struck up their final set of the day. The boat was rocking and the people were all carrying on, thinking it was great fun. But not Violet. She rushed to the lower deck, with my great-grandfather in tow. He was only a small boy at the time and had become separated from his mama. He remembered her telling him if the worst happened, they could swim. Anyway, all the people on the upper deck scrambled to the starboard rail to get a final view of the band. The *Lady Jane* tipped"—Hal held up his flattened palm, slanting it at an angle, and let out a whistle for emphasis—"and finally the idiot passengers were frightened! They tried to fix it by pressing port side"—he turned his hand the other way—"but they overbalanced her and she toppled." Hal slapped his hand down on the table and took a breath before going on. "It gets worse. The boiler dislodged, crashing through the bulwarks and opening a hole. People were burned. Everything collapsed."

Arthur felt sick. The shocking image Hal had painted was clear in his mind. His eyes were drawn to the photo again, to the long dress Violet wore. How would a person swim in that, if given the chance?

Would Ella have had a fighting chance against the river if she hadn't been wearing her puffer coat?

Hal broke into Arthur's thoughts. "My great-grandfather survived because of Violet Gray. Never saw her again though." He tapped his fingers on the table between them. "They say she haunts the bay yet, lighting a candle for her love to find his way back to shore."

They were lovely in their lives, and in death they were not divided

At the crack of dawn, Arthur trudged through the local cemetery. He hadn't slept a wink; Hal's story had replayed itself like a movie in his mind, and that combined with the howling wind had left him feeling like a child who'd heard a ghost story. Technically, he supposed he had. Hal had implied that Violet

Gray—the woman he'd just spoken with—had perished over one hundred years ago in a boat disaster.

No.

Impossible.

He had to see it for himself—Violet's grave. He wandered about in the misty morning and finally, after what felt like an eternity, he found it.

There were two adjoining graves, Violet's and Edward's, with a single headstone. The inscription read, *They were lovely in their lives, and in death they were not divided.*

Arthur stared at it in a haze, remembering that Violet had muttered those exact words. Then, she'd laughed wildly and begged him to find the truth. *I lived a lie,* she'd said.

But what was the truth?

Arthur's heart ached to find out.

Purser of the Lady Jane

By 8:45, Arthur stood outside the museum Sybil had mentioned the night before. It was located in an old brick building on the main street. The sign still said Closed, so Arthur bought himself a coffee and a bagel at the bakery next door and plonked himself at a little table outside and waited. The morning was warming, the sun bright, all the eeriness of the day before dissipated. The shops were quaint and old-looking, with pretty coloured canopies, and he found himself thinking how much Ella would have liked Graymouth Harbor.

It wasn't long until a middle-aged woman wearing a long flowery dress strolled up with a key in hand. She was heavy set with tight curls that frizzed in the damp air. She waved a hello to him as she slipped inside. Arthur gave her exactly two minutes to turn the sign and flip the lights on, and then he followed. A bell jingled as he went in.

She looked up from the counter in surprise. "Good morning. It's Mr. Hale, isn't it?" He nodded and a firm hand shot out to shake his. "I'm Greta Taylor, local historian. It's not too often we have someone come in so early. What can I do for you?"

Arthur got straight to the point. "I was recently told the story of the *Lady Jane* disaster—"

Greta smiled knowingly. "Ahh, you've had a run-in with Hal.

It's his favourite old story, especially if someone new comes to town, which of course leads into his Violet Gray haunting theory, which in turn leads people here. Not that I mind him drumming up business."

Arthur blinked. "Is there any merit to it, then? The . . . ghost part?"

Greta shrugged. "Who's to say? I will give him this though—people have reported sightings of a candle burning in the old house. But only a specific few, mind you. Only men, which is interesting in itself, since history usually places women as the one to see ghosts in all their so-called hysterics." Greta led him past displays of Victorian household rooms. "We can appease your curiosity, though. Easy-peasy. The *Lady Jane* disaster put our town on the map."

Arthur followed her to the back of the building where glass cases held memorabilia and artifacts from the tragic day. Sturdy frames on the wall housed newspaper articles, hand drawings of the steamboat, and a few more photos similar to the one he had in his pocket.

Arthur squinted at them.

Sure enough, there was the one of Edward and Violet. No, it wasn't quite the same though, was it? Arthur moved closer, scrutinizing. There were differences in this one: it encompassed a wider angle, taking in more in the distance, and Violet's head was turned, catching only a blurry profile. Something had caught her attention behind her. Arthur scanned the crowd near the boat. There was one person who stuck out, who was seemingly looking at Violet as well—a young man wearing a white shirt with a simple waistcoat.

"You had to hold very still for photos back then, Mr. Hale. Otherwise, they came out blurry."

Arthur started; he'd almost forgotten Greta was there. He pointed. "Do you know who this man is?"

"Certainly." Greta carried an air of confidence as she gestured toward a pillared stand in the corner. "That's Adam Rixon. He collected the fares and tickets and kept the money. Interestingly, we have his lantern here. Come see."

Arthur looked. Beneath the glass was a brass kerosene lantern with an etched chimney. It read Purser of the *Lady Jane*.

"The Rixons were English born but emigrated here in the

1860s. Unfortunately, Adam perished aboard the *Lady Jane* that day. It's amazing this lantern survived. Would you believe it turned up at an auction in the 1980s?" She rubbed a hand lovingly over the glass case. "That's the thing with history, there's always something to be unearthed."

"And . . . Violet Gray . . ." He licked his lips, searching for words. What he wanted, he realized, was confirmation. "She died that day, too?"

Greta raised a brow. "Supposedly." She turned to the far wall, where a list hung behind glass. "This is a victim list, which was published in the Graymouth register that summer. You will find Violet Gray's name on it."

It was.

Gray, Violet—19. Arthur also found other names. Laurier, Edward—32 and Rixon, Adam, purser—26.

"You said 'supposedly,'" Arthur said. "Is there something else you're *not* saying?"

Greta's mouth curved up at the corners, and Arthur could tell she enjoyed her job very much. "How perceptive of you, Mr. Hale. Since you've asked, we do have some written accounts of that day from survivors and one has always stood out to me. The handwriting is almost illegible so I won't make you suffer through it. But the story goes like this. A piano tuner, named Thomas Lister, alleges that he grabbed his daughter under one arm and his wife under the other arm and flutter kicked to shore. Once there, he realized the girl he'd thought was his daughter, was not."

Horror filled Arthur. Even though Ella had drowned while he slept, what if he'd had the chance to save her, but had saved another woman instead? Would that have been worse than never having the chance to save her at all?

He realized Greta was looking at him, eyes wide, ready to deliver her next line. "He claimed to have saved Violet Gray."

Arthur rubbed at his temple. "So, I assume, since her name is on the victim list, no one ever confirmed that he did, in fact, save Violet Gray?"

Greta's eyes danced. "No one ever saw her again, unless you count the ghostly sightings, of course."

"Of course."

Maybe it was the tone in his voice; Greta was looking at him strangely now. "But if further information were to surface . . . wouldn't that be something?"

Yes, Arthur thought.

"It's always the little things," Greta went on. "Like these hand-written accounts. Sure, they are only one person's version of a story, of history, but they are so enlightening. Some of the best artifacts are journals or diaries."

Diaries. Arthur had a flash of the worn book Violet had been holding. The book she'd taken the photo from.

He barely remembered to say *thank you* to Greta; he could only think of Violet's last words to him. *Tell them the truth.*

The truth. The truth. The words thundered in his head. She'd shown him where the truth was from the beginning. What he wouldn't give to know Ella's truth too. Why had she gone out so early in the morning? They could've walked the dog later . . . together.

He may not ever know Ella's truth, but maybe he could find Violet's.

It was only as he stumbled toward the door that Greta gasped. "It wasn't just Hal's story that had you curious, was it? Why didn't I see it before?" Her nails dug into his arm. "You've seen the ghost of Violet Gray."

Tell them the truth

Arthur hurried back to the Victorian house on the cliff. He was both surprised, and yet not surprised, to find it faded, rotting, abandoned. He climbed the cliffside carefully, taking it all in. In the sunlight, he could see it was just as washed-out, as dull, as the other forlorn houses. Why had he thought it any better?

Arthur's chest twisted with sorrow, while at the same time his heartbeat sped up in anticipation. Would he see Violet again? Arthur had never been one to believe in ghosts, but now he found himself fervently hoping that Violet *was* a ghost. If she was, then Ella could be a ghost, too. And if he could find Ella, well . . .

But no, that was silly. If Violet was truly a ghost, then she was here because she had unfinished business.

Ella did not.

Would it really matter if Arthur knew the gritty details of Ella's death? Not likely, he admitted. Perhaps it was time to stop replaying the events as he imagined them in his head, time to stop feeling guilty that he hadn't been there.

The heavy door creaked open with a push and Arthur slipped inside, feeling the whisper of cobwebs across his face. The entryway was musty, vacant, a tomb. He let out a slow breath.

Was he mad? Had he imagined it all? He walked to the parlour, light-headed. There were no furnishings besides a mouldy sofa and matching chair. No tea tray, no fire burning in the grate. The windowsills were covered in a thick layer of dust, the old curtains threadbare. Arthur tore them aside to let in the light, the warmth. Had it been him who'd closed them?

No one had been here yesterday.

No one had been here in a long time.

Except him. He could make out the imprint where he'd sat in the chair, the trail his bare feet had made across the hardwood.

The hairs on his arms stood on end. Greta's words echoed in his head, *You've seen the ghost of Violet Gray.*

Arthur rubbed at his arms, his mind turning. Whatever had happened, whatever he'd seen, there was only one thing left to do—the thing Violet had asked him to do.

Find the truth.

Like a madman, Arthur darted about the room, searching for the missing book. When it was apparent it was not in the parlour, he rushed back into the dimly lit hall, wondering which way to go. The grand staircase reminded him of what had brought him here in the first place—the candle in the upstairs turret window.

He took the stairs two at a time, pausing in the upper hall to look around. There were five doors, all open. When he spied three curved windows, he went into that room. The view of the bay was incredible; the sunlight dancing on the placid blue surface took his breath away. And there, in the centre window, sat a lone white candle in a tin holder. It was practically brown with dust.

Arthur knew without a doubt this had been Violet's bedroom. Even the wallpaper, dainty purple violets in greenery, had likely been chosen by doting parents. But there was nothing in the room any longer, save a built-in bench that wrapped underneath the windows to create a sitting nook. Discovering that the seat of the bench opened, Arthur looked inside each compartment, but there was no book.

He settled on the bench, admitting defeat—the book had likely been removed along with everything else. For a while he watched the water, his mood etched with a melancholy—from Ella, as always, and from these old homes that were once vibrant with life, and from Violet, too, the young lady who'd had a secret to share.

Tell them the truth.

The words seemed to whisper from the walls, and Arthur startled, spinning around. But there was no one there. He did, however, notice a slant of sunlight across the floor, revealing one board that sat a little higher than the rest.

Arthur's heartbeat sped up again.

It took him only seconds to pry up the loose board. And then he was looking at the little blue book Violet had held in her hands.

Arthur plucked it out, his hands trembling. There was nothing special about it, although the cover appeared watermarked. Inside were hand-written entries in scrawling penmanship, the first entry dated 1879. Quickly, Arthur tried to remember the date of the *Lady Jane* disaster. What had Hal said? June? Yes, that was it. June 30, 1881. Arthur flipped the pages, barely breathing.

He found the date three-quarters of the way through the book.

He sank to the floor and read.

Festivities on the pier

June 30, 1881.

Edward is to come today on the ferry. There will be festivities on the pier, though I must admit I'm not feeling very festive. Father insists we're to have our photographs taken in front of the *Lady Jane* and I'm intrigued at that part. And the prospect of ice cream. But later, we are all to set sail for the mainland for wedding arrangements. I feel ill at the thought, and almost wish I would come down with something deathly so that it may excuse me from the event altogether.

How awful that sounds! What some girls wouldn't give to be in my place, to be betrothed to the handsome and rich Edward Laurier. How well I know this. Even as I write this, my cheeks burn with shame.

I will say no more; there is naught for it. Father has arranged it, and whatever lies in my heart shall soon have to be snuffed out like a candle.

I must go, I can hear Libby on her way to style my hair before she leaves. Father has dismissed the servants for a few days while we are to be away, and I have never seen such excitement.

It couldn't end like this

The next pages were stuck together. *No, no, no,* Arthur thought. *It couldn't end like this.* But no—they weren't stuck exactly. Only watermarked like the outside cover, probably damp at some point and dried together. With gentle force, he was able to wrest them apart. There was no date on the final entry, and the writing was looping, almost erratic. It took a while to make out the words.

I am going now, back to the sea

Everyone is gone. I am here—alone in my room, in this house—and no one knows it. I creep around like a ghost. I'm not thinking correctly. Father would say it's shock, if he were here. He'd have Libby spoon me up some laudanum. But no, I must keep my wits about me. And I must put the events to paper.

The *Lady Jane* has capsized in the bay, a day ago. So many are dead. I can see the searchers out my window yet, trolling the waters, reeling in the bodies. I would be dead too, if it weren't for Thomas Lister. He thought I was his Mabel, and I can never unsee the look of utter despair on his face when he realized he'd saved the wrong girl.

I should be in a watery grave, with my parents and Edward and . . . oh, not once have I written his name.

But what does it matter any longer? Father insisted I marry Edward, for his money, for his station, for everything that seems trivial now. But my heart belonged to Adam Rixon.

My love.

We should have run away and never been here on this ill-fated vessel, but he would never have asked me to do such a thing, and I was too weak to stand up to Father. The truth burns in my chest, too bright, while the whole world has faded. If I could rewind time, I would tell the world I loved him, and Father and Mother and all the naysayers be damned. I lit a candle for Adam, our usual sign, but this time he has not come. That is how I know he's truly dead.

The worst thought I have now, is of living a lie. How can I face a world where I am dressed in black crepe, where everyone thinks I'm mourning Edward and my parents, and no one knowing what lies in my heart?

No, I cannot bear it. I would rather join Adam.

I am going now, back to the sea.

The ghost of Violet Gray

Arthur looked up from the entry, his eyes blurred with tears. There was a noise outside, something that drew him to his feet and back to the window. Later, when he thought back on it, he wouldn't know what that noise was.

But there, below, like an apparition, a sparkle in the bright sunlight, he saw Violet in her billowing white dress, walking back into the water.

Strangely, she looked like Ella again, too.

He thought perhaps she turned and waved to him, smiling before she disappeared beneath the depths, but he might only have imagined it.

Later, when he dropped the journal with Greta at the museum, he felt a little as if something lifted from his chest and flew off . . . rather like the little sparrows that had flown out of the grasses when he'd first seen the ghost of Violet Gray.

Rage Against the Sea

Adria Laycraft

I will live at the seaside and have a life of my own," Emmy cried, shoving the engagement scarf her father had foisted on her back into his hands.

"And how will ye survive, foolish child? Don't tell me you're off to become a whore, now?"

"Pa!" Emmy's face burned hot, and she thought she might steam like the kettle. They'd been at it long enough the argument had become heated and unreasonable . . . and loud. It made her gut churn and her heart pound, but she knew she must stand up for herself. "You know I've been offered a position at the castle, and I will take it!"

She shook with anger, righteous anger. She had never yelled at her father before. Her shout rang in the silence after, rolling like a wave. For the slightest moment, she saw a flash of something other than anger in her father's eyes, but it was gone before she could name it.

"Go then," he cried, flinging the scarf down and stomping off out the open door. "It's good ye mother's dead so she can't see ye leaving." His voice carried back to her, and she knew all the neighbours were listening and judging and gossiping. Guilt struck her like a knife to the gut. She couldn't stay, though. She had no interest in marrying the baker's son, no offense to the lad.

She had studied and trained under the local teacher, Mistress Jenny, to be able to go and teach children of rich families. Emmy did not belong here, living this life. She had a chance at something better, and she would take it. Her father had become a bitter old man, unreasonable with expectations of her, and now, trying to keep her here with this unsuitable marriage proposal. She blew air out her lips as if she really was the kettle releasing steam.

With shaking hands, Emmy took out her best dress, her linens, and her smallclothes. Underneath, she found the blanket her mother had made her learn stitching on. A child's blanket, really, too small for a bedspread, but big enough for her to snuggle under, even now.

It was a soft rose pink with a dainty flower print and squares of gingham patchworked on the back. Emmy scooped it up and held it to her cheek, despite the mothball scent, and closed her eyes to drift a moment in her only memories of her ma. The images were vague, bits and pieces of recollections like touching her mother's cheek, of her humming Emmy to sleep, and of waking to be comforted by the soft tones of her parents' voices. Sometimes she worried they might slip away, these old memories, so she indulged in them to keep them strong and alive in her heart.

There were three other important items: her lesson book, Ma's bible, and the hand-painted book of flowers her grandmother had made, with neat printing describing each plant and how to use it. All three books would be used in her classes and must be taken with her.

Once she had the bag packed, she fingered the blanket again. Could she squeeze it in? It would make it overstuffed and much heavier, but at the last minute, she folded it in, tucking and shoving to get the bag closed. On the bed, she left her everyday work clothes, the men's britches and a smock that kept the worst of the muck off. They were ragged and stained and stunk like pig. She wished she had time to burn them.

Emmy stepped out into the sunlight. Across the lane, Goodwife Meggie pinned washing on the line, her old hands working quickly with long practice. The crone cast a quick glance at Emmy and pursed her lips.

"He's gonna miss you, lass, and I'll bet me whole cottage ye'll miss us, too."

Emmy glanced up the lane towards town, where her father was surely now in the pub getting much sympathy and many a free beer.

"No, he won't," she said. She lifted her chin and hefted the bag. "And I won't either."

As the carriage brought her to the castle gates, she marvelled at the towering stone rising above her. She stuck her head out each window and craned her neck to see everything she possibly could. Behind them the road wove upwards to the bluff and on inland, crossing a narrow spit of land that widened out to become a point of rocky sea cliffs and castle walls. Sand stretched in either direction, and bright waves curled and spread over the beaches in rhythmic patterns.

From up on the headland, her heart had thrilled at the expansive view over ocean and shoreline, the smell of salt water, and the call of shorebirds. If she felt any pinch of sorrow at not having a proper goodbye with her pa, she quenched it with all the glory around her.

They rumbled to a stop. Gulls screamed as they circled above, riding the brisk sea wind. Emmy's hair lifted as she disembarked, and she threw up a quick hand to hold it. Already, even on this lee side of the castle and down low at the first gates, she could hear the thunder of waves striking the shore. It was cold in the shadow of the walls and towers, and clouds came to shroud the sun.

"Surely you can drive within," she said, seeing the gate was clearly large enough, but the carriage driver dumped her bag at her feet and turned to climb back into his seat without a word. The man snapped his whip even though the horses were already in motion, rolling their eyes at her as if she was some ghost. She sighed, hoisted the bag, and turned to find two dour-looking guards glaring at her.

Thinking quickly, she decided to go with charm.

She curtsied. "Hullo, I'm here to teach the children," she offered, bright as could be.

The older of the two frowned. "Ye might be a spy."

"What? No, I . . ."

The younger spoke over her. "I'll take 'er to the chief." He stepped closer, reaching.

"Wait!" Emmy set the heavy bag down and struggled with trembling hands to dig out the small hand-written letter she had received. "Here, here, it's a letter, it has a seal!"

They studied it, and her, for several more moments, the older guard looming over her and actually poking his dirty finger in her open bag while the younger tried to take the letter. She held it out of reach with one hand and snapped her bag closed with the other, putting on her sternest mistress face and pulling out her teacher voice.

"I am here on assignment and by invitation of those you serve, good sirs," she declared, fisted hands on her hips now. Both men's eyebrows rose. "I suggest you either assist me with my bag, or find a page boy to do so."

The younger guard pouted, and the older fare snarled. "Won't win ye no friends with that attitude, missy," he warned. "Besides, ain't no page boys around to help, they's all off at war, see. And we canna leave our post. So, you better just lug that bag outta here before I decide I want a better look."

She had lugged her bag, at that, now regretting her decision to add the blanket, sentimentality aside. Within moments of crossing under the arched rock and back into some semblance of daylight, the darkened skies released their cold rain. To her right was a small single cell, its barred door standing open, and the nearby guard's gate room was also quiet. To her left stood the inner gate, and beyond, the climb to the castle proper. She wondered what welcome waited for her there.

Exhausted and uncertain about the steep, wet stairs, she dipped into the cell for a moment's reprieve from the rain. Tears pricked her eyes, all elation from earlier gone. She could not let a couple of lowly gatekeepers and a grumpy carriage driver ruin her triumph. She would rest a moment, gather her strength, and pray for the rain to stop long enough for her to find her way to someone in charge.

Within the cell, she set her bag down and sat upon it, leaning back against the wall. It was dry, somewhat chilly, but out of the wind too. She cooled her forehead on the rock. It was quiet, peaceful despite what it was. With mild curiosity she realized she could not hear the sea.

The rain slackened, and she was growing cold, so she hefted her bag and began the long climb. Now she could hear the roar of the wind. No, wait, it wasn't the wind alone, it was also the churning ocean beating the shoreline around three sides of the castle. She crested the stairs and stepped through an archway onto an open green space. Across the way, at the other end of a stone path, firelight danced in windows, voices rose over the wind, and the smell of cooked food wafted out to her.

She had arrived, wet and likely bedraggled, hauling her own suitcase, and without any clear contact, she realized from a quick reread of her letter. Would she find welcome within? She drew in a deep breath, let it out slow, and pursed her lips in a way that made her think of Goodwife Meggie. She would prove that crone wrong, and build herself a good life, one suitable for her small stature and feisty spirit. Emmy squared her shoulders and crossed the yard, only hesitating momentarily before entering the hall.

It was warm and smoky within, and full of men all seemingly talking at once. A large fire burned in the hearth, and braziers glowed throughout. Platters of red creatures with giant claws and the strangest looking fishes she had ever seen loaded the tables, and many people sucked on pieces of the claws like they were sweets. The smells were overwhelming, a churned-up mix of food, saltiness, unwashed linens, people, and dogs, all permeated by wood and oil smoke. It had a tang she wasn't used to; one she could only ascribe to the strange creatures on the food trays. She watched a large man scoop up what appeared to her to be a giant, red, spider leg made of some hard shell, and snap it in half, pulling the pieces apart to reveal a hunk of pinkish meat that he slurped out of its casing.

He seemed to sense her watching, and suddenly she was in his sights. Without taking his gaze off her, he took a long draw off his ale, set the stein back on the table, and rose.

"Who are you, missy?"

His voice carried over the other chatter, and many turned to find out what was happening. Emmy strode over, fumbling her letter out, and presented it to the man.

"I'm here to teach the children, goodsir," she said, again with a curtsy. Couldn't hurt. Never know who you were talking to.

He didn't look at the paper more than a glance, handing it back to her with a shrug. "Probably the wives' doing. You know there's a war, right?"

She nodded. "Down in the southern parts, past the Fell River."

He gave her a look of scorn. "Well, that was then, now we face a possible siege. War doesn't stay where ye want it to, lass."

"Why are you telling me this?"

"Are ye crazy? You should return home while you can."

Emmy reeled. She couldn't go home. "No, I agreed to teach the children here. I sent a reply, and they sent a carriage to bring me." She waved about, trying to make light of the situation and agonizingly aware the whole room was listening now. "Besides, what a pleasant place to be stuck, if we must be, wouldn't you agree?"

They all burst out laughing. The whole room. She was aghast. They clearly thought she was a fool.

"Well, lass, it will be of interest to see how long you hold that belief." He turned and called out to one of the serving crew. "Take missy to her room, and then bring more ale."

The rest of them cheered, and Emmy followed a wave from the kitchen door, still hefting her own bag.

⌒

"Oi, you've come, then," the cook said as Emmy was presented. "Heard 'bout that, I did. Right, then, put 'er in the old mistress's room, Dot."

The young girl who had waved her in, named Dot apparently, gasped at Cook's suggestion. Cook gave her a quelling look. "It's all we've got. So, be nice and donna scare her with yer stories, right?"

Dot nodded, eyes as round as beach pebbles. She couldn't be a day over twelve, the poor lass, and by her apron's stains she worked as hard as any adult here. Emmy's heart fell. It didn't matter where she went, this was a common thing . . . more work than hands to complete it.

She followed Dot out a back way, through the kitchen gardens where they struggled through muddy puddles, up more stone stairs still slick with rain, and finally into hallways and rooms constructed of wood. They were within the strong castle walls, safe from the sea and attack, and finally she would be able to rest.

Dot lifted the heavy latch and leaned hard to push the door open. Emmy followed her in and dropped her bag beside a massive bed while Dot went to tug the draperies over the open window. It did nothing to block the sound of the crashing waves below. "The window's cracked open a bit, I'd leave it for air, miss," she said, "but I like to draw the drapes to keep the draft out." She curtsied twice, her gaze skittering about, and scuttled over to the hearth to light the kindling already set there. "Bed's all fresh, made it meself," she went on, "and after you're settled, you can come back down and I'll fetch you some eats, right?"

"Thank you," Emmy said, curtsying back, as Dot paused in the doorway. Dot giggled, then, as she looked to the now-covered window, blanched, and stuttered.

"B-b-b-be careful," she said. "It's nothin' but rocks and sea below 'ere. Don't ..." She swallowed visibly. "Don't sit in the window sill," she whispered, and then she was gone.

Emmy stood for one long, surreal moment, gazing around at the ornate furniture, including bed frame and headboard all carved with leaves and small woodland creatures, upholstered chairs set by the fire, a fine writing desk in the corner, and a massive wardrobe that was laughable when she thought about the contents of her bag. Maybe, once she saw pay, she could buy another dress.

She touched everything, circling the room. The bedpost was ridged oak leaves, with small smooth acorns hiding within. The chair back, the frame also carved wood, had a cushion of fine fabric she couldn't even name. No rough sacking here.

The immature fire settled, needing more fuel, and she selected from the abundant pile of sticks and stacked driftwood. Someone would likely come every few days and replenish it for her. What luxury! And who knew, perhaps he would be handsome.

The writing desk was walnut and had compartments and drawers. She pulled one open to find some dust and hair, long blond hair just like hers, as if someone had kept a hairbrush within. Emmy sat on the stool, running her hands over the desktop. She would prepare lessons here, maybe even write her own poetry. Hope thrilled through her.

Rising, she twirled around, her skirts lifting. How beautiful to live in such a place, with the lovely ocean sounds coming in the window. On a hot day, the breeze would be wonderful. Of course, they faced long winter and spring before that might come. The leaves were turning now.

Curious, she gathered the heavy drapes aside and peered out. Night had come, and the last of the light caught on the foaming whitecaps out at sea, the wind still driving the earlier rainstorm.

She realized she could feel the pounding surf under her feet. Her lips tasted of salt.

Which made her hungry. Time to learn her way around this new home. But before she drew the drapery back over, she leaned out, putting her head into the wind, and looked down.

With a gasp, she pulled right back, shoved the window shut, and stumbled away until the bed was at the back of her legs. She sat, hard, breathing fast, and little spots danced in her eyes.

The height was immense, and clearly the rocks below were not accessible ever, based on the sheer rock cliffs around them. Well, that, and the skeletons that lay amongst them.

⌒⌒

"Aye, the superstitious will tell ghost stories, but there's no truth in 'em, eh?"

Emmy nodded. Cook handed her another scone, which she gladly took. It had been a long day. "Who were they?"

"Both mistresses, the first one, a right sweetheart, and the last," Cook said. "That one, I think she got herself in a bad way, ye take my meaning?"

Emmy nodded again. Heaven protect any woman who found herself pregnant without a husband.

Emmy was warm, fed, and full of stories about who was who, what title or place they had, and which ones to avoid. Dot was scrubbing dishes with another girl, and the other women continued to come and go from the greatroom, each laden with trays of scones and fruit, or steins of ale, or returning with more dishes. Three lads came tearing through, snatching up warm scones off the hot tray only to juggle and curse and blow on their fingers. Cook shooed them out again before returning to her mulled wine.

"The children are mostly darlings," Cook said. "I'll send Dot on the morrow to show you the family wing. They take their food separate, see, the wives and the young'uns."

Emmy could see. The greatroom was loud, full of rude, drunk, armed men, and she thought she heard a fight breaking out.

"Go on, then," Cook said to Dot, "you've done enough for today. Take missy here up to her room and then get yerself to bed, y'hear?"

Dot nodded, dried her hands, and waved for Emmy to lead the

way.

⌎⌍

Emmy woke to the sound of constant surf. The coals of the fire weren't much to see by, but moonlight shone through the open window from a now-clear sky. She sat up, heart thudding in her throat. She had left the drapes closed. Had someone been in while she slept? Even if it were just Dot, the thought was unsettling.

As she slipped from the bed, she realized she heard someone crying over the waves and wind. Must be coming down the chimney from another room, poor soul. Her room held no guests. She checked the door and found it had a lock, so she engaged it, slipped more wood onto the fire, and crawled back into bed. It would be nice to block the breeze coming in, but she couldn't bring herself to approach the window.

She dozed, the never-ending cycle of sucking water to smashing wave not lulling her as she had daydreamed of, but instead jolting her awake again and again. Emmy tossed and turned. Hopefully the sounds would become known and normal, like the roosters and barking dogs back home.

Home. She cried a little, knowing she was just overtired and overwrought. This was home now. She couldn't expect everything to be perfect, or for her to feel settled on her first day. With this small comfort in mind, and the light of dawn touching the sky, she slept at last.

⌎⌍

The next morning, far sooner than Emmy was ready for, Dot arrived with breakfast. The girl set a new fire while Emmy ate. Then, once Emmy was in her best dress with hair pinned, Dot brought her to the children in their well-appointed dayroom in the family wing. It, too, opened on one side to the sea, and the crashing surf made her feel she needed to half-shout her introductions.

There were five boy children sat at the table, from about five years old to maybe nine. Dot curtsied and was gone before Emmy could ask where the rest were . . . and where the girls were. Perhaps they came later, since they were supposed to start with arithmetic, and many nobles felt girls had no need of learning numbers.

"Did you see the ghost last night, Mistress?" It was the youngest. Samuel. The eldest two snickered.

Emmy smiled and ignored the question even while the vision of the skulls in the rocks flashed through her mind. She encouraged them each to use the pebbles she had brought to complete simple addition and subtraction so she could get an idea of what level they were at.

"You'd be our fifth mistress, now," the oldest one said. Jeremy. "In as many months," he added, gazing at her expectantly. "The second lady even went home, and she still died."

"Yeah, fell outta a tree, broke her neck," the second-eldest said. "Aren't you scared?"

"No," she replied firmly. No matter how she might feel inside, it was her job to be the calm adult in the room. That's what Jenny taught her. She was nineteen, after all, and these were just tall tales told when someone died. "I am here to teach you, and teach you I will. Why would I be afraid of that?"

"Because they all died, mum," another piped up, helpfully. "They all take a fall." William. He wasn't much older than Samuel. "Five is a lot." He counted out five pebbles, then subtracted one away, then another, and another, and two more, until none were left.

❧

The girls did arrive in time for reading and writing, trailing bits of thread from their needlepoint lessons. And so began Emmy's new routine, six days per week, Sundays off. Occasionally, one of the mothers would slip in the far door and listen for a few moments, but they never spoke to her. Once she tried to approach, and the woman's eyes widened in fear before she, too, fled.

"They think ye may be cursed," William said. "My ma cries a lot about Mistress Beatrice. They were friends."

Emmy crouched in front of the boy. The others were playing tag about the room, paying them no attention. "I'm sorry she lost a friend," she said. "Did you like her, too?"

William shrugged. "Mostly, but not when we had to do writing. She said I was hopeless."

Emmy had to agree that he was hopeless at staying within the lines, for all his trying. "Doesn't matter," she said. "You know your letters, and how to read them too, so being neat is only important if you're going to be a scribe."

William's face brightened. "You really think so, miss? Because I got mad at her, and then she died. And Ma was so sad."

Her heart broke a little. "It's not your fault, William, I promise. It's still hard, but it's not your fault." She thought about how, after her own ma died, she had thought it was her fault because she'd been naughty. Her pa had assured her it wasn't, and couldn't ever possibly be, her fault. Emmy missed him with a new, deep grief then.

❦

At night, Emmy woke often, always to the slap of water striking the rocks. Ever on, the roar of the surf swelled and ebbed with the tides, but it never, ever silenced, never quieted completely. There was no relief, no respite, and with each passing night she was becoming more deprived of rest.

The weeping continued, also, and sometimes it contained words wailed in agony. "I want to go home," was the clearest line, with mumblings and moanings about lost dignity and endless grief. She tried calling out to the voice from the safety of her bed, but it had no effect, as she received no answer.

One night, after too many startles awake, she got up to rekindle the fire. She paced about, muttering to herself in a vain attempt to drown out both the surf and the crying.

"I made a promise. I canna go home, no, not after yelling at my own pa." She slumped down in a chair. "I'm here to teach. Ghosts aren't real. And if they are, they canna hurt you." Back on her feet, she paced the room, avoiding the window. "The sounds will become normal. I'm safe here." She regarded the rucked-up bedding, and then turned away. "The pay is fine, Cook and Dot are nice, the children are sweet, people will see. Pa will see. Maybe he could come visit." She started crying again, her own sobs matching the mystery woman's.

She found herself rocking in one of the fine chairs, her head in her hands, repeating, "I can't, I can't, I can't." She stopped with a gasp, pulling her hands down to dig fingernails into the fabric as if that could cement her to something sure.

Then she remembered a place that might hold some peace.

Emmy wrapped herself in her blanket, and then her shawl, and crept down to the castle proper, across the greens, and down some more, until she came to the tiny cell. The guards should be outside the gate, and sure enough, the nearby guardroom was empty.

She slipped inside with a sigh. This place, the one point farthest from the walls looming over the rocky cape, this was her escape. She gathered her feet under her and closed her eyes to wish it all away. If only she could just go inland for a night's sleep, and a day at the shops.

These idle ruminations only made it worse, though, when time came to climb the stairs, perform her duties, always in those upper rooms with windows wide to the ocean. The whole place was cold stone and salt, and relentless noise, an endless pounding, like some exquisite Chinese torture drilling at her head.

"Do the waves quiet, in the summer?" she asked Dot once, and the girl scowled and shook her head.

"Some days I want to just rage against the noise, ye know?" Dot said. "But she never quiets, the sea. It goes on and on, and I never get used to it."

Emmy felt such despair, but she had agreed to come and live there, she had a job, an obligation, a duty. She would have to tough it out.

She also had too much pride to go home. After the fuss she had made, returning would make her look like a dog with its tail between its legs. Goodwife Meggie would smirk. Maybe come spring, she could give notice with some excuse of missing family. Maybe the weeping girl was getting to her with the repeated cries, so full of anguish and longing and despair. Emmy wanted to ask Dot about the chimney, and whose room might be above or below her, but there was something about it that made Emmy think maybe she didn't want to know, and she never brought it up.

On and on the torture continued, always the rhythmic roar that never ceased, when she woke, as she taught, in the gardens helping weed, always it was present. Even on the calmest days, the roar continued unabated, ruthless, pounding against her soul.

At the end of her first fortnight, Emmy woke from a dream of her pa to find herself at the window, hands gripping cold stone, the glass opened to its widest while salty rain lashed her face.

She covered her ears and focused on her favourite memory, the one of the soft tone of her parents' voices when she had woken in her bed, only a small child then. That memory, the sound of loving voices, was so unlike any ocean or wind sound, and different too than ordinary conversation. This was quiet intimacy, comfort in knowing her parents were right there. Her favourite part was when the fire cracked, and her ma laughed. Emmy remembered that sound better than her mother's actual voice. She could almost smell the lavender pouches her mother would tuck under the pillows and in the rucking enveloping her in safety.

Emmy stayed awake in the chair by the fireside for the rest of the night with her hands over her ears, wrapped in her blanket that still held a hint of mothballs to it. She hummed tunelessly, unable to remember the exact notes of any song in that moment. All she could think was to keep the sound of the ocean out of her ears.

At first light, Emmy gathered her courage to face Cook and admit she could not stay and teach. Cook would tell the mothers, help her arrange a carriage, and give her some hot tea and breakfast, saving Dot the trouble of bringing it up.

But when she reached the commons, the place was a tumultuous flurry of men calling orders, women asking questions, and dogs barking. She snagged Dot running by with an arm full of linens.

"What's the hurry?"

Dot teetered from foot to foot, her colour high. "War has come to our very doorstep, Emmy," she said, breathless. "We are under siege."

Instead of teaching that day, Emmy helped settle the bedraggled soldiers that were now camped on the green, and ran for more bandages like the ones Dot had been carrying earlier. Their men had suffered a horrid retreat across the moors while the advancing army continued to batter at them.

When the soldiers' demands on her time seem to ebb, she fled towards her sanctuary. She had misjudged her timing, and two guards were coming up from the gate. Not wanting any sort of confrontation, she turned to a different set of stairs as if she had meant to go that way, and escaped upwards to find herself on the inland wall.

She could see the besieging army sat in wait, their fires dividing the sky with parallel lines of smoke, white against the grey. They moved about like ants on a hill, and they blocked the access to the mainland at the start of the cape.

More rain threatened, and even from here she could still hear the water. It echoed through the stone beneath her feet, a vibration as if the castle shuddered at the assault. She shuddered too. There would be no carriage to take her home now.

Fishing boats could not reach the castle by sea, but food was grown and raised within, and the stores were stocked full . . . they were trapped, but safe and well-fed. Everyone said they would outlast the waiting army, that their enemies had no easy way to catch fish, and that they would face winter weather soon. But Emmy knew it was part bravado. There were sheep, flocks of 'em, up on the headland, plus deer, coney, pheasant, and so much more, to say nothing of supply wagons arriving from afar. She could see one approaching the camp now.

Her gaze travelled down the rugged coastline, this way, that. Could she slip through, unnoticed by the perimeter guards of both the castle and the besiegers? It might be a foolish plan—who knew how far she would have to walk the wide beach to find a way up the cliffs. She could walk for days. She could run out of fresh water and find none to drink.

She spent the night in the cell and returned to the children in their upper room the next morning, blinking against the sound of the crashing waves below. A new bluster darkened the sky, and the awful sound of the angry ocean swelled to unprecedented heights.

As always, lessons on counting and arithmetic were first, but instead she taught the children songs, justifying it in her head because music was math, after all. It helped distract her, somewhat, and the children loved it.

That night the cell had an occupant, so she was forced to return to her room. She tossed and turned, willing sleep, but every time she began to doze, the wind would whip up into a scream, and the frothing water below would slap and hiss, churning out anger at her foolishness, her belligerence. Why didn't she listen to her father? Or the advice from the man when she arrived? Now, she could not go home, could not leave this place of torture. She couldn't even send a messenger.

She wrapped her blanket around her head, desperate for anything to muffle the haunting sounds. She had locked the window latch tight, and closed the drapes, but again she woke to find the curtains pulled back and the salt spray shimmering on open air.

Emmy leapt out of bed and relocked the window, banging at it to see if she could somehow jam it even tighter. "By God, leave me be," she cried. She sobbed and shuddered. She wanted to scream. It seemed she woke so many times in a night now, she wasn't sure she ever slept more than a few moments altogether, and her thoughts were becoming blurry.

She tugged the drapes, thinking she would sew them shut if she had to, and crawled back into bed, weary beyond belief. She cried little sobs along with the weeping lady, fully understanding now why one would want to cry every night here.

She survived the next day, a Sunday, by sitting out of sight near the green where the soldiers were camped. They made so much noise, she couldn't hear the surf. She dozed, her head against stone and her shawl tucked around her, until dusk brought a cold wind.

Back in her room, she lit a roaring fire and tucked into bed. She woke while the fire still sparked and snapped, but it did nothing to drown out the sea, or the wailing. She rode a wave of exhaustion, dozing in and out, as the firelight died.

Then she woke, again, and she was sat on the window sill, one leg hitched up over the ledge. Emmy screamed and scrambled from the precipice, scraping her legs and fingers in her haste, and falling into the room onto her backside.

That was enough for her.

She lit a candle with shaking hands and pulled out her bag and her belongings, and knew immediately she could never take it all, not and carry it herself. With a little sob, she began pulling on everything she owned over top of each other, all her underclothes, her smock, her second nightdress, and her one fancy dress. She wrapped her shawl over it all and then looked at what was left.

Her precious books. Her ma's bible, her teacher's book of lessons, and her grandmother's hand-painted book of flowers. A tear dropped on the cover, and she quickly dabbed it dry.

There was no way she could take them. Even if she could carry the weight, they might get wet on the coming journey. She would have to start over. On a whim, she went to the desk and wrote a note to Dot, asking her to keep the books safe, and she would return when she could. She knew Dot would understand.

Emmy looked at what was left. She would need provisions, a knife, her flint and frayed cotton for tinder, and the pouch of coin she had earned. And there was her blanket. How would she take anything, though?

Then she saw the solution. She used her blanket to bundle leftover bread and apple from the day before, added her table knife, hair brush, tinder kit, and her few coins, and tied it by the corners. Castle folk wouldn't question if they saw her, she often carried her blanket and wore her shawl when she sought refuge in the cell.

She snuck down and waited for the guard change, slipping out the gate in a moment of inattention and striking off the carriage track immediately to take cover in the gorse brush and sea grasses. The sand should be a handful of steps below. In her study of the besieging army from the wall, she had seen that they blocked the narrow strip of land between the castle and the headland, but not the beaches to each side. No one could do much but walk for miles trying to find a way up the sea cliffs, so there was no need to guard the beach. Since it was dark, she could slip down to the sand and walk away, no one the wiser.

Now she crept downslope only to have her foot sink into churning water that surged and drained, before surging again. The beach was bigger, she had thought, and a way was clear. But now the moon sailed free of the clouds, and instead of sand there was a vast expanse of waves and foam stark against the dark water. Far distant, where the besieging army kept guard, was a narrow strip of beach up under the base of the cliffs.

How did the beach change so much? She understood tides in theory, but to see it like this, so vastly different than what she had seen from the wall . . . well, it was astonishing. The water below her surged again, and she scrambled up, hoping no one would notice the brush trembling and shaking with her passage.

She crawled along, inching her way towards the enemy encampment. If she were found, she'd be jailed as a spy, and likely used like a whore. Her father's accusation flashed through her mind. Maybe she would be better to just fall into the water and let it drag her down.

"No," she breathed, while she crawled over jagged rocks, catching her shawl on reaching branches and shoving her bundle before her.

After an endless time, she made it to the sand. In fact, the strip of beach might be a bit wider now, she thought. Soon the dawn would come, and her chance would go with it. She could hear voices and smell woodsmoke, that's how close she was now to the besieging army.

The ocean roared, and she wanted to roar with it as she made it to the sheer cliff and began walking.

Light came too soon, and pounding rain with it, making random rocks shower down from the cliffs above at regular intervals. The surf ebbed away until the beach was huge again, but the cliffs were her only shelter from being spotted, so she moved on, her bundle on her head in hopes that would save her if a big one came down. She also needed to stay close to search for a footpath up off the beach.

When she finally found an animal trail, she climbed, slid, slipped, and scrambled until she stood on the headland far above the sea. The castle was a distant speck, and looked like nothing more than sea cliff from here.

She looked down and her head spun. A temptation came over her to just tip forward and end it all. No more struggle, no more grief, no more cold and wet. The ocean surf roared in with the next wave, and the old familiar weeping rose up with it.

Emmy thought she might lose her mind. She fell to her knees as a fresh spate of rain and wind lashed her. Rage gripped her then, flooding her with heat, burning her cold skin. There at the crest of the bluff she faced her rage . . . against the sea, against fate for taking her mother, against reality that meant war and conflict, against the loss of her job, and against whatever had happened to those other mistresses that created this awful curse.

The heat burned through her like a firestorm. She tipped back her head and wailed.

What was the point of returning? She felt the real fear of nothing better than life on a pig farm. She remembered her Pa's face, that flash she had seen. It was grief. Then she felt shame for leaving him all alone. The fact that he was alone brought her rage on again.

She sobbed and wailed, pounding the hard soil with her fists and crying out at the furious wind and rain. And when her rage drained away, like the tide had below her, she came to terms with it. She could see more possibilities for her future. She gasped and gulped, and the wind seemed to calm along with her.

She stood again and gazed down over the sea. It was quiet, just for a moment. The tide seemed at its lowest point. Perhaps it was turning, a moment of stillness, the barest hint of peace.

Then the wind lifted, waves leapt up and roared inwards, sweeping the beach, and the weeping returned. There was a strong desire, a *need* to jump to make it all stop.

"No," she whispered. She stepped closer to the edge, startled by how steep a grade she had climbed. Her head spun.

"No," she said, louder. A new rage came over her then, not the rage of grief, of loss, but an anger at this curse that would not let her be. It had ruined her job and now tried to take her life.

"You can't have me," she screamed at the waves.

She scooped up her bundle and held it under one arm, then covered her ears. She retreated a step, but also, she sank into childhood memories of soft voices, her parents in the next room, the crackle of the fire, the squeak of the woodstove door as her pa added a log. The fire popped. Her mother laughed.

Emmy stepped back again, the memory strong and alive. She was loved, she had a home to return to. Yes, there was grief, as any life had. She continued making steps back and back, then she turned and walked steady over the headland and into the moors.

After a while, she took her hands from her ears. There was no sound of the surf, no sobbing woman. She had broken the curse. Emmy fell to her knees and wept with relief.

❧

"Hi, Pa."

He was bent over the kitchen garden, pulling weeds. She was

so nervous, she held her blanket bundle in front of her like a shield, gripping it hard. It had taken her three days and nights to walk here from the top of the cliff, and she must look a sight. Her once rose-pink blanket was grubby brown, torn, and even singed on one corner.

He turned.

"Emmy!"

In two quick strides, he scooped her up, blanket bundle and all, and swung her around with a whoop of joy. He set her back on her feet, swiping away tears he'd never admit to, and took up her face in his hands.

"You came back. Did you hear about the new job for ye, then?"

She was crying too, but she laughed, dropped her bundle, and snuggled into his embrace. "Job? What job do you speak of?"

He laughed with her and squeezed her tight. "I thought ye must've heard about the need for a new mistress here."

"No, Pa, I just came home," she said, frank and honest, and contrite. "It was awful there, and I missed you." He gave her another big hug. Across the lane, Emmy saw Goodwife Meggie grinning at her. Yes, the crone had won her bet, to be sure.

"Well, there might be work for ya, wouldn't that be a treat, eh?" Pa turned and pulled her towards the house. "Come on, then, I'll put the kettle on."

"Pa, what happened to Mistress Jenny? Did she move away?" Mistress Jenny was the one that had taught her and certified her for teaching.

His sad face warned her, but not near enough for what was coming. "Ach, she took a fall, poor soul. Died of a broken neck right instant, they say. Only three days ago, now. Was the strangest thing."

Emmy had stopped dead in her tracks. "A f-f-fall?"

Her pa pulled the door open and waved her in. "Yeah, out the second story of the tavern. People kept hearing someone crying, too, but no one's sure who it is."

The sound of surf whispered in her ears, and she smelt salt. The curse had taken a life in place of her own. But was she free?

Weeping started.

A VIEW OF WATER

DINO PARENTI

1

The boy died in a muggy Los Angeles July.

By the time Christmas ads were bombarding radios and televisions in the States, the parents had moved to a new house on the northern coast of Belize.

She was Alma, thirty-five, a dental hygienist. A sneaky kind of pretty that once exposed could never be repacked.

He was Diego, thirty-seven, a renowned concert pianist. Not as handsome as Alma was pretty, but neither was he a homely man. He wore his disproportions regally, in the vein of a janky mutt who'd spent a few stints in shelters.

Emmitt was six, their best elements compressed into a gem of his mother's wild black locks and father's dimpled grins.

Not long after Emmitt's passing, a mutual friend confided to Diego of an artists' house situated on a bluff within a secluded cove in Belize. Its original bohemian owners decided their twilight years were better spent in Denver growing pot and doting over grandchildren than risking malaria, and they'd just put it on the market.

"It's one of those multi-level *architectural* magazine homes," the friend had boasted after slurping a second daiquiri, "replete with cantilevers and big open spaces, but with a touch of whimsy. Pottery-shard mosaics, car-part garden sculptures arrayed about it. So *very* Alma. You know, hippie shit."

He'd always had a crush on Alma, long before Diego was in the picture.

Drunken slight to Alma aside, Diego was intrigued. Despite the heat issues—it gave Alma headaches and made his skin peel—

the impulse to relocate, far enough from the pain of their So-Cal lives that they didn't have to smell it anymore, was too adamant to ignore.

A place that fit their need for isolation and rediscovery.

⌒

Alma fell instantly in love with the house on their initial visit to Belize. The quirky sculptures and open floor plan. The small, natural crescent harbour of sandstone plinths. So thunderstruck she was by it that she was willing to overlook its proximity to the ocean she always professed to dread.

"It feels . . . like a lover's embrace," she said, eyes squinted upon the striated surf, as if auguring beneath its surface for gems only she knew the existence of. "It's so glorious."

And while not exactly to Diego's taste—so much ubiquitous sun hurt his eyes—it inarguably suited their needs. He just quietly asked the realtor for the deed and took the liberty of signing both their names.

The only access to the property was a single-lane dirt road that snaked through three miles of jungle before hitting a highway leading to a small town of young tourists and ex-patriot Yanks and Brits. Familiarity at hand if it came calling, but they wouldn't spend much time outside their new home.

Their first day there, Diego grudgingly let Alma convince him to toss their cellphones into the surf.

With all contact to their prior lives severed, Alma christened the house and surrounding cove *Curación*, the Spanish word for healing, a word that took Diego a month to properly pronounce.

"You keep accenting the wrong syllables," Alma, after a perfunctory sigh, would frequently remind him.

2

There *was* one other way into *Curación* by land.

Alma and Diego were barely there a week when they spotted the first surfer on their beach.

Diego saw him from the music room while tuning his piano. The room extended beyond the bluff, sporting a 180-degree view of jungle and ocean panorama. That had sold him to *Curación* more than anything else, especially after Alma opted to convert the separate guest beach cabana as her personal artist studio. That left him the entire main house to stage his quarter-million-dollar Steinway grand piano.

But the surfer's unexpected intrusion rendered their sanctuary moot, and so Diego dropped his tuning lever and marched down to the surf.

Alma stood cross-armed in the doorway of the studio, glaring at the interloper with a white-eyed, unblinking disapproval that crippled most retorts and excuses.

Diego plodded to where the surfer's towel and bag sat on the sand and waited for him to ride in his latest wave. He wasn't even out of the water and Diego was already grilling: "How the hell did you get here? This is private property!"

The twenty-something in his teal wetsuit and samurai man-bun shrugged and pointed towards the western bluff. Explained to Diego how someone in town told him about the cleft through the rock and of a paradise cove beyond.

That it was his last day of vacation and he'd wanted a special memory.

"That so? Show me this cleft."

The surfer gathered his things, smirking as if to humour the conspiracies of crusty old boozers. Diego felt the ageist slight in the younger man's expression, and though he wasn't yet forty, he caught enough in the mirror to realize the assumption. Grief kneaded the skin with rough hands. Lathered on tough courses of grime and decline.

They trudged down the beach to a narrow artery concealed behind boulders and drooping foliage that punched through the southern peninsula of rock. One look through the sluiceway told Diego everything: during low tide, it offered a straight shot from the other end into their cove.

The tide was already rising, so Diego handed the surfer the four hundred dollars he had in his wallet and sent him through.

"Don't come back here. Keep quiet about this tunnel and this cove, or I'll bribe the local *policía* to tune your ass up."

The following morning, armed with a concrete drill and several sheets of heavy gauge diamond mesh found in the garage, Diego walked the twenty yards to the opposite end of the cleft at lowest tide and bolted the steel mesh across the opening.

Despite a slathering of sunblock, he still suffered patches of second-degree burns.

3

A month in, and with no further interruptions from the outside world, Diego offered to hook up a sound system in Alma's cabana so she could enjoy music while she worked on her ceramics. He wanted to do her a kindness, especially since she was less likely to ask for it herself. It also allowed him to demonstrate his worth. His skill and ability outside the soft, at-hand comforts of city life.

Alma watched him work. While he kept clothed outside to prevent peeling, inside he worked shirtless. Their less processed diet had already yielded results for them. Linens no longer pinched and delineated less flattering topographies, but fluttered against trimmer tummies like loosely tacked spinnakers.

As he ran speaker line along false beams, Alma said, "Maybe I can do something for you in return?"

Diego simpered from the stepladder. His few attempts at intimacy following Emmitt's death came off less like performances as they did dissonant, pre-concert tune-ups. They've yet to try in *Curación*.

"I was thinking of making a piece of art for your music room," she said.

Diego paused his unspooling of wire. Waited for a smile to at least appear level before nodding and accepting. By then Alma was staring out at the golden waters, mouthing silent stratagems.

That night, Diego was startled awake by a nightmare. He'd been having anxiety dreams since arriving in Belize, as if the clean ocean air had finally ruptured whatever the smog and congestion of L.A. had congealed.

Emmitt and Alma were playing with a Ouija board. Diego wasn't a fan of his five-year-old son being spoon-fed superstition, often scoffing at Alma for leaving Emmitt's teeth under his pillow for the tooth fairy. Alma came from a line of supposed *Santerías* and *brujas*, and though not a practitioner herself, she saw no harm in Emmitt playing near the fantastical and supernatural.

In the dream, they were back in their L.A. house. Emmitt and

Alma on the lawn off the back patio as they sometimes did, surrounded by candles, Ouija board between them that had been handmade by her father from a glue-up of mahogany planks and burned-in characters and sigils. Both were mumbling questions just out of Diego's earshot. Behind them, they had staked fishing poles into the grass, the lines fed over the low rock wall surrounding the saltwater lagoon that came with the house, and which never had fish.

Diego was practicing on the patio; an odd occurrence since he never would've exposed such an exquisite, expensive piano to the elements. As he ran a line of Chopin, he heard Emmitt and Alma giggle seconds before a column of fire geysered from the Ouija board, shooting flame fifty feet into the air.

Emmitt and Alma were instantly engulfed.

Diego screamed, but as if welded to it, he couldn't budge from the piano bench.

And so, he watched.

Watched his son and wife, blackened under orange flames, as they continued guiding the planchette across the Ouija board's surface, asking questions as their flesh curled and molted from their bones, just as both their fishing poles caught simultaneous bites, bending sharply towards the pond. Something too large for so small a body of water, however deep it was in the centre, spinning out line until the reels smoked . . .

Diego rolled out of bed, gasping. Upon gathering himself, he shuffled to the kitchen for some water. In passing the music room, he saw Alma standing in the middle of it, gazing at the only wall without windows. An orange gibbous moon gilded her form in the dark room—an anthropomorphic lava flow, veined in filaments of fire.

Before he could speak, Alma nodded. "My gift to you is going to be a mural. A mural made of sea glass."

She all but proclaimed it, then drifted back to bed, whispering more indistinguishable tactics to herself, sounding to Diego how she and Emmitt did while shrouded in flames.

Instead of water, Diego downed a shot of whiskey, the whine of fishing reels still squealing in his head.

☙

Diego kept dreaming of Emmitt and Alma, though seldom as

horrific as the fire dream. More evasive and frustrating. In one dream, they were fishing at the fishless pond again, looking back every now and then to giggle at Diego, as if swapping secrets they never could've known about him.

In another dream, Emmitt plopped the Ouija board on Diego's piano on the day he died, steering his planchette while the party guests watched, this as David played *La Campanella* by Liszt on a loop until the flesh started shredding from his fingertips.

4

Almost a full year since Emmitt's passing, and the days in *Curación* meandered into each other like overlayed filmstrips. Diego and Alma only occupied the main house together to eat and sleep, otherwise they were ensconced within their respective creative spaces.

Often Diego would glance out the window while fiddling on the piano for some composition loath to show itself, and see Alma at water's edge, one hand bunching up her skirt while dredging the wet sand for sea glass. Back in L.A., he couldn't get her to set foot in the saltwater pond, let alone go to the beach. Not only could she not swim, she feared the ocean in general. Its vast, unseen, and perilous nature beneath its reflective, inviting surface.

Now she was knee-deep in swirling saltwater daily, with a nary a scrunch of apprehension on her face.

One hot afternoon as he sat at the piano, fog-headed and uninspired, his fingers sliding atop the keys as if employing a Ouija board planchette, he found himself staring at the mosaic Alma had begun, working exclusively at night after he went to bed.

The upper left corner of the wall was already covered in amber and sea-foam green tiles the size of nickels. The translucent shards caught the light, lobbing it back softly, but the image itself remained abstract, and he wondered if she had a plan, or was simply winging it. Before he broke big as a concert pianist, Alma essentially supported them both with her small dental practice, with hardly any time to work on her own creative ceramics. When

Emmitt came along, there was simply no time to work on her art, while he practiced his morning-to-night.

His fingers absently plunked a C-chord, but it sounded off, down-pitched despite its recent tuning. Perhaps the humidity was warping the soundboard, distending the strings just out of 440 hertz.

When he looked out at the shore again, Alma was looking right back up at him from under the brim of a floppy hat, as if snagging onto the same discordant notes ferried in the breeze.

5

In their second month at *Curación,* they drove to the nearby town for fresh supplies.

The place was small but lively. Bustling hole-in-the-wall bars, eateries, and street vendors. Fried plantains, moped fuel, and brackish water jousted in the air for olfactory dominance.

Alma needed new sources of glass. She'd scoured their limited beach and found as much as she could, which wasn't in the tones of blues and reds she claimed to need to continue the mosaic.

While she wove through street kiosks in search of coloured glass, Diego shopped for toiletries. Upon cleaning out one vendor of his aloe moisturizer, he caught himself admiring a pretty mother with her little boy browsing headscarves.

Despite the heat, the cold punch of memory iced his veins: Alma and three-year-old Emmitt at the time, perusing the glass case at a candy shop. For such a quietly perfect moment, the tableau had churned up hot inadequacy, as if his family was a borrowed suit too pricy for his chequebook.

So lost in his reverie and gawking that at first, he failed to note Alma staring at him from between fluttering Incan rugs. His posture wilted at once. To compensate, he pointed haphazardly at a mirror within a kiosk.

Before she even got to him, he was rambling about how cool the circular mirror would look in the bathroom.

She stepped to it, and Diego stepped behind her. Though the frame was a lovely, bleached wood, the glass was tarnished and wavy, twisting all it reflected.

"I'll buy it if you want," said Diego, smiling. Suddenly he felt horribly self-conscious of his dimples. They reminded him of nail holes on walls from which once hung family pictures.

Alma thought a moment, then shrugged. "Nah. We deserve a cleaner likeness."

Diego watched her stroll away, her body limber and receptive to the sun, leaving him to blame his creative doldrums solely at the mirror and on the vendor eyeing him from the side as if he might start ripping items off the shelves and smashing them.

After dumping supplies into the truck, Diego wandered the market some more, the air in his chest stuffy and stale. In those moments, he felt the most aware of how wrapped in clothing he was compared to all the skin on display around him fortunate enough to tan and darken instead of sear and blister.

Eventually he came upon an old bearded local minding a spot under a canopy. Strewn about his table were all manner of electronical components—ham radio sets, reel-to-reel tape recorders, receivers, speakers, gutted amplifiers, and televisions.

The old man, Hispanic and sun-bronzed to the gums, smiled warmly and nodded, and Diego returned the gesture. Behind him leaned several bowed bookcases of technical manuals which gradually morphed to encyclopedia sets, to books of local history, and finally to volumes of black magic, Santeria, and even the occult.

Diego ran a hand along the cool edge of an old stereo amplifier. He loved recording equipment, especially the outmoded stuff, despite his use of computers. The metal felt honest, analog, quenching to the touch.

But it was upon regarding the books that a strange inspiration flooded him—a kind of hunger only sated by the quirkiest of fare—and he drew out his wallet.

Later, when he found Alma inspecting a table of seashells, her eyes immediately arched at the canvas bag Diego carried. "You bought something? *You?*"

"What? I can succumb to an impulse buy like the next man," he said, patting the bag before starting for their truck.

6

A few days after their drive into town, Diego watched from the music room as Alma bent over something along the shore. He grabbed the theatre binoculars that had somehow made the journey to Belize, and focused in from behind the concealment of curtains.

In her hands, a pair of pliers that were working free the teeth from a beached reef shark. A pile of about a dozen bloody triangular bits were already amassed on a napkin by her knee.

For another twenty minutes he spied dumbfounded until she finished, cupping her bounty back into the studio.

Afterwards, he sat at the piano and wrung his brain for inspiration. The last time he'd played for anyone was during his birthday party at the L.A. house. The day Emmitt died. The memories seized him suddenly, like blankets whipped off beds to reveal swollen humps of things lurid and grotesque.

The guests eating up his expert playing, including a couple of female musicians new to the philharmonic, who hovered around the piano like seagulls circling a beach picnic . . .

Alma and Emmitt huddled away from the others, both grumpy over the day's unusually moist heat, engaged in a game of secrets; Emmitt cupping his hand to Alma's ear and pointing in the piano's general direction, whereupon she would reply in turn . . .

The fading concentric rings of the saltwater pond, winking under strands of patio string lights . . .

The images resurfaced now and then, months removed and in a different country, in transient zoetrope flashes that Diego's mind promptly slurped back up.

He studied the mural. It covered a solid third of the wall by then but was no less vague in its imagery. A wooded space? A landscape scene? It's browns and greens undulated in alternating bands like sine waves. Earlier he'd examined up close the latest work Alma had done overnight. It read different from afar—more uniform—until he realized she had started using buttons from her clothing in lieu of glass.

Verifying through the theatre binoculars that Alma was still down in the cabana, Diego went to the closet and fished out the canvas bag from their trip to town.

Back in the music room, he drew the piano bench up to the east window where he could keep watch on Alma, and pulled out the books he'd bought from the vendor. Back in L.A. he never would've dared wasted a dime on such foolishness, but down here in their seclusion, the world took on a fresh tint. The humidity and salted air opened up a secondary set of pores, as if his skin rotated them over like an array of replacement shark teeth.

He had one chapter left in the book on electronic voice phenomena and hadn't decided yet whether to follow it with *Parapsychology for Dummies* or the tattered volume of *On Contacting the Dead: from Ouija Boards to Ghost Boxes.*

7

One especially warm night, Diego was awakened by a voice drifting from the music room. He got up and draped on a linen shirt to investigate, the material scratchy against his dread-prickled skin.

Leaning his head in, he saw Alma, long after he thought she'd finished her mural work for the night. Her back was to him. The full moon washed her in stone and bone, and the first thing he noticed was how thin she had gotten. Even in shorts, he saw the more pronounced jut of hip, the deep concave swale between shoulder blades.

She appeared to be cradling something in her arms. Cooing to it, as if were a pet or a child.

"Sweetheart?" he said, and immediately she froze like a video frame still. Even seemed to judder for a split-second through his sleep-grimed gawk.

She ran her hands down her sides as if to wipe them of sweat before turning to face him with unfocused, sunken eyes. Her cheekbones evoked the sharp edges of a coffee table that could maim shins. And yet her beauty still peeked through in fleeting twinkles from the rifts and hollows, especially the tiny cleft in her chin, which raged like a third eye whenever they fought or made love.

Her head slowly turned then, and something of a grin pushed through. "I need a new source. For mural tiles. The shark's teeth were nice, but I don't expect one to beach itself for me every day. That's asking a lot of a hunter."

"I . . . suppose," was all Diego managed.

"Incidentally, the high tide's been creeping close to the cabana's door. I wonder if maybe berming some sand would redirect or funnel the water?"

Diego just nodded, and as she walked past him, he grazed her shoulder. It felt like lukewarm skirt-steak left all day on a countertop.

From the music room he watched her trudge across the sand and into her cabana. Then he looked at the mosaic, now about halfway done. The new spot of red on the bottom right of the wall exploded like a gunshot wound.

The shark teeth, arranged in something of a concentric floral design, dyed a bright vermillion.

The image needled a chill through his belly, and when he absently tried to close his shirt, he realized that all the buttons were missing.

⌒⌒

At dawn's first light, Diego set off for town, telling Alma he needed things for the piano.

When he returned several hours later, he waited, assuring that she was occupied in the cabana, before sneaking in a ham radio, a receiver, a couple of reel-to-reel recorders, and other assorted mechanical odds-and-ends. Only later did he realize the folly of being clandestine: what he was going to make would be done in the same room Alma was crafting her mosaic in. She was going to see it.

Maybe he just wanted a head start, he told himself. He had everything he needed, and what he couldn't find, the old man minding the tent claimed he could get within a week if the price was right. Diego had doled out hundreds on the table like a poker dealer.

8

The next morning, hung-over from downing a bottle of chardonnay while working eighteen straight hours on his own project, he happened to glance at the beach and saw Alma crouched over a body on the sand.

Even as the low sun further stirred the agony in his skull, he pushed through the binoculars nonetheless to verify that it was not only indeed a human body out there, but that Alma was doing what he'd hoped his mind only tricked him into believing she was doing: yanking out the corpse's teeth with pliers.

Diego dropped everything and hurried down.

When he got to Alma, she was already wiping the pliers against a hand towel draped over her forearm in the vein of a hotel maître d.

In her hand were at least two dozen extracted human teeth. The bloody roots evoked tiny tuning forks.

"I found him floating where the waves broke," she said. "I'm guessing that he hit his head paddleboarding by the reef."

The wind contoured the shirt against her body, slipping apart at one point and yanking open because the buttons were gone. She was naked beneath. Her skin, normally a glowing mocha, had turned sallow and loose. She hadn't shaved in weeks.

Diego crouched by the wet-suit clad body. Middle-aged, bald, and chunky. The gash on his head certainly could've been caused by coral.

Alma picked through the teeth. "I think they'll hold the dyes well." She gazed at the surf, a smile pitching first port, then starboard. "It's so . . . glorious."

She walked back to the cabana then, and Diego remained knelt by the body, staring at its bloody grimace as if expecting the corpse to offer testimony.

He buried the surfer in a deep part of the jungle, then hid the paddleboard until he could figure out what to do with it. The notion that Alma had been bone-dry after supposedly hauling the body in from the surf was mere whisper against his aching body.

In the shower later, tiny parmesan shavings of skin curled at his toes before draining away. Even in the shade of mango trees, the sun had still found him, raking his shoulders and neck with its claws.

He worked on his device that evening until it was nearly completed.

Alma, finally appearing to work on her mural after 2 a.m., looked at the piano through a cocked head. Its top lid and music rack had been removed, the strings and bridges exposed. Electrical wires were connected to every string, spilling over the rails and hooking into some manner of radio setup. The hammers that would've otherwise been situated within the action connected deep beyond the keys, were now arrayed above each black and white key from a 2x4 screwed directly into the side rails. These, like the strings, had individual wires likewise running back to the same hodgepodge radio setup.

She glanced at Diego.

"It's nice having a distraction," she said, her smile level, then started gluing human teeth to his wall, some dyed the colour of persimmons, others cleaned to polished bone.

9

When Diego went into town for their next supply run, the antenna he'd ordered had arrived, along with blank tape reels.

Aerial stored in the truck, he returned to the market instead of going home. He wasn't sure what he wanted—a different kind of air, the frequency of other people, an opportunity to flirt, even if his odds towards success seemed slight. Like Alma, he'd started losing weight, neglecting health and hygiene, obsessed with converting his piano into a receiver.

A musical Ouija board to speak with his boy. To ask Emmitt questions.

Wandering the market, he caught his reflection in the same round mirror he almost bought for Alma on their first market visit. He wore a tattered, very unalluring t-shirt. All his nice button-shirts had been sacrificed to the mosaic, the totality of which only hinted to familiarity in the reptile regions of his brain, fuelling a fight-or-flight response he didn't understand.

Eventually he found himself in one of the more jumping cantinas. He settled at the bar and stirred a mai tai for the better part of an hour, listening to various hacks playing bad covers of Beatles and Elton John ditties on an off-tuned upright piano while others sang along, equally deaf to tone.

A barrage of memories tracer-fired through his brain during shrill choruses of "Rocket Man".

Himself playing Beethoven on his birthday while flirting with the woman all but draped across the closed soundboard . . .

Emmitt, grumbling and wiping sweat from his brow, wandering towards the low stone wall and the saltwater pond beyond . . .

A brief glimpse of Alma, who'd retired early because of a

migraine, peering between the drapes of their bedroom with the theatre binoculars, staring at him and the woman at the piano . . .

The lone scream of a woman shortly thereafter, followed by men hollering and the splashing of someone jumping into the saltwater pond . . .

The distant approach of firetruck sirens . . .

The honk of a sputtering moped outside the cabana snapped Diego back to the present discordance of sozzled patrons mangling Billy Joel's "Piano Man".

He couldn't tell how long he'd drifted. The duration of the spell. He sipped at his flat drink and at length struck up a conversation with a couple of surfers upon overhearing them lamenting the lack of primo peak sets.

After swapping general banter and bonding over their mutual California upbringing, Diego casually mentioned a secluded cove not too far away with excellent breakers. There was no forethought, no overt machinations beyond a simple need to share something distinctive with other human beings. He even drew them a crude map to the cave on a cocktail napkin, plus the best times to ride, usually at the break of dawn.

The two young men thanked him and even paid for his drink, and for the first time since arriving in Belize, Diego felt a sense of inertia. Of potential.

❧

Back in *Curación*, Diego hauled the antenna out of the truck, and in crossing the yard from the carport, finally registered what he'd only noted subconsciously before: Alma had thoroughly stripped all the garden sculptures of their mosaic tiles.

Later, before the tide got too high, he hunched down the cleft through the southern peninsula and took down the mesh barricade.

With the day's remaining light, he installed the antenna on the roof above the music room.

10

It took two days, but the surfers came.
They came, and they died.

No sooner had Diego checked the beach at dawn through the binoculars than he spotted movement along the water's break.

Alma, naked, wading waist-high through the swells, gliding through them like a knife through foam.

On the beach, spread out a dozen yards to either side of her, a pair of bodies parching on the sand.

Diego didn't run down to the beach this time. Apprehension had slackened his muscles, hooked weights to his reflexes.

He glanced long enough at the first corpse to catch the bloodied mouth and head. The blond buzz cut of the more mild-mannered of the two surfers whose fate he'd inked in a dark cantina two days earlier.

Alma had returned to the shore, one of their upright boards beside her as the water waked against it.

Diego joined her, and for a while they looked out at the water together. The tide was ebbing and the surf skulked, soft and glassine. He couldn't look at her. Looking felt like fake confession to someone else's interpretation of affront, and they'd moved too far to spare random contrition a moment's thought.

Eventually Alma spoke.

"People keep washing up on our beach. It's not easy dragging them out of the surf."

Her buttonless linen shirt stretched and flapped behind her gaunt nakedness like a windsock.

"Last night the tide reached the threshold of the cabana and smothered the porch. I'm worried the water will eventually slip over. Ruin the bamboo flooring."

Diego nodded. "I'll take care of it."

After she retreated to the studio, he went to the storage shed and fetched a shovel. For the next four hours he dug and trenched and buried the two surfers beneath, forming a berm of three-foot-high sand that should redirect water from the door.

That night, he showered under the coldest water he could stand, shrieking with each curl of skin that sloughed from his back and shoulders. His *Mestizo* shade, so much lighter than Alma's more indigenous hue, reminding him now of its flaws, and he wept while smearing handfuls of aloe onto the screaming red meat.

Unable to sleep, he sat on the bedroom floor while Alma worked on the mural, adding clean human teeth along the bottom above the floorboards. That they were undyed made it more unnerving for Diego, their arrangement in oblong patterns like a herd of sheep, or thought bubbles without words.

After she left, he returned to the piano. He checked that all the lines were connected, all the hammers poised perfectly above each key before turning on the ham radio and the random frequency sweeper the ghost books called a Shack-hack.

Pulling the piano bench to the radio, he sat down, teeth gritting as raw, red skin sandpapered over muscle, then gripped the microphone.

"Emmitt, are you . . . out there? Somewhere maybe, listening?"

He was drifting off an hour later when the ping of a G note juddered him fully awake.

‖

Diego sat at the piano bench while Alma grouted dyed teeth to the wall.

At length she turned and panned over his contraption.

"Your project is . . . interesting. Is it what I think it is? Some kind of radio?"

It wasn't a direct query on its efficacy, but Diego figured it was as close as he was going to get.

"It is indeed," he said, and pointed to the easel. On it, a chart of piano keys he'd drawn on poster board. "Twenty-six uppercase letters plus twenty-six lowercase letters, equalling fifty-two white keys. The ham radio's been modified to randomly scan frequencies. You ask a question into the microphone, and if . . . there's a response, the corresponding letter is hammered on the corresponding key. It's a rather expensive . . . ghost box."

He expected sarcasm, or at least lukewarm chuckles, but Alma just nodded and glued. "And did you get one?"

Her tone was too neutral. He didn't care for it one bit. "One what?"

"A response?"

For nights on end, he'd been trying to reach Emmitt—to get a word, a sign, anything—and only two letters kept getting played: G3 and G5.

"Just . . . letters. *K* and *R*. I figure Emmitt, because . . . he couldn't spell yet ... But it's probably just interference from KREM. It's one of the biggest radio stations in Belize."

He hated confessing that, but would've hated feigning a victory even more.

Alma smiled. "If you say so."

The wall was nearly filled. Diego was no closer to figuring its meaning, yet he didn't like at all what it suggested.

"Thirty-two adult teeth cover roughly the area of a credit card," Alma said, slathering glue on a blank square of wall. "About twenty credit cards fill a square foot. That's about six-hundred-and-forty teeth, or twenty mouths per square foot. This wall is one-hundred-and-eight square feet. About one-hundred-and-three square feet is already done, leaving me about five square feet worth of teeth to go. Or about ... a hundred more mouths."

The ham radio crackled and feedbacked. The dissonance buzzed the room like warring mosquitos.

"You're crazy," Diego said.

His words lingered like their own kind of radio static.

Alma frowned as if posed a question of serious philosophical merit.

"I don't think *crazy* applies. *Crazy* is a crutch for lesser developed imaginations."

Diego chortled, and he felt the lie of it sizzle his skin—grossly peeled and baked red, as if he'd been flayed down to the musculature. Sometimes when he'd squeeze the radio's microphone, blood would wring from the creases in his hands. "What does this mosaic mean?"

Alma shrugged. "It's a secret. One that Emmitt told me."

"I don't believe you. Anything Emmitt told you he would've told me, too."

Alma grouted another tooth in place, this one dyed dark brown. The centre of a red flower, and for the first time something concrete as to her intentions nudged at Diego.

"You're cruel," he said.

Wiping smears of dye against her shirt, Alma cocked her head back at Diego. "How so?"

"All that," Diego said, finger wagging side to side, indicating the bottom of the mural. The part with the undyed teeth. "Is that supposed to be ... the wall?"

Alma looked at the area curiously. "What wall?"

"Are you serious? The rock wall. The one bordering the pond. The one Emmitt easily climbed over."

The wall should've been higher. He'd always told her that. And Alma had always promised to call someone to have it heightened, or at least augmented with tall wrought iron. Because Diego was too busy with concert season to deal with such things.

And as if Alma had read his thoughts, she said, "*You* promised to teach him to swim."

As with all their discourses since Emmitt's drowning, she never expressed anger. Never really expressed much emotion at all. Diego supposed it stemmed from the trauma of it all, though he suspected resentment played a massive part in her apathy. Emmitt had been *his* responsibility in that moment, as she'd gone to bed to sleep off a migraine. The implication was clear, but Emmitt was also both their responsibility for his brief lifetime, and for that they would forever share culpability, and so Diego bit back on escalating things further.

"Can you . . . at least tell me the secret?"

Another frown. "Emmett told it to *me* on the day he died. He asked me never to share it. Most especially with *you*."

"Goddammit," Diego growled, rising to his feet and splaying hands in frantic circles towards the wall. "Are you gonna tell me what this whole fucking thing means or not?"

Alma adhered another tooth. Diego noticed her hands then, smeared red and black, suggesting some horrible chemical burn. With one of these hands, she gestured near the floor.

"Well, this down here *isn't* the rock wall if you must know. But *you* inspired it nonetheless. Incidentally, can I have some of your extra leader tape? It'll make for a great black tile."

Diego glared at the mural's final unfinished corner, maddening like a loose fingernail he was forbidden from yanking off.

12

The next time Diego went into town, he struck up a conversation at the cantina with some abalone divers. After gauging their sense of adventure, he told them about a hidden cove he understood to be a boon for molluscs. Incredulity dampened, enthusiasm stoked, and maps sketched, they parted ways.

The abalone divers showed up to the cove the next day, shortly before noon. Two men and a woman, replete with camping and snorkelling gear. Their giddiness at having found so secluded and perfect a paradise practically glowed from their skin as they prepared for their first dive.

The following morning, all three of their bodies dotted the beach in the equidistant humps of skinned buffalo on a prairie.

Diego had spied from the music room as Alma harpooned each as they emerged from the surf at dusk.

Watched her wander out into the surf to fetch two of the bodies the currents were already drawing out to deeper water.

After lining up the corpses, Diego followed her through the binoculars as she approached each one in turn, pliers in hand, starting with the furthest one, slowly moving her way back to the one closest to the cabana.

Teeth collected, she went back inside. Diego went out, grabbed the shovel he had waiting by the door, and went to work, adding to the berm what he'd already started, lengthening it to help further redirect the tide from the cabana's front door.

That night, still weeping from his shower and the fresh handful of skin the sun had scoured from his shoulders and back, he beheld Alma's completed mural, especially the final finished corner. The backs of two heads, one adult and one child, as if gazing up at some hilltop. Alma had made that clear enough, at least. The black leader from his tapes conveyed without any doubt hers and Emmitt's shared raven locks.

For a fleeting gulp of thought, Diego comprehended the entire story in every detail, but like a wave plowing through a sandcastle, only lumpy, hissing echoes of shore remained.

13

"On this went. For weeks, then months, and eventually years— people emerging onto the secret beach from the cleft, only to wind up the medium of two reclusive artists. It's garnered quite the urban legend status amongst divers and surfers in town: the monsters that live and consume tourists in a secret placed called *Curación*."

The young surfer snorted. Maybe it was the fantastical nature of the tale told, or the inevitability of her fourth mojito.

"That's . . . insane," she said through a slushed smile, her Aussie accent even more pronounced behind the booze.

Diego pulled on a cigar while mirroring the young woman's smile. He'd introduced himself as Bob. Sometimes he used Sam. Simple, wholesome American names. "I don't deny the absurdity of it," he said, zipping the hoodie that covered almost every inch of saddlebag hide to the top. "But the house is still there, and the cove is just as hard to find. And if you believe the stories, the berm before the studio is now as high as a van, and it stretches to the tideline. And, once in a while, it's been said that a man of lobster-red skin continues to dig and mound sand to this day."

A guffaw between a dog's yawn and a donkey's bray tumbled from the surfer's mouth. Mona, she said her name was. Along with a wetsuit coloured so loudly it would've popped out on Bourbon Street during Mardi Gras, Diego safely assumed that self-consciousness was not an issue she suffered. As it was, the bar was half-empty and they sat in a dark corner furthest from the others.

Mona crab-held the top of her dewy glass, using her middle-finger to point at the sunbaked man across from her. "And how do *you* know all of this?"

A coil of grey smoke spooled from puckered lips. "You live long enough in a secluded place, you learn all its dirty secrets."

"Is that so," she prompted. "So, have you been to this place? This . . . *Curación*?"

Diego reclined in mock offense. "You don't make it to your fifties by taking unnecessary risks."

Mona aped *Bob's* recoil. The surprise on her face suggested she thought him ten years younger than she'd initially assumed. She probably thought the sun had been no help to him, nor his clumsy flirtation attempt on a woman half his age.

"And do you know how to get there?"

Diego dragged the stogie across the press of lips, implying smile and grimace at once. "You obviously weren't listening. I'm still alive. But if you insist on rolling the dice with *your* own life, I can certainly sketch you a map? The waves there are . . . glorious."

This time Mona gave him all her pearly whites, letting the

smile frolic while Diego quickly drew his map on a cocktail napkin.

Mona peeled off a twenty and slid it on the bar to cover their drinks. "I assume you're a regular here, Bob?"

A ribbon of smoke snaked from both corners of his mouth. "Not much else to do in the lost parts of the world but drink and surf."

"And disremember your old life," she said behind a wistful smile.

Diego noted for the first time since they started chatting her earnest, candid state of mind. "Disremember indeed."

With a burlesque curtsy, Mona thanked him and promised to buy him another drink next time if his boasting of the waves in the cove panned out.

She strutted out in tight speed-skater strides. Maybe it was for Diego's benefit—a kind of tip for his time. More than likely, it was for any number of surfer bros downing tequila shots and tracking her peacock flourishes out the door. Diego didn't care. By then he'd become absorbed by a particular older woman at the bar, the casual way she leaned against her man. A flower adorned her blonde hair. A red hibiscus.

Not unlike the gaillardia the woman wore at his birthday party back in L.A. while leaning over the closed soundboard of the piano as he played—this as Emmitt wandered in the direction of the saltwater pond.

And disremember your old life.

An odd expression for someone as young as Mona, Diego thought. *Disremember* in lieu of *forget*. As if to suggest . . .

Emmitt had caught them in the pantry earlier—him and the gaillardia woman—close together, hands about places he'd only seen his father and mother explore.

. . . intentionality.

The woman jolted at seeing Emmitt. She plastered on a tight grin and fumbled for a pack of napkins before walking back to the party.

Yes, that was what had happened, thought Diego. *I didn't intentionally* disremember *anything. Here, I'll show you . . .*

Emmitt asked, "Who's that?"

Diego, hands absently running up and down his sides, at last knelt before his son. "That is the new cellist in Daddy's orchestra.

One of the best in the world. Her name is Kristin Rizzoli. She's going to be famous one day."

Emmitt, obsessed by water in the way Alma was, only fuelled by curiosity instead of fear.

But sometimes . . . Sometimes you have no choice but to forget. At least for a while, until your mind is ready to bear the weight. Because sometimes, that takes years.

The hubbub and yelling and sirens had rousted Alma from an Ativan slumber, and she ran towards the fading, concentric rings in the pond where Emmitt had gone under and had been pulled back out lifelessly by one of the guests. As others held her back from running into the pond herself, her eyes kept darting to Diego, frozen at his piano.

To the young woman standing behind him with a red flower in her hair, rubbing his shoulders in comfort.

Sometimes it takes years to make sense of the screams.

The screams from Alma that began as grief-wails over Emmitt, but boiled fast into rage at her husband's distraction and inertness, and it required a sedative shot from a paramedic to finally quell.

Years to untangle fact from fiction.

The same messages kept arriving on Diego's improvised grand Ouija board, even well after KREM had gone defunct. Even so, he kept claiming it was simply bounced signals. The same pair of notes, two octaves apart, *could've* been a radio jingle.

K *and* R . . .

Kristin Rizzoli . . .

Her cottage sat on a low terraced hill a mere three blocks from their house, girded by gaillardia around which white, calcite stones were bordered for contrast.

Years to clamp all the links of a chain together.

A week after Emmitt was buried, Diego stepped out of Kristin's house to see Alma's car parked on the curb. He'd told her he was going on a store run for groceries, but there she was, closing the trunk. They made brief eye contact before she got in the car and u-turned it back home. Once the shock wore off, Diego told himself he was going to confess everything upon returning from the store.

Years to gather up your pieces and put yourself together again.

When he got home, it was to firetrucks and cops. Just like with Emmitt. The housekeeper who had been cleaning the upstairs claimed she'd seen Alma stepping into the pond. She had filled two backpacks with the white calcite rocks from Kristin's front yard to weigh herself down before sinking like a stone, dying two days later after a short coma.

Years to amass coherently what you'd forgotten, not *disremembered.*

Such a beautiful smile, Diego thought of Mona. Gorgeous, full teeth.

Alma will certainly think so.

And maybe Mona had even meant it about returning tomorrow to buy him a drink like she promised . . .

And like that, the memories congealed, exhausted distinctiveness, and funnelled down the drain, and Diego blinked the tangible world back into focus, remembering emotions without sources. Names without motives.

She was Alma Samantha Mendoza, fifty-one, an artist. A sneaky kind of pretty. Deceased now for almost two decades.

Her husband was Diego Robert Mendoza, fifty-four, former concert pianist, current contactor of the dead. Not as handsome as Alma was pretty, but neither was he a homely man, even with skin like a buckskin loveseat abandoned on a roadway.

They were about to start redecorating their kitchen. A mosaic backsplash behind the stove, design yet to be determined.

HUMAN, STILL

B. ZELKOVICH

I *am a mermaid*, I think and dive beneath another wave. I slice through the murk, swept in a kelp forest of my hair. Pressure builds in my ears, presses behind my eyes, still I plunge ever downward.

I ignore the panic in my lungs and kick deeper and deeper into the dark. If I kick hard enough, think it loud enough, maybe this time it will come true. This wish, my childhood fantasy. *I am a mermaid.*

Ariel in reverse. The girl whose heart longed for fins more than feet. I think there's nothing I wouldn't give up, no song I would not sing, to make this fantasy reality.

I pull against the water and repeat it over and over in my mind—*I am a mermaid.*

My lungs burn, a furious heat that swallows my chest and climbs up my throat. I scream, a stream of bubbles pouring from my mouth. The last of my breath.

I am a mermaid. The dark and the deep is where I belong. And yet . . .

My traitorous legs kick away from the dark, tilt me up toward the pale dot of sun and the promise of air. Tears dissolve in salt water, disappointment anchors in my gut.

I am a mermaid, I think. And, *I am dying*. Someday soon I will be a carcass, sinking to the silt to nourish crustaceans.

I am dying, just not today.

I break the surface, gasp my coward's breath. The sun is warm on my face and I know. Human, still.

Today, I am not a mermaid. I am shivering and gasping, soaked and treading water. Another day of blinking, blubbering, breathing. I'm tired.

I thought there was nothing I wouldn't give up, but that isn't true. Not yet.

So, so tired.

I will be a mermaid.

Tomorrow, I'll try again.

SARAH'S KITCHEN

LISA CARREIRO

S arah was in her rocking chair with her needlework resting on her lap when the ghosts first appeared.

Seven phantom men opened the front door and lurched into the dim parlour surrounded by a haze of sea-green fog. Thunder crackled as though in the distance, a muted roar like a squall blowing nearby briefly filled the parlour, and the floorboards creaked like a ship at sea in a storm.

Sarah gaped silently as her late husband and six sons shook rain from their coats on that clear evening and stamped seaweed from their boots. Her husband paused and blinked at her, as though uncertain whether the old woman who stared at him in disbelief really was his wife, and one of her boys whistled for his dog whose bones lay long buried in Sarah's backyard. The ghosts lumbered through the dimming parlour for only a few minutes before they faded, one by one, into the unearthly fog.

Sarah dropped her needlework and staggered to where they'd disappeared. The last of the dissipating fog drifted out through the still-open doorway. Sarah's heart banged in her chest. She couldn't swallow the lump in her throat. She forced herself to the doorway and stared out into the twilight.

Waves crashed on the nearby rocky shore as the tide rolled in. An owl hooted and a distant dog barked. No human voices carried across the dimming evening, and not so much as a phantom flickered beneath the glowing gas lights. Even the boy who lit the lamps had gone to the next street.

Sarah waited, unable to call out, afraid to venture to the beach, uncertain whether she'd simply fallen asleep and dreamed, again, of her lost family.

Her dreams had never been that vivid though.

Her dreams had been glimpses of their faces, of her boys as toddlers, of her husband laughing as he brought in more wood for the stove.

She finally knelt where they'd walked and touched the rug. It was dry and clean, yet when she shut her eyes, she heard the squall. She smelled the sea. She felt the chill so intensely that she shivered for most of the night.

Sarah never told a soul. She feared that if she did, her neighbours might speak of the unsettled spirits of fishermen lost at sea with no bodies laid to rest in consecrated ground. They'd cluck their tongues, whisper behind their shawls, and shake their pompous heads.

Ten minutes from Sarah's house, several cracked, moss-covered headstones stood in tall grass near a rocky cliff. Every few days Sarah walked among the graves and paused beside each one. Her third baby didn't yet crawl before she died with a fever Sarah couldn't ease. Two sisters perished bearing their own babies, another sister was lost to fire, and two brothers were killed in a faraway war. And early on a summer morning twenty-seven years earlier, Sarah's husband of thirty-three years sailed into a calm blue sea with their six sons, and never returned.

Sarah never cried, never prayed, and barely breathed while she stared at chiselled letters she couldn't read. But she knew who was buried where. And she knew the stone with no bodies at rest beneath it. In rain, fog, sun, or snow; whether the sea was placid or stormy, Sarah stared at that stone and listened. She was certain that her husband and boys called to her from the water, their voices carried to shore on waves and wind. Yet when she turned toward the ocean, she could no longer hear them.

When the seven ghosts returned the following spring, snow blew in behind them though the pre-dawn sky was clear, and their muddy bootprints briefly stained the floral rug in the parlour.

Sarah called from her room and ran down the stairs. When she reached the bottom step, the one that creaked, her apple-cheeked youngest turned to her. He was still sixteen with no beard. His smile turned to bemusement when he saw his white-haired mother with her hand over her mouth, smiling through tears.

The others stumbled into the kitchen where her husband opened the cold stove and grunted. He gave a wordless cry of frustration as he slammed the stove door shut. The boys joined in his keening, and they all disappeared before Sarah reached them.

She stood in her empty kitchen and called each one's name over and over again. A bootprint of icy seawater chilled one of her bare feet, but the puddle evaporated within a minute.

The cat peered at her wide-eyed from beneath the tall hutch. On its scalloped top shelf, one mug had been moved—just a thumb's width—but Sarah understood.

They were hungry and cold, these men who'd climbed out of the sea. They wanted fire to thaw frozen hands, drink to wash salt water from parched throats, and food to fill long-empty bellies.

Sarah stared out the window, watching the sky change from black to pink to blue, and waited for her ghosts to reappear.

The phantom men didn't return until late in the summer. They tromped into the house on a clear morning just like the one they'd sailed away in. Sarah reached the kitchen ahead of them to add wood to the small fire in the stove. It flared and the dry wood crackled.

Her husband's gaze met hers. His once-sparkling green eyes were milky, dull, and joyless, but Sarah wasn't afraid. The men's phantom pipes clattered against their teeth. Tobacco smoke and fog swirled through the kitchen while Sarah boiled water. They laughed wheezing noises and kicked off seaweed-covered boots but disappeared before Sarah opened the flour canister.

After that morning, she kept a chunk of molasses bread or a crusty loaf beside a pot of cold coffee or sweetened tea for the next time her family slipped in. She piled seasoned firewood by the stove, even in summer. Along with extra sugar and flour, she bought the raisins and molasses she hadn't needed for more than twenty years.

Without any pattern her ghosts returned. Three months might elapse between visits, or ten days. They'd stamp through the doorway, sometimes waking Sarah from deep sleep. She'd jump from bed to the stairs to greet them, usually to find the parlour empty. Now and then, though, one or another son blinked at her aged face as he faded into the fog. They rarely came in the day, but one winter afternoon, Sarah's husband peered out a window at her when she returned from her errands. He was gone before she'd crossed the parlour.

Seven months after she'd seen her husband through the window, Sarah woke to the men's footfalls. She hurried down the stairs and into the kitchen as fast as she could; no easy feat where her hips and back ached with age. While the ghosts spoke their dead's language and her eldest poured seawater from a boot, she stoked the fire and doled out the previous night's bread; thumb-sized morsels on teacup saucers. But as quickly as she thrust saucers into ethereal hands, they faded. Two saucers shattered on the floor. Sarah poured cold coffee into cups and handed them to the remaining men. The last two boys had barely wrapped scarred blue hands around cups before they, too, disappeared.

Sarah stared at the broken shards, the spilled coffee, the dropped bread. She swallowed her tears. She picked up her broom to sweep up the bits of broken crockery and fallen bread while she called out her husband's name in time to the sound of the ebbing tide.

Every morning after that found Sarah in her rocking chair by a blazing stove, year-round. A kettle of water sat ready at a furious boil; a pan on the back of the stove brimmed with golden corn bread or browned buttermilk biscuits. She dozed with a blanket across her lap at night and knitted scarves and sweaters for her family during the day. Any morning before the sun rose, neighbours could see the glow of a fully lit kitchen and an oil lamp burning all night in a parlour window. She rarely stepped out to do errands, but when she did, they whispered when she passed, lowered their eyes, and never stopped to visit.

The morning after the shortest night, before the sky over the sea was even pink, Sarah woke to the opening door. Her family entered, wheezing harsh laughing sounds. The men clamped their ethereal pipes in their mouths and then fumbled with phantom tobacco pouches. Sarah dashed to the hutch for cups.

Each ghost sat in his usual seat: her husband by the window from where he watched the sea and sky, now with an orange stripe cast across a low cloud. Her eldest sat beside his father smoking his pipe and nodding. The youngest sat nearest the hutch. A hint of whiskers darkened his upper lip. The others cozied up to the stove even on that warm morning, empty eyes searching the room.

Her husband actually smiled while he grunted meaningless words. His scarred hands blurred as he gestured while he spoke. The boys near the stove leaned forward and breathed in woodsmoke from the stove and steam from the kettle.

Sarah set handfuls of corn bread on one plate in the middle of the table. Then, trembling so much she spilled scalding drops on her bony hands, she poured water into the teapot, all ready with a spoonful of leaves. She didn't wait for the tea to steep, only poured cup after cup after cup, crying out as her husband faded before he opened his mouth to utter another preternatural sound.

Her eldest reached for the corn bread, only to slip away like a dream.

The second and third, as close as twins, reached out to hug the mother they finally recognized but then, with a glance to each other that told Sarah they understood, they too disappeared.

The fourth simply closed his eyes and left her.

The fifth reached for his tea with a desperate motion, swiping his spectral hand through the steaming cup, and uttered an eerie cry before he faded into a blue wisp to become part of the fog that had followed them in.

But then her youngest, her apple-cheeked boy; he who'd begged to follow his father and brothers to sea, curled diaphanous hands around hot teacup, lifted it to his mouth, and sipped. His cheeks bloomed with fresh blood, hale and ruddy in the brightening morning. His ethereal hands grew substantial and calloused. His face aged from boy to man and creases from work at sea in sun lined his eyes. His eyes cleared. His lips grew dark. Seaweed dropped from his boots and faded, but the boots and feet and boy himself remained, smiling up at his mother as he reached for some bread.

Sarah draped a scarf across her son's shoulders, pressed her aged hands on his salt-dried cheeks, and leaned down to kiss his forehead.

SEAWEED AND GOSSIP

LEA STORRY

"Are you coming?"

I look up and see Mom, in her moss green bathing suit, standing in the doorway of my bedroom. Childhood bedroom.

"Nope," I say, turning back to my laptop. "I've got to finish this job application."

"You never stop working," sighs Mom. "You haven't been home in years. Don't you want to join us old gals for some seaweed and gossip?"

I'm almost one of those old women now. At forty-nine, I'm home in Nova Scotia, single and living with my parents after losing my job. My mother's summer ritual of bobbing in the ocean with her lifelong friends will not put money in the bank. I need to find work and some grey-haired mermaids are not going to fish something out of the Atlantic for me.

After being laid-off during the pandemic, I have nothing to show for my career as a journalist except a few articles. The terror of not having a job makes my heart pound like winter storm waves smashing into the beach. I wobble in my chair.

"You spend too much time on the computer," says Mom. "Take a break, Serina. Besides, we don't get many summer days like this."

I glance out the window. Grey clouds hide the sun, covering what should be a July blue sky. But the ocean is flat, calm. A dark blue mirror. Come to think about it, it's exactly like the morning I said goodbye to a boy, a crush. Childhood crush.

I sigh, pushing my chair away from my desk. Childhood desk. "Fine," I say. "But I'm not getting my hair wet."

Mom nods and shuts my door. I pull my black bathing suit out of one of the suitcases squatting like a brown toad in the corner of the room. I left Alberta a couple of weeks ago, yet I can't bring myself to unpack. This is the place where, as a teenager, I had formed dreams of life and love. Only for them to turn into shipwrecks, sticks and bones abandoned years later.

With my bathing suit on, I head into the narrow hallway, leaning into the bathroom to grab a towel. I wind the rough and faded red terrycloth around my waist, cringing when my fingers sink into my soft belly.

"I haven't worked out in two weeks," I mutter.

At the beach, Mom parks the car and we get out. The bluish rocks leading down to the dark calm water are strewn with clothing. A t-shirt here. Jeans there. Shoes everywhere.

"Serina!" calls out a voice from the sea. "How nice of you to join us!"

I grunt.

"Don't mind her, Phan," says Mom. "My girl is grouchy."

"Nothing some seaweed and gossip can't fix," says Phan, turning to float on her back.

"Get in here," yells Janelda, water droplets flying off her wet hand.

Since I've been back, I've only glimpsed the ocean from my home. Childhood home. I used to sit on this beach, a long time ago, with the boy. He's long gone. Well, long gone from my life. I haven't thought of him in ages.

The salt air smells familiar to me. The perfume of my youth. The sea was the backdrop to my years of dreams so high they could touch the sky and skin so soft and smooth the sand could never roughen it no matter how hard it tried.

I step from stone, to stone, making my way to where the sea meets the shore. I don't dare seek my reflection, looking up at me from the shallows. I take a deep breath and let it out before stepping into the black water. The air is cool just like the ocean. The water feels like velvet swirling around my legs. I plunge my shoulders into the Atlantic, and my body shivers, shaking me from my toes to my chin. I take a few strokes out to where a group of seven women and all their lumps and bumps are suspended over waving seaweed.

"You know, Serina," says Phan, rolling onto her front like a seal. "My mother used to say, 'If we all threw our problems in a pile and saw everyone else's, *we'd take our own back.*'"

"It's true!" says Janelda. "I don't want your husband."

Phan splashes water at her friend and all the women giggle.

"My man would never want you!" says Phan.

I bite my lip. Silly old ladies. My childhood was filled with thoughts of becoming a big-city newspaper reporter who came home every night to a man who made me laugh and made me supper. No man has prepared anything for me recently except my taxes.

I tread water, using my limbs to create little whirlpools all around me. It's the riptide you have to watch out for here. It sucks you from the shore and sends you out, out, out into the wide and vast sea. Your body could be discovered miles away or never found except by the creatures that consumed you.

The boy and I often asked each other which sea animal we'd be. He said he wanted to be a lobster with great clacking green claws. I said I would be a whale that jumped high and dove deep. The boy laughed and said that I was a shark, a combination of beauty, grace, and sharp teeth.

"You never know when they'll strike," he said, "and tear you apart."

This shark grew legs. Once I was done high school, I headed west for the big city near the mountains. Where I've lived until I was forced to trade rush hour for the rush of the ocean. After losing my job, my savings went quickly. I had tried to scrimp and make do without, but at some point, it wasn't enough. I had to come home.

"Earth to Serina," says Phan.

"Oh," I say. "Sorry, were you asking me something?"

"I wanted to know if you've seen anyone since you've been home?"

"So far, just you folks."

While driving to the beach with Mom, we had passed large cedar-shingled houses with long white balconies and pink, orange, and yellow flower-filled gardens. Green lawns sloped to gleaming metal docks that met the sea. I bet the owners of those grand homes never worried about anything. I bet they didn't have to avoid old friends. Childhood friends.

"You're back!" said an old schoolmate to me the other day at the grocery store. "We should go for coffee and catch-up."

"I'm swamped," I said, scurrying away like a crab chasing the tide.

How can I tell her I've returned to this small seaside town with nothing to show for my years away? No job. No partner. No money. I can't even buy a cup of tea without adding up the bills in my head. Is this the $3.50 that will pull me under? I feel like I'm drowning when I'm on solid land.

The other week, I had driven by the boy's house. Childhood house. It was evening and a porch light was shining into the darkness. I remembered watching the boy close the back door softly so he wouldn't wake his parents. It was late at night and the boy and I were walking to the beach drenched in moonlight. The boy was the first person, besides my parents, to tell me he loved me.

Mid-January waves were crashing on the shore ice. The stars above us were bright in the clear sky. The wind was blowing snow into the water and into my ears. Still, I heard him whisper something into the air.

"I love you."

The shark with the sharp teeth didn't bite on the words, didn't lunge for them. Instead, she let them float around her until the riptide grabbed them and took them into the depths. Today, even if she dove deep, deep, deep, she would never be able to pull his words, childhood words, up and to the surface.

The sages who drift in a ring around me now, are a reminder of what's to come. Wrinkles, creases, and pops and cracks. There is nothing graceful in growing old. My life is, almost, half over. I've learned so much and yet, nothing at all. I am now part of this drifting coven of women.

Georgia, her white hair in tight tiny braids, glances at me over the ripples of all our moving parts.

Georgia is the boy's mother.

She starts talking about her granddaughter.

"Lienna's so smart. Had her pick of five law schools. She won't have trouble finding a job when she's done."

The group clucks in agreement.

Lienna is the boy's daughter.

If I had stayed, would the boy and I have children? Would I have had babies with him? Probably not. I nurtured a career instead.

I hurt the boy when I left. On a dull late summer's morning. Just before the days fell into autumn. The fog hovered in the hollows along the shore. Dew dripped off the wild pink roses that grew thick by the sea. The water was playing dead, laying still as still could be.

"Don't break my heart," he said, sitting down beside me on the seagrass, a stone's throw away from the Atlantic. "Please don't."

"If I don't do it now, I'll do it tomorrow or the next day."

"You'll regret it," he said, shaking his head. "You'll regret leaving."

"Sharks don't feel regret," I said, smiling at him sideways. "They act on instinct."

I took the boy's hand and held it in mine. His fingers squeezed my fingers so hard I thought they were going to bruise black and blue. Together, the boy and I watched a piping plover wade into the ocean and then retreat to land. Only to walk back into the water. The tiny sand-coloured bird dipped its short, black-tipped yellow beak into the sea, searching for something to eat.

We stared at the bird until it flew away. That's when the boy and I noticed the Atlantic was done with sleep. The ocean was waking up. The waves rose higher and higher, showering us with cold salty spray. I wasn't sure if I was crying. If the water running down my face was from the ocean or my tears.

Then I got up and left.

That memory, childhood memory, swirls around in my head. The women before me start spinning like sea witches. More memories from my younger years flood my brain. My chest tightens, and all my thoughts are dragged into the riptide of youth.

I paddle through the gaggle of women, trying to outswim the emotions pouring into my body. I close my eyes and sink. Deep under the water, where I can't feel the seaweed tickling my feet, the blackness of the ocean envelopes me. The current is lightly pushing against me. Pressing into my shoulders. Hugging me close. Forcing me into stillness.

The thing about sharks is that they have to keep moving. They don't have gills that flutter like fish. Sharks have to push forward to keep breathing.

I've always been on the move. I work. This is what I do. Researching. Interviewing. Editing. Writing articles. It's always been my coping mechanism. A tactic. A childhood tactic. If I stop, I'll sink, fall to the bottom of the ocean where there is no light. I'll never be able to make it to the air again.

I've never allowed myself to stop. To take a break. To go back to this beach. To give my lost and wandering memories space to be present. To remember the boy.

I open my eyes under the water and see my bubbles floating upward into a blurry golden light. I push towards it, breaking through as the sun strikes the Atlantic. I take a deep breath in and swim back to the women still treading water over seaweed and gossip.

"His divorce is final," says Georgia.

She's smiling at me.

ON A NORTHERN SHORE

NIKOLINE KAISER

What I really wanted to say was that a monster is not such a terrible thing to be. From the Latin root monstrum, a divine messenger of catastrophe, then adapted by the Old French to mean an animal of myriad origins: centaur, griffin, satyr. To be a monster is to be a hybrid signal, a lighthouse: both shelter and warning at once."

- Ocean Vuong, *On Earth We're Briefly Gorgeous*

The Baltic Sea licked at the rocky shore, and Nora had to, yet again, suppress the desire to jump right in and take a wild, cold swim. She'd be crushed at best, sucked down by the current and drowned at worst.

Three months, here, to start. Eight on the contract. She had supplies for six months, and had made sure to bring enough entertainment to keep even an energetic child active. A whole box of sketchbooks had been shipped ahead of her, but she had kept herself to just one canvas, almost too big for the easel that she had dragged along on her own.

"You're ridiculous," her sister had accused, but Nora hadn't cared. She had brought plenty of books as well, heavy volumes, classics she'd always meant to read but never gotten around to. She knew she wasn't going to get through them all. What else was she supposed to do out here, but paint?

Six months' worth of food and entertainment. Three months until someone came to check on her. Unless she put out the distress signal, of course. Nora hoped it wouldn't come to that, and not just because it meant something was wrong. She wanted to be alone, to feel it aching in her bones. Alone without being lonely. She had only ever heard of that in dreams. She wanted to find out if it could be real.

❧

"There's no Wi-Fi but you're going to have radio-contact, and I'll check in every day," Will had said.

"Is that really necessary?"

Will frowned. "Usually, we recommend a few times a week, but for this place I like to do it every day. It doesn't have to be every twenty-four hours on the dot, but I want frequent signs of life. Accidents tend to happen more frequently here."

"I've been warned about that." Nora wasn't superstitious. She was sure that if you put up the statistics, this lighthouse wouldn't be more accident-prone than most others. It was just that people had decided to pay attention to this one given the history here.

"You don't even have to talk to me, there's a Morse-code function on the radio. I'll show you what to tap so I know you're okay." Will was younger than she had expected. When she had first spoken to him on the phone, the voice had been deep and gravelly, and she had imagined some grizzled old sailor, settled down by the shore to watch out for all the wayward keepers of all the wayward lighthouses. Instead, she had met a man in his thirties, about her own age, with black curls and skin that looked far too soft for all the outdoor-work he did. She had liked Will, even if she thought he worried too much.

"Do you believe in ghosts?" he asked, once they were in the boat to the small island that would be her home for the next many months.

"No."

"Good. The previous guy did."

"What happened to him?"

"Thought he saw something and fell out of the window. He's all right, but he was hospitalized for a long while. That's another reason I want you to check in every day—if we hadn't done that with him, we wouldn't have known anything was wrong for another two days and he'd have died."

The wind was harsh against her face; she knew she had to get used to it. It broke against the sea, spraying salt on her lips.

"I read up about the history of this place." She had to shout a little, to be heard. The sails whipped overhead with loud cracks.

Her voice felt hoarse already. She couldn't wait to be silent for a long while, to not have to speak, to ask. To answer.

"Yeah, so you know what people see. Most people say it's her. Luna."

Nora did not believe in ghosts. Still, the name sent a shiver down her spine. She'd read the article, seen the grainy, browning photograph that read *1853*. *Liam Hendricks with his sister, Luna.* Twins who hadn't ever been away from each other for more than a few weeks at a time. Inseparable to the point of rumour and gossip. She had even gone with him when he unexpectedly took the position as lighthouse keeper. Gone with him to the lighthouse where he would kill her. Then himself.

The lighthouse had cut through the horizon, a long, black line that had turned grey and then white as they approached. Nora had seen pictures of it, but it couldn't compare to the real thing. The sight knocked the breath out of her more than the wind ever could. *How beautiful,* she thought and wanted so badly to paint it, but she didn't think she knew how.

Will was kind enough to help carry her things from the boat and up to the lighthouse. She knew she had brought too much, but he didn't complain, not even about the weight of the books or the paint supplies. He showed her around the place; it was a twenty-five-minute walk to circumvent the entire island, thirteen minutes to walk across it. Going around the island was only possible when the tide was low, otherwise it cut off access to the beaches on both sides. Unless you wanted to risk the climb, or go swimming. Neither of those came recommended, if you valued your life.

The island was shaped like a fat teardrop, the small bay and bridge that served as a harbour on the southern curve, the lighthouse nestled on the northern tip, as far out to sea as you could come without toppling over the rocks.

The beach beneath the cliffs by the lighthouse held pure, white sand. Luna's body had been on that beach. She had been thrown from the top of the lighthouse and had soared downwards. Nora did not know if her body had hit the sea or the shore. She knew only that her death had been instant. That's what the article had said.

Will went with her into the lighthouse, showing her where everything was, how everything worked. She had been shown

before, of course, in another place, for her training. The man who
had been her teacher had been shocked to see a woman arrive.
His name was Karl, and he'd looked twenty years older than the
seventy he was, though he moved as if he was still thirty.

It had amused her how much he had floundered at first. He'd
gotten over it quick enough, but still, he'd had questions. "What
does a lovely young woman want to do in a lighthouse alone for
eight months?"

Her hands had been purple-black with spilled oil, helping him
clean the small motor that kept the light going. "What does
anyone want to do that for?"

"It's the way of old, lonely men. Widowers and misanthropes."

"Which one are you?"

"Both."

"Maybe I am both, too."

⌒⌒

Her predecessor had taken good care of the lighthouse, but
she could see the few windows caked in dust and grime, and knew
already that the hinges on the door creaked like an old man in a
bad mood.

Will led her up the stairs, showing her the Vega lights. She had
surprised herself with how much she had enjoyed reading about
the lighthouse's history. It had first held a hollow wick lamp,
using whale oil. Nora did not want to even imagine the smell of
it. Then, there had been a parabolic reflector. The modern lights
were all LED, but much of the old machinery was still intact. It
had been removed where necessary, to make way for the new
technology, but the rest had been left to stand, obsolete and
slowly rusting.

Nora liked it.

She liked the kitchen, with the blue, painted cabinets, liked
the storeroom in the basement that felt like stepping back into
the 1800s, even though Will had assured her it was properly
insulated and clean. The more she saw of the lighthouse, the
more she fell in love with it.

I could stay forever, she thought. She looked down from the
very top of the lighthouse, down at the beach below. The ocean
washed up driftwood, a sheen of white shells.

"There," Will said, turning off the bright lights, cutting off her view. They both took a few seconds, eyes struggling to adjust to the sudden darkness.

"You're all set," he said.

Her first month was uneventful. True to his word, Will let her do the Morse-code to assure him she wasn't bleeding to death at the foot of the lighthouse, though twice he called to tell her a bad joke. That was all right; it was nice to hear a familiar voice, especially one that did not expect her to hold a longer conversation.

She picked up the news of the outside world from the radio too, snippets of current events that she found herself caring less and less about. She responded when she was hailed by passing ships. She found the channels that played classical music twenty-four/seven and carried the radio down with her to the western beach, a sketchbook tucked under her arm. She tried, desperately, to draw the lighthouse, but all of it seemed inadequate. As soon as the shape of it was down on paper, it looked too ordinary, like just another building.

Instead, she tried to sketch the birds she saw, catching them only in glimpses until she learned to throw uncooked rice for them to eat. They soon grew used to her presence, bearing it for the food, unknowingly posing while her hair whipped in the wind, and she furiously turned her pencils to nubs against the paper.

The island was always cold, and Nora quickly found herself using every single sweater her sister had forced her to pack. Most of them were scratchy wool, ones she'd told herself she would only use when the nights got really cold later in the year, but soon it became second nature to don one as she got out of bed, letting herself be enveloped by warmth both itchy and necessary. Her skin cracked in the wind, her lips bleeding almost every day. She stopped using hot water for her showers, determined to beat the cold before it beat her. It helped; both to keep her alert, and to remind her that she had a body. She could not get too lost in her own head. She made lists to remember to eat. She napped during the day and stayed up most of the night, though she did not have to; there were systems to alert her if the light went out. By the end of the month, she could climb the ladder to the top of the

lighthouse in her sleep, could find her way around the island
blindfolded, and knew down to the second when the tide would
reach the first rock on the Northern beach, where poor Luna had
died.

She was—not happy, she thought. But she felt quiet, in a way
she hadn't for a long while. Being here had helped, like she had
hoped for.

That was why she took out the easel and big canvas, after a
month and three days. The kitchen was just large enough to hold
it. She'd found old newspapers dating back at least twenty years,
stacked beneath the bed, and she spread them out to protect the
floor. Her sketches of the lighthouse still hadn't borne fruit, but
at least she could make a base, start with something.

The familiar feeling of a paint-brush in her hand made her
tremble; she had to take a deep breath. *Settle. You know how to
do this.* Claire had shown her, that first time, light strokes and
warm hands. *You can do anything, make anything. That's why
it's beautiful.*

It was growing dark by the time she had finished with the
base. She put down her brush, flexing her aching hand. It had
been a while since she'd painted; longer than she had been at the
lighthouse.

She climbed up the stairs, then the ladder; there was a control
system just below the actual head of the lighthouse, and she could
do everything from there, not needing to climb the rest of the
way. But it had become a ritual for her now: she would get up
there, moving carefully, a small flashlight clipped to the collar of
her jacket or sweater. She would check that the old motor was
fine, though it was not needed for the Vega light. She would move
her hand, gently, over the light-station itself, and think she was
fortunate that this was not a modern lighthouse, where you could
not climb up here so easy. Where it had never been necessary,
because it had never been built for the ways of old.

Then, finally, she would look down at the beach below, still
visible because the ocean held its own kind of light, reflecting the
setting sun and the coming stars. The white sand glowed and the
cliff-side seemed to reach both up and down, as if indecisive on if
it wanted to kiss the earth below or the sky above.

A woman stood on the beach, tall and stately. Her long blonde
hair was halfway out of her elaborate up-do, and though she was

too far away to see it, Nora knew there were streaks of tears down her face.

She stumbled back, hitting the light, hand coming up to cover her mouth. The woman had turned around, had looked at her.

Her body trembled for what felt like hours, and it was growing steadily darker and darker. She only managed to force herself to move when she remembered she had to turn on the light, that this was literally her only job. Slowly, she pushed forwards, crawling on hands and knees. For the first time she was afraid of toppling over the side of the lighthouse, when before her feet had always been sure and steady. She looked down, again.

There was no-one on the beach. Of course not. She blinked, hands clenching. She was tired, or the isolation was getting to her. Will had made her read up on that too, how being too long on your own could make you hallucinate people, familiar and strange alike.

The woman had been familiar—Nora knew exactly who she was.

She climbed down, ignoring how she was still trembling, and started up the light. The faint humming of the system helped ease her somewhat. She checked and rechecked that the light was working, and then went down to cook dinner, taking more care than usual. Perhaps she needed to eat more, better. She had skipped lunch today. She had to be more diligent about looking out for herself. There was no-one else to do it, here.

The next morning, she awoke to the smell of paint hanging thick in the air, and it had given her a headache. There had once been a time when she never thought she would go unused to the smell. That had been before Claire left.

She checked that the base she'd painted was dry and then put on a jacket over her sweater, before opening the kitchen window. It was freezing cold, but she'd brought several pairs of gloves with her, and it was an easy thing to cut the fingers off one, so the brush was easier to wield. She painted light sky-blue in broad strokes over the canvas, not caring when it dripped onto her pants or stained the glove.

The canvas was big, and by the time she was satisfied with her progress for the day, the sun had crossed over the lighthouse and found the other side, and her stomach was rumbling in protest. Neglected for too long. She packed up, feeling light-headed, her mouth dry as the desert. She closed the window, shivering. When the radio turned on, her fingers were almost too stiff to respond, despite her gloves. She fumbled and then pressed the button to answer by voice.

"Hi, it's me. Not dead yet."

"Oh!" Will sounded shocked. "I'd forgotten what you sounded like!"

She had too—her voice was rough with disuse, unfamiliar to her own ears. "It's gotten colder," she said, nonsensical, because of course Will would know that. But now she was speaking again and she didn't know how to stop.

"Yeah. Are you all right? Do you need anything?"

She shook her head, though he couldn't see. "I'm fine. I like being here. A lot."

"Good, that's good." He did sound pleased. Perhaps a little relieved, as well. "And no sightings of ghosts?"

Her heart thumped loudly in her chest, echoing in her ears, in the quiet of the room. In the quiet of the entire, solitary lighthouse.

"Hello? Nora, you there?"

"No ghosts," she said, voice faint. "It's just me." Outside, there was the sound of a sharp shriek.

"You and the seagulls," Will said. "Ready for another joke?"

Two more days passed. She left the painting alone, pushing the easel to the corner and waiting for heat to seep back into the kitchen. Heavy rain fell, followed by hail, and she was forced to stay inside, unable to go out and find things to sketch. She found packets of cocoa powder in the storage and made a thermos of hot chocolate, bundling herself in layers upon layers, and brought a book with her up to the machinery. It was warmest there, the heat from downstairs moving up and coalescing, finding a home right beneath where the light shone out to all at sea.

The day before, Will had patched a call from her sister through. She hadn't been able to hide her worry, though Nora had insisted she was fine.

"Your voice sounds like you're sick," she kept saying. "Use it some more, won't you? Talk to the birds or whatever, I don't care."

That was how Nora found herself reading aloud from her book. The heavy rain made it dark as evening in her little spot, and she could imagine she was a child again, her and Claire bundled under blankets and reading to each other with just a flashlight and a lot of courage.

There was a small, cold gust against the nape of her neck, like an intake of breath, and Nora's voice stuttered, stopped. Her teeth clipped together. She was sure, so very sure, that someone was sitting right behind her. She could not move.

Something downstairs made a loud clatter followed by another and another. She jumped up, panic forcing her downstairs, almost falling. *Like the others,* she thought, wildly. *Drop down and break your neck, break your body, your bones.*

The easel had toppled over, knocking into one of the chairs, and then the painting had toppled from there to the floor, hitting the table on the way. There was a long stripe of blue paint on the table, though the paint should have been dried by now. Nora carefully picked it all back up, checking that the canvas hadn't broken, that the easel was secure.

The wind must have knocked it over, though the window was closed. Or she'd knocked into it while making her cocoa, or . . .

Claire's laughter rang through the air, bright and almost-real. *I know you don't believe in ghosts, but there is more between heaven and earth, Horatio, than is dreamt of in your philosophy!*

The radio clicked on, soft music crooning through the room, and fear struck Nora near-blind again, until she remembered the timer she had set. She put a hand to her head, breathed deep.

It was not until much later, when she climbed back up to do her routine, to start the light, that she had the thought that the easel had been knocked over because she'd stopped reading aloud. Because she hadn't gotten to the ending.

❧

Two months had passed, and the rain and hail had given way to snow. Nora bundled the radio, the thermos, and a book into her backpack; it was only just cresting dawn outside and she had determined to go on a hike around the island before everything iced over and made a trek too dangerous to try.

She timed it with the tide, reaching the Northern beach just as she had walked herself warm. She did not mean to stop there, but she did. The radio was crackling to life, nearly inaudible buried in her backpack and over the sound of the whistling wind. Her hands shook as she pulled it out. She hadn't set a timer today.

The buttons she used to send the messages in Morse-code were being pressed, invisible fingers playing over them. Nora lowered herself to the sand, shaking all over. She put the radio by her feet. The wind howled in her ears and the ocean licked at the sand only a few inches away. There was a message.

Who are you?

This, Nora thought, was the weirdest Ouija-board she'd ever come across. But it was the same message, repeating over and over again. She was sure of it.

Should she just answer out loud?

"I'm Nora."

The next message came immediately.

Why are you here?

"I'm the lighthouse keeper."

You are a woman.

Nora frowned.

"Yes. I'm the lighthouse keeper."

A long silence passed—she almost laughed. *Silence.* As if an actual voice was speaking to her, as if this was real in any way. She had officially lost her mind.

Minutes passed, and the water crept closer. Nora would have thought the ghost had left, except she felt keenly that she was not alone on the beach. That someone was waiting. And then suddenly she was too curious herself not to ask.

"Who are you?"

The answer that came back was not surprising at all, but it still knocked the air from her lungs.

Luna.

☾

"Hello? Will?"

"Oh, are you calling me now?" Despite the words, he sounded delighted to hear from her. Nora smiled. It felt foreign on her face.

"I am. I was just wondering—you're coming here soon? It's almost been three months."

"Yeah. Anything in particular you need? I'm still waiting on a list, aside from the necessities."

"I'd like some history on the island and the lighthouse."

"Oh?"

"I've really fallen in love with this place." Her words sounded stiff, too practised, probably because they were. She was desperate for Will not to know that she wanted information because she was starting to . . . she didn't even know. If he asked her about ghosts again, she would still tell him there was no such thing. She still could not explain what she'd experienced. Nora hadn't been back to the beach since the message, though the temptation had been there. She didn't think she was going crazy, but then again, crazy people never did. "I just . . . would like to know everything."

"I'll see what I can find, but there should be quite a bit because we keep stuff like that around the office for every location we oversee. It's not a problem."

"Thanks, Will."

She mixed a new batch of paint after that, a deeper blue that fit with the ocean as it had looked on that first day she had arrived. She had thought about the painting every day, but she had yet to go back to it since it fell over. Instead, she had spent her free time reading aloud, over coffee in the kitchen, in her bed, even up above, leaning against the light and trying to ignore the way the wind would rip at the pages. She wasn't doing it for herself. Someone else was listening.

It was the day before Will was set to come with new supplies that it happened. She had turned off the radio for the night and was sketching the small bedroom, when it suddenly clicked back on.

Again, a message.

Why?

She licked her lips, staring at the radio, as if it could explain the sounds it made by sight alone.

"Why what?"

Why are you here?

That had already been answered. But Nora thought she knew

what question was really being asked.

"I lost someone I loved. I need to be alone."

She waited for an answer. Seconds ticked into minutes, and outside the ocean beat up against the heavy rocks. There was no reply.

Oh, she thought, heart sinking. She had not meant it like that.

She did not sleep a wink that night, lying awake and listening. Any minor sound made her strain her ears, but it was only the wind outside, the gentle lapping of the waves, or her own heartbeat. In the morning, she went down to the small water-bridge to greet Will. He was visibly startled when he saw her.

"Have you slept at all?"

"Not last night," she admitted. He didn't push more. They busied themselves hauling what he'd brought back to the lighthouse. Some more food, more cocoa and tea, a few letters, and a heavy folder stacked with printed out papers.

"From the historical archives," Will said, once they were all done. She'd put on a pot of tea while he spread the papers over the table. It was strange to have him here—her physical space suddenly occupied by another breath, another heartbeat. It made her uncomfortable, in the same way a new bruise was sore; yet also in the way it reminded you that you had a body, that there was a *healed* after the hurt. It helped that it was Will, whose voice she had become as familiar with as her own.

She nearly spilled the tea when she saw the old photograph staring up at her. Liam Hendricks stood tall and regal, with a full beard and his light hair pulled back at the nape of his neck, one arm rested on the back of the chair, half-hidden by his sister's form. Luna was smiling, just slightly, an unusual thing for such old photographs. Nora had read they required the subjects to sit still for a long time so that the image would not be blurry. It had made many of the people in them look far more severe than they had actually been. The twins really did look like each other, she thought, by the eyes and the set of their shoulders and the tall cheekbones.

"I found some more about those two," Will said, following her gaze. Nora did not meet his eyes when he looked back up at her. "I figured you'd be curious."

"I am. Thank you."

"Nora . . . I don't want to impose, but I hope you know that you can talk to me. It gets to be a lot, out here, and I do have some counselling training exactly for that kind of thing. I'm not saying you need it, but it's there. Lots of the others have used it. Some of them didn't, even when they maybe should have."

She gritted her teeth. He sounded so much like her sister, then. *Maybe you need to talk to someone? A professional?* But she had been so sick of talking. All she had ever done was talk and talk, answer every question with explanations that only grew more exhausting, for talker and listener both.

"Thank you," she forced herself to say, again. "I appreciate it. I'll keep it in mind."

Luna Hendricks had been engaged twice, first to a notable businessman in America and then later to a childhood friend recently returned from overseas. There was a photograph of the latter, probably before the engagement; he stood tall amidst a group of sisters, all of them light-haired and freckled, and it took Nora a moment to recognize a young Luna among them. She stood next to a girl of the same age, their hands just a hair's breadth away from each other, as if they had been touching. Or as if they wanted to touch.

The first engagement had ended due to a small scandal, the details of which Nora could not decipher. The second had ended when the young man and four other members of his family had perished in a fire. Liam had taken the position at the lighthouse only three months later. Was that why Luna had come with him? Out of grief for her long-lost love?

It did not explain why Liam had killed her. All speculation about it was just that—speculation. He'd grown mad being alone with a hysterical woman. He was jealous because his sister didn't love him enough. She had tried to kill him first.

There was a copy of his suicide note too. Nora trembled and her vision blurred for a moment. It had been written with a shaking hand. A transcript was included, but despite the sloping cursive, she found she could read the original text without issue.

I sought to be a lighthouse for my sister, a shining beacon of hope and safety. Instead, I have failed my purpose and she lies dead at my feet. For this I have no recourse but to take my own life and pray that God above offers me forgiveness.

His signature was unreadable, splotches blacking out most of it. Nora wanted to cry, could feel it building up in her throat like a hand reaching up to choke her from the inside.

The radio turned back on, buttons tapping a question. She ignored it, grabbing her jacket and climbing up. It was growing dark. She had to turn on the light.

One of the letters Will brought her was from Claire. Nora had seen it right away, but she had placed it neatly on the other end of the kitchen table and refused to look at it again while she did her research. When she came down the next morning, the letter was on top of Liam's note; she was sure she had not moved it there.

"All right," she mumbled, unsure who she was talking to. "All right, I'll read it."

It was drivel. She knew she was being unreasonable, but every single word made her teeth ache, as if she had bitten into a lemon. Claire was happy. Her pregnancy was going so well. She missed her. Being on the other side of the world was hard enough, but now she couldn't even call. Why would Nora choose this? She couldn't understand. She blamed herself. She wanted Nora to come back.

Back to where? she wondered. It had been made clear that she did not fit into Claire's life anymore, not after that conversation. For the first time, thinking about it did not make a deep sadness ring within Nora—instead it made her angry. Angry enough that the letter crumbled in her hand. She put it down before she tore it up completely.

Driven by sheer stubbornness, she brought out her sketchbook, found a whole new vantage point, and sketched the lighthouse again. She kept going, ignoring the icy wind on her face, ignoring how her hand turned pink from the cold. She kept drawing; she was not satisfied. Whatever this lighthouse was, however physical she knew it to be, it seemed it could not be captured on paper. She should have become a photographer instead, able to capture the truth of a single moment, the lines and colours in their real format. Whatever artist interpretation was going on, it was failing spectacularly.

Still, she kept at it, as if possessed. The sounds of the ocean rang in her ears, and she did not turn on the radio except to assure Will she was still alive. The few times she caught a faint press of a button or the note of the musical channel, she ignored it until it went away again.

Worry hung thick in the air, all over the island. She ignored that as well. She spent nearly every day outside, trying to draw the lighthouse and failing.

Night came quicker now that winter was setting in, and it was only when Nora stood up to go inside that she realized how long she had been sitting, every muscle aching and cold, so very cold. Her teeth chattered, and she wrapped her arms around herself, hoping to catch some semblance of heat.

She looked up at the figure standing at the top of the lighthouse, hair falling down her back, skirt whipping around her legs. She stared at Luna, whose hand was clenched around one of the pillars, half of her torso out over the edge. There was a light on in the kitchen, though Nora had made sure to turn it off before she left, surely Liam was there. He would come up at any moment, appear behind his sister, and push. Surely, he was already on his way.

Luna looked at her, and from this distance Nora could not tell if her eyes were grey as the sea in storm, blue as the sea in morning or green as the deep afternoon, when the seaweed and algae reached out to colour its way across the surface. Her sketchbook dropped from her hand, falling to the frozen ground just as Luna let go, her hair free in the wind as she fell, and fell, down.

It was sheer madness that made Nora run down to the beach. The tide stopped her, cutting off her path, and for a mad moment she was tempted to jump in and swim. But if the cold of it didn't kill her, then the current would, and she stopped herself just in time. The beach was empty, anyway, no body crashed on the still-visible sand or carried back and forth by the waves. No, no, there was nothing. Of course, there was nothing.

She stumbled back in a daze and spent several long moments searching for her dropped sketchbook, with no success. Inside, her radio was going crazy, and she made it in just in time to answer the ship that was hailing her. Thankfully, it was one used to the route, one who knew there should have been a light on. One that believed her lie about falling and needing to hobble back, one kind enough not to comment on how frazzled she sounded.

"It's all right," the kind, kind sailor said. "You've already got it back on. No harm done."

She blinked, staring at the radio. She had done no such thing, but he was right. The soft, sweeping light kept blinking through her window, reaching across the ocean and calling ships home. Steering them away from cliffs and dangers. A warning and a beacon. She barely registered him saying goodbye.

There was a beat, after the conversation ended, and then the radio turned back on.

Who is Claire?

"My childhood friend. She's gotten married. She's moved far away."

How far?

Nora wanted to laugh. So very far. For a moment, she couldn't speak, her tongue frozen. The cold had become a part of her now, setting up shop in her chest and bidding her be silent, be still.

"Very far," she responded. "I told her that I loved her, and it made things awkward."

You love her?

"I am in love with her. She did not take it well."

No one had taken it well. Not that everyone had taken it *badly*, but everyone'd had so many questions. *Why, when, how long have you known, why didn't you tell me, who are you, are you into me, is that why it didn't work out with, how didn't I know . . .*

So many words, and none of them meant anything.

I lost my love too.

"Yes, in a fire. I read. But why hadn't you married him sooner?"

A long stretch of silence, confusion in the air. Then, Nora thought she heard laughter, but it was only the wind outside, crashing against the ocean.

He?

Oh. *Oh.* Nora wanted to laugh, but instead she was crying. A scandal. Of course, she hadn't married that other man. *A scandal.* And that was why her brother had dragged her away with him, so she could not cast more shame on their family with her ways, with her love. With her.

"Is that why you jumped?" she asked, and then it hit her. Liam had not been up there, hadn't pushed. He hadn't taken his sister away from society until the fire, until . . .

I missed her so much. I couldn't go on.

And how to explain that kind of love? Nora hadn't even been able to explain it today, to people claiming to want to understand. She'd not had the words, not in the face of *conventional* and *should haves*. And she had lived it, was living it still. How could Liam hope to explain it to people, explain who his sister was, when all her life they had refused to see? Better to take the blame. Better to leave the story as that.

"Is he here?" she asked, looking around as if she could see them. "Is your brother here, too?"

Why would he be? He protected me. I have failed to protect him.

Everyone thought he'd killed her. Everyone accepted it. Because in the dark you could not see the cliffs, but when the light shone so brightly, you could not see the lighthouse either.

"I know, now," Nora said. "I know."

The radio had turned off. Maybe, Nora mused, with all the sadness and humour in the world, maybe it had never been on. Maybe she was losing her mind. That wouldn't be so bad, she thought, as the wind carried through the closed window and touched her cheek, light and cold, like the faintest brush of fingers.

❧

The contract she'd signed was for eight months, but there was a clause to end it with a week's notice. Nora gave Will a heads-up in advance—six months was enough, she reckoned. The last three had been especially lonely.

"I'm both surprised and not," he admitted. He'd come a day early to help her pack up, bringing cardboard boxes and two extra suitcases. "I thought you'd last a shorter while, I have to admit, and then when you powered through, I thought you'd go the full eight months."

"I probably could," she said, more a musing thought than a brag. "But I feel like it was time to get back home."

"Yeah, I get that. Time for someone else to deal with the ghosts here."

No ghosts, she thought. *Not anymore.*

"Oh, hey, I thought you were painting the lighthouse? But this is beautiful. You've got real talent."

He'd spotted the painting, which she'd hung in the kitchen; after so long working on it in there, it seemed to fit. And so, there it was, the canvas filled with all the hues of the sea, dragging towards the white sand of the Northern beach. The man and woman stood hand in hand, curls mingling in the wind; she had written their names on the back, just *Liam and Luna,* and hoped no one would think it inappropriate enough to take it down. No one could see their faces and recognize them anyway—they were turned away, looking forward. Their eyes towards the sea.

DAUGHTER

ELIN OLAUSSON

The woman who calls herself Lucy says that the world wasn't always as it is now. There used to be animals other than seagulls and gnats. There used to be people. I don't know if I should believe her stories, or if she tells them merely to amuse me. Maybe it's not important. However crowded the world used to be before my time, it isn't crowded now. There's just Lucy and I, the island, and the house. Everything else is water.

My bedroom window faces east, in the direction of the greenhouse and the bay. Lucy stands out there every morning as the sun rises, grey hair flurrying around her like seaweed swaying in the waves. The gulls are unafraid, but they've never attacked her. Close up they are big, heavy-looking, but in the air they become weightless. Unlike us, they spend long periods away from the island. I've tried asking Lucy where they go, but whenever I do, she gives me that look that means migraine and sadness.

I've just made my bed and put the cardigan on over my nightgown when she comes inside, bringing a gust of salty air. Her footsteps are heavy because of the bad leg.

"Put the kettle on, girl." Lucy slumps into a chair and drops a couple of potatoes on the table. They are misshapen and small, but we are lucky to be able to harvest at all. That's what Lucy always says.

"Did you see them?" I ask. Lucy narrows her eyes, lids drooping even more than usual. She knows I'm not talking about the gulls.

"That wasn't why I went outside. Now let's eat."

Breakfast is my least favourite meal of the day, and not only because it consists of algae and little else, but also because as soon as it is over, Lucy makes me take my medicine. She stores the jar under a rock outside, and just the sight of that jar makes my stomach churn. The medicine looks like soil, but wetter, and it smells like something rotting on the shore. Once I walked in on her as she prepared it, but she ushered me back into my room before I could see what went into the jar. Herbs from the greenhouse, I suppose, and kelp and seawater. But there are other things, too, metallic and vile. The taste of the medicine grows in my mouth, like a poisonous weed, but Lucy says I have to drink it. One teaspoon every morning, or I will stop breathing.

"Here. Just drink, it's nothing you haven't tasted before." She holds out the spoon and I take it, put it between my lips. I've tried to trick her once, spit it out when she didn't see, but after a few hours my chest started to tighten. By the evening it was so painful that I longed for breakfast, but I couldn't let Lucy know what I had done. Now, I swallow the brew and force my body to keep it down. Lucy puts the jar back on the lid and returns it to the hiding place outside. Her movements are slow, nothing like the gulls or the insects that scatter in all directions when a rock is lifted. *You'll have to prepare yourself for loneliness, Noë*, she told me once. I've known loneliness all my life and I don't want more of it.

"Can we go down to the sea-window today?" I ask once I've put the mugs away in the cupboard. Lucy sighs. Sometimes she makes sounds I can't stand and this is one of them.

"I should never have showed you the sea-window. It would have been for the best if I'd sealed it up after Herbert left."

Her voice goes heavy when she mentions Herbert's name. He was her husband, though I'm not really sure what a husband is. Once, I asked her and she told me that it is something that I will never have to concern myself with. Just like all the other things from the past.

"You can't seal it up!" My chest hurts at the thought, even though I've had my medicine. "I only want to watch them. There's no harm in watching."

"You sound just like him," Lucy mutters, but in the end, she unlocks the steel door and leads the way down the stairs. The walls are slimy from the damp, and the stairs creak and waver. If they ever collapse, the sea-window will be lost forever. We have to pass through another steel door before we enter the room Lucy calls the laboratory. It smells sickly, like my medicine, and there are strange things lining the desks and counters; objects made out of metal and plastic, with buttons and shattered screens. There were heaps of notebooks here before, filled with scribbles in unfamiliar handwriting, but Lucy has used them all as kindling.

The sea-window dominates the room, stretching from one wall to another. The glass is as thick as one of the large slabs down by the shoreline, but I can never shake the feeling that it's going to burst. Still, I'd spend all my time in front of it if only Lucy would allow it. Down here, the sea looks nothing like the dark, stormy surface the gulls soar over. The sunlight softens the water, makes it seem warm and inviting. Starfish attach themselves to the window and jellyfish pass by, cod, mackerel. Once, at a very long distance, I think I saw a whale. But studying fish isn't why I come to the sea-window. I only want to watch the Daughters.

"They don't like being spied on," Lucy says. She's pacing the littered floor, clearly eager to go back up. "Can't say that I blame them."

"Why are they called the Daughters?" I ask her, though she's told me before. Sometimes her stories confuse me, because there are so many things about the past that I don't understand.

"It's just a name." Lucy huffs. "It's the Daughters of Ran, really, but that takes too long to say."

"Ran." I like how the name slips off my tongue, short like my own.

"She was a sea goddess in the lost ages. I don't know the full story; it was some colleague of Herbert's who came up with the name. These creatures have been called lots of things, fairy-tale names, but Herbert and his team wanted something completely new." Lucy sits down on one of the swivel chairs. Her face is turned away from the sea-window.

But I keep my eyes on the water. I barely blink. It takes a long while until something shows, but when it finally does, I gasp. Three shapes, three Daughters swimming toward us. Their faces are human, they've got arms and chests and bellies, but instead of legs they have fishtails. Long hair spread out around them, black and red and ghost-white. I move closer to the window, eager to study every little detail. Their faces are narrow, foxlike, and their eyes are strangely large and translucent. I close my fists at the sight of their intertwined arms. I've seen enough Daughters to know that there are lots of them, and they always come in pairs or groups. They don't ever have to be lonely.

The sea-window is dark on the other side, Lucy says, which means the Daughters can't see us. Still, when I shift, I get the feeling their eyes track the movement, and the one on the left turns the corners of her mouth up in a smile or something like it. She looks a bit like me, with thick, black hair and skin many shades darker than Lucy's. As I watch her glide through the water I wonder if she has a name. Do Daughters talk at all? I barely know a thing about them, and Lucy doesn't share my fascination. I wish Herbert was still alive. Lucy would be happier with him around, and he could tell me things about the Daughters.

The black-haired creature laughs—at something one of her friends has said? I try to imagine their voices but I can't. They could be tinny or chirpy or nightmarish, monstrous. Lucy's yawny sigh turns my gaze to her, and the look she gives me reminds me of childhood, of nicking food supplies and being found out.

"Are you satisfied? This leg is killing me. I tell you, one of these days I won't be able to make it down those stairs."

"You don't have to come with me," I blurt. "I can come down here on my own."

"Oh, no." Lucy throws a quick look at one of the broken machines before turning back to me. "There are things here you don't understand. End of discussion."

"But—" I glance toward the sky-window. The Daughters are gone. It makes me sad.

"Come on." Lucy leaves the room, and I follow her reluctantly, like a defiant shadow. She moans and complains on the stairs, and I can't help thinking that she only has herself to blame. She could easily give me the key, but she won't. It's as if she doesn't want me to have access to the sea-window at all.

The Daughters are on my mind for the remainder of the day, especially the black-haired one. The one who looks like me. There's something there that bothers me, something that makes my heart ache and beat faster all at once. I don't look anything like Lucy, but I look like that girl in the water. My sleep is fitful and sweaty, and it's harder than ever to swallow my medicine the next morning.

"You have to," Lucy says. She stands in front of me, holding the jar in both hands. "For your breathing."

That's when the thought lands in me, like a nestling-feather falling to the ground. I can't breathe unless I take the medicine. It's just like the sea-creatures, who can't survive outside the water. Just like the Daughters.

What if I'm not like Lucy at all? Herbert studied the Daughters, filled notebooks with findings about them. What if he wasn't satisfied with watching them through the sea-window and found a way to bring one ashore?

The thoughts thrill and chafe. They make perfect sense and no sense at all. As I water the greenhouse plants, I think about the creatures I saw, their intertwined arms. Maybe I have been like them all along.

That night, as we drink our weak mint tea, I ask Lucy for how long I've been on the island.

"What sort of question is that?" She has her bad leg propped up on a pillow and winces when she moves. "You've always been here."

I should feel sorry for her because she's in pain, but mainly I'm disappointed because it means we can't go down to the sea-window until she's better. "But I don't look like you," I say.

Lucy's forehead creases. "Children don't always look like their parents. Now, why don't you go get the bird book and read us something?"

I ignore her attempt to change the subject, though I love the bird book. It's older than Lucy, with stories about hundreds of birds that look nothing like gulls. There are colour drawings that I could gaze at for hours, drawings from the time when the world was a lot bigger than just the island.

"Were there people in the past who had black hair like me?"

Lucy sighs. "Oh, of course. There were all sorts of people back then."

"And the flood killed them," I say, hoping she'll tell me the story. It's one of my favourites.

"Yes." Lucy goes silent, as if the memories have snatched her away. "There had been floods before, but none like that one. It devoured everything. Some people believe the gods were angry and sent the flood to wipe us out. But I think the sea just wanted to grow."

I don't understand the part about *some people believe the gods were angry*. If Herbert and Lucy and I were the only survivors, who are those other people? Like always, Lucy's stories confuse me, but I know she'll get a headache if I ask too many questions.

"Now fetch the bird book," Lucy says. "Read to me about the eagles."

⁢⁢⁢⁢⁢⁢⁢⁢ᘓᘔ

I toy with the idea of refusing the medicine every day for the rest of that week. Nothing shows on my face as I mash potatoes for supper or collect rainwater for our tea. Lucy is as she's always been, slow, solid. Her outlines are so much sharper than mine, as if I'm carved from some strange material. Daughter-material? I've started seeing them in my dreams, their crystalline eyes, the scales coating their lower bodies. At night, once Lucy has gone to sleep, I study my naked legs. If I look close enough, I can spot the marks, the traces. The proof that I am not human.

Then one morning, Lucy has a fall when she's heading outside to fetch the jar. She sinks down on the threshold with a whimper, and I run to her, grabbing her shoulders. Through the sweater they feel stiff, hardened by aching muscles.

"You should rest." Lucy protests but I guide her to the bedroom. Make her lie down.

"Your medicine." Staring into my eyes, she reminds me of a bird. A screeching gull or an eagle. "Noë, you have to take it."

"I will." I smile the way I used to when I was little, showing teeth. The smile digs into my face.

"Don't forget." She looks eager to say more, so I nod and leave before she keeps talking. I go outside and grab the jar, then head back inside and remove the lid. The smell makes me nauseous like always, and I stare down at the muddy concoction, knowing it's for the last time. Leisurely, I fetch a spoon from the drawer and dip it into the jar. Make sure I do everything right, so Lucy won't understand what's up. I wash the spoon and bring the jar back outside. There's a wild feeling in my chest, as if a swallow is tumbling about in there. This is the day.

Lucy claims she's fine, but she doesn't get out of bed. Her face is marked by headache, and she moans when she thinks I can't hear. I bring her tea and water, and I read from the bird book. I harvest potatoes, onions, and lay seaweed out to dry. In the afternoon my chest starts to throb when I draw a breath. By evening it has grown to a cutting pain, and every word I read out loud stabs my lungs. But it's the last time I'll ever read to Lucy, so I force myself. She's quiet, tired. Her face eases when I go through the page about the white-tailed eagle.

"I saw them once when I was a little girl." Her voice cracks, is about to turn into a memory. "I couldn't understand how something so big . . . could fly so high."

She's fallen asleep before I've read the final sentence. I put the book down beside the bed and blow out the candle. As I leave the room, I take one last look at Lucy. She isn't my mother but she's something similar, and I'll never forget her.

The gulls have gathered by the waterline when I head down to the rocks. They watch me with their pale eyes, and I would have asked them to look after Lucy, if my chest didn't hurt so bad. I stare into the dark water, picturing the fairy-tale world below. The wind pinches my skin as I slip out of my dress, my heavy cardigan. I wonder if the transformation will be quick or if it will take hours, if growing back a tail is painful. Then I dive into the water.

At first, I see nothing, as if I've gone blind. The waves tear at me, push my limbs in all directions. And then—I see them. The Daughters. They are all around me, hundreds of smiling faces, eyes meeting mine. I recognize the girl who looks like me, and I smile back at her, though it's difficult with the water slipping in between my lips. Not a quick transformation, then. But I'm used to pain.

The Daughters come closer, touching my face and arms. Their hands are scaly, clawed. Through the sea-window, I never noticed the claws. My lungs are about to explode, and I kick my legs, desperate for air.

The one who could have been my sister shakes her head. When her smile widens, I see fangs, and I realize why Lucy didn't want me near the sea-window. I realize a lot of things, in that one moment until I'm gone and Lucy is alone on the island, in the world.

Sink Your Sorrows

to the Sea

CHANDRA FISHER

An aching, empty tug pulls my feet onto the rocks. It's cold here, sad and devoid of any meaningful life. Only scraggly grasses and lichen clinging to the salt-crusted stone. There's no life in the tidepools. No birds wheel overhead. The wind drags her fingers through my hair, tugging at my skirt, lacing through my top, urging chill-bumps to rise on my skin, my arm hair to stand at attention.

The locals tell a story of this lonely, unnamed stretch of coast. No men dare to come here, and only the women who've lost.

Which is most of us, truth be told.

And I among them.

My feet are cold, the uneven icy touch of the rocks beneath them both steadying and slippery. It's only a ten-inch drop to the water below, and it looks shallow enough. But the October air is bitter and I don't know if I can step in.

The bars in this small town are like bars anywhere, filled with people getting drunk enough to do something stupid enough to stave off whatever loneliness keeps them awake at night. Although last night, I was mostly sober when I was followed into the bathroom.

But you've heard this story before. If you have woman friends, you may have heard it more times than you care to revisit it. It's not the important part, anyhow.

The important part is the woman in the waiting room of the

clinic.

Last night, after it happened, I went straight to the emergency medical clinic. It's a small enough town that I walked there, my white lace dress torn and my feet bare.

The woman in the waiting room had long wispy grey hair. Knitting needles clacked in her weathered, age-spotted hands, deftly meting out cream-coloured lace, millimetre by millimetre.

"Whatever it is, you can sink it into the sea. I know just the place."

Something about my face must have spoken to her, and the instructions she gave must have spoken to me, because here I am, barefoot on the freezing rocks, unsure if I can do what she told me after all. I scan the horizon, and just as she promised, about two hundred yards out, a battered white rowboat sits on a sandbar, gently rocking in the lapping waves. The knock of the oars in the oarlocks can be heard even above the wind and the water hissing against the shore.

I look down at the parcel in my hands. I know the contents of the white paper bag. I tied it closed with dental floss because it was the only string I could find. My medical bracelet. My underwear. A drink ticket from the night before.

I'm here. What have I got to lose?

I squeeze my eyes shut tight and lower the toes of my right foot into the waves.

He brought you ribbons for your braids and matching ones for your dress. He helped you with your chores, keeping you company and lightening your workload, when he probably should have been helping his own family.

You couldn't send him away. Even if you'd wanted to, he was so handsome, and so smitten with you. It was beautiful to be desired, and the embers in his eyes let you know that he certainly did desire you.

When it wasn't chores, it was walks by the sea. On sunny days, you held one hand, carrying your shoes in your other as your toes found the heat of the sand and your hearts found the heat of one another.

Promises were made.

His battalion was called to the front that spring. He left with tearful goodbyes, and you vowed you'd wait for him, and you faithfully kept that vow.

At summer's end, the letter came that broke your heart.

You soaked the paper with your tears and nearly shredded it with your wailing. Your father shouted at you, complaining about the scene. Your mother watched you with empathy but didn't speak against her husband. You took the letter and ran.

You found yourself in the barn. You found a rope. You climbed into the hayloft where the sun's rays had caught the amber flecks in his brown eyes, where his thumb had gently caressed your cheek, where the promise of when you turned eighteen was spoken aloud for the first time.

Your birthday was less than a month away now.

You only made it out of the barn alive because you couldn't find anything in the hayloft to tie your rope to.

When you made your way back to the house, only your mother was there. She knew. She understood your loss the way only another woman can. She told you about the beach.

You knew the spot. He'd pulled you from the sand before your feet could touch it. He said there was something bad there, something evil, something he could feel in his chest. Maybe it was the tide coming in, he'd said, but it didn't feel safe.

It didn't, because it wasn't. But your mother sent you there.

You took your tear-soaked letter and wrapped the ribbons he'd given you around it. You found the little white boat and rowed out past the breakers.

The sun was hot overhead but that hadn't stopped the day from feeling dreary. The listless heat lay across your hair like a shroud.

You should have been making wedding plans with him. Instead, you gathered the last of your tears on your fist, wiped them onto the letter, and sank him into the sea.

A gasp fills my lungs with icy air as my feet move through the water. I'm closer to the little boat now, and there's a chill in my chest that has less to do with the sea or the late fall breeze and more to do with the memory you just handed me, his letters and a frayed old barn rope. I swear I can feel them in my hand now, the paper soft, the rope rough. But when I look down, it's just my own white package in my hands, my bare feet and the hem of my white lacy dress soaked in salt water.

Seaweed curls around my ankles and the wind grips my hair.

I push onward.

You become a woman and everything that happens on the toilet is a find-and-seek game. Every time you sit on the throne, you're looking for something: a speck of blood, a shiny clear streak of egg white, a plus sign. Sometimes you're seeking with joy in your heart, and sometimes with fear, but every time you tend to your own relief, you're seeking.

You found what you were looking for after a long year of searching; a year in which he almost gave up. *You* almost gave up. After you found the egg white, you did not find blood. The not finding was as thrilling as the found, and shortly thereafter you found the plus sign.

You felt divine. Not in the sense of feeling nice—"It was divine, darling"—but in the true sense of divinity, a goddess unleashed. You felt powerful. You felt awful. Not in the sense of feeling terrible, but in the true, original, literal sense of the word: filled with awe.

Two souls inside your body. Two lives within your boundaries.

But the seeking didn't stop there. It never does. Once it begins, there is no end to it. And one day, a few months later, you found something that struck fear into your heart.

Blood.

Blood when there should not be blood.

Later, soundwaves confirmed what you already knew to be true: the things you'd already found, the egg white and the plus sign, were gone. And now instead of seeking, you had to wait. You had to wait while your body curled around the soul exiting you. You had to wait through the pain. More blood. A truly frightening amount of blood.

You soaked it up with towels. You put the towels in a mesh laundry bag. You soaked the towels and the bag with your tears, blood and salt and agony.

When it was over, you couldn't bring yourself to wash the towels.

Instead, you brought them to the shore. The midwife told you about the boat, and though you were not a sailor, you figured it out. You rowed and rowed and rowed, pouring all of your agony, all of your loss, into the muscles in your arms.

The sea was grey and lifeless, calm. You thought you might never feel calm again, and in that moment, you envied the sea.

When there was nothing left, you leaned over the edge of the little boat. You waited a long, long time. You don't know what you expected. Maybe a flash of light, a storm, some recognition of your loss. Nothing changed.

The mesh laundry bag and the towels, the blood and the tears. In another life, those things might have become your daughter.

You hoisted them over the side of the boat, and sank them into the sea.

The salt air is tanged with copper now, so thick I can almost taste it, and half my tears are for myself and half are for you and the daughter who would never be. You deserved better, and I can't believe fate was so cruel to take it from you. The breeze picks up now, and the white boat rocks a lullaby in the waves.

She would have loved it.

The wind keens, and it sounds so much like the wail of a newborn that I whip my head around, looking for a child crying on the shore. There's no one there; just as I noticed before, this place is lifeless.

And how far I've come. The shore is as far back as the boat is ahead, and I'm soaked to my waist. A shiver runs from my tailbone to the base of my neck as the salt kisses me between my thighs, my sex naked because my underwear is in my hands. I imagine the water is washing me clean again, making me new.

I turn to the boat. How much deeper? I can certainly swim, but the ocean is not a swimming pool.

I push farther out, and in only a few steps, the ground disappears beneath my feet, the depth of the water pulling me under.

I grip my packet tighter and kick for the surface, emerging with a gasp. My dress floats around me, swirling and bobbing, luminescent in the moonlight like a lace jellyfish.

I look to the shore.

I look to the boat.

I swim onward.

☙❧

The air conditioning hit you full force, a relief on your sweaty skin. You started to shiver in seconds. You pushed down the aisles of red, white, and rosé until you found the perfect cab sav to soothe the savage beast.

It was one of your usual bottles, your routine predictable and comforting.

It was a new kid at the checkout.

Kid. He was probably twenty-five. You chastised yourself as you dug in your purse.

"Nineteen seventy-five," he said, without a glance your way.

Your fingers hovered over your driver's license, your brain short circuiting. You'd meant to be ready to pass him your ID, but he didn't even ask for it. Now you needed to replan your course of action, correct your fingers and reach for your credit card, and the stumble took you longer than was socially acceptable.

Even though there was no one in line behind you, no one waiting, you felt the anxiety of taking too long.

You tapped your card on the reader. He passed you the bottle.

On Monday you took your son to the doctor. Just a routine checkup, because you were a good mom and you worked hard to make sure your kids were well and provided for.

Through the stethoscope chest listening and the reflex tapping and the tongue depressing, the doctor didn't even look at you. "He's eating all right, Mom?" "And how is his sleep, Mom?" "He's getting along all right with his peers, Mom?"

You didn't even have a name anymore.

Did you even exist anymore?

At home, you dug out old pictures of you from a shoebox on a high shelf in your closet. The glossy chestnut hair and tanned skin, the bright eyes, the drunk girl rallying cry of your university years. Boudoir shots from earlier in your marriage that hadn't been looked at in ten years. You barely recognized that girl.

You told your husband you were going for a drive to clear your head.

He didn't answer.

Down the coast and to a stretch of sand that felt like you did; hollow, invisible, forgotten. Like called to like, and you found yourself in the water, a bottle of wine in your hand. As you walked, the rocks jabbed at the soles of your feet, but the cold and the alcohol numbed you enough that it wasn't uncomfortable. You were walking away from the shore, toward nothing. The night was clear and calm, the moon glinting off black water, and something grew in the distance.

A boat.

A low, drunken chuckle escaped your throat as you climbed in, remembering summers of your youth, camping with friends, joy riding in stranger's boats, delighting in the thought of their empty gas tanks come morning and finding freedom in the wind in your hair as you soared over the waves.

The rowboat wasn't quite like that, but neither were you anymore.

You rowed out. You looked at the photos tucked in the pocket of your denim jacket, swigging the last of the bottle of wine. One by one, you rolled the photos and slid them into the empty bottle.

You held the bottle over the bow of the boat, watching bubbles rise as it filled with sea water. The girl you were was gone now.

You sank her into the sea.

℮∽⊙

My arms pull against the spasming of the cold, and my numb fingers reach the boat with a thump. I open my mouth to cry out with pain, and the water flows into my mouth. I expect salt; instead, I taste red wine. Knowing I'm sharing a drink with you gives me strength to drag myself from the waves, forcing my fingers open around the packet as I drop it into the bottom of the boat, my limp body following.

For a long moment I gasp and shudder on the floor of the boat, letting it rock me as I stare up at the stars. The Milky Way urges me onward, and with my hands aching with cold, I reach for the anchor chain and haul it up.

It doesn't take long. The water must only be deep enough to make me work for my goal. The anchor hits the bottom of the boat with a thick, hollow sound. My hair hangs damp and loose around my face and drips more salt water into my dress. At some point, I started crying. Funny, I haven't actually cried since it happened.

I tug the paddles through the oarlocks, white paint flaking into the water. The wood is old and soft and spongy beneath my grip, and water is leaking into the bottom of the boat. I look back at the shore.

The smart thing to do would be to paddle back. But sometimes grief picks unintelligent choices for you, choices that wouldn't make any sense to the casual observer, but choices that would make anyone who's grieved nod with understanding.

And I have to sink these sorrows into the sea.

I stop shivering.

Some part of my brain knows that when you stop shivering, that's when you're in trouble, but my heart is in charge now, and she bids me *row*.

I have no way of knowing how long I paddle. I row and row with no plans of stopping until it feels right. Every woman I know has suffered incalculable loss. It's just that we don't say it out loud. Or maybe we do, in therapist offices and to our closest friends, in anonymous chat rooms and late at night over too many drinks. And right now, I am rowing for them, for every woman who's promised to confess a dark secret only to reveal a hurt so profound it's left me breathless.

There's a change in the colour of the water, a change in the way it reflects the stars. It's darker here, and some part of me knows it's deeper.

Older.

My arms won't row another stroke, and I know this is the place.

I retrieve my white parcel from the bottom of the boat. For a moment, I pass it from hand to hand, huffing hot breath onto each hand in turn, trying to loosen my fingers which still form the shape of the oars.

I lean out as far over the edge of the little boat as I can without tipping. I want to say something, something meaningful, something that will make all my hurt, all your hurt, disappear. Something that will erase the fact that any of those things ever happened to us.

But that's not real. That's not true. There are no magic words, and we are only amalgamations of every experience that has brought us to this point, and as the waters lap at my little white parcel, my fingers open of their own accord, softly, unfolding like petals.

The moonlight casts the water suddenly transparent, and I watch the parcel sink down, down, down. When it's almost out of sight, I see something else.

Something rising.

I think it's seaweed, but as it rises faster and faster, I see it's a rope. The rope from your barn. I lean forward further, to get a better look, and my hand sinks to my wrist in the water and your rope coils around my arm.

I don't even have time to shriek as I'm pulled beneath the waves.

Your rope threads itself across my shoulders. Your letters and pictures swirl up from the depths like glorious fish, swimming in a sepia toned school. They're followed by a tattered manta ray—no, an old towel, stained burgundy with wine or blood or both. Everything, everything, all the fear and loss and agony and every memory tossed into the sea threads itself through me, attaching to my arms and my torso and spine.

I don't think to breathe. I look up, and a trail of bubbles escapes my mouth, moving up and up toward the surface, toward the moonlight, toward the stars.

For a moment, everything goes dark.

And then, I rise.

Through the water I am propelled like a fish, until I burst forth from the surface like a bird, like an angel, on wings made of memories, an apparition of sorrow and strength made flesh. Saltwater and wine and blood pour forth from my lips, as I join this forsaken sorority of wounded women with a scream of agony.

ᗴHE ᗡEEP ᗴND OF ᒪONGING

HAYLEY STONE

very morning since our fight I've come down to the shore searching for any changes.

Blades of fresh algae stretch across the beach, drying black beneath the cold eye of the sun. Gulls circle in crying gyres. The ancient wreck where we met still reclines in the inlet, hull seamed with rust, mast broken on the rock.

You aren't here.

I want to apologize. I must tell the waves a hundred times how sorry I am, how I didn't mean what I said, how I was wrong to try and make you into something you're not. I'm listening now, my love, but all I hear is the pounding roar of the ocean in my ears, and the sibilant hiss of water over harsh sediment as the tides leave.

If you're out here and you still want me, I'm yours.

But I need a sign.

❧

Cal's decided you don't exist, never did.

My dear husband scoffs at the very word—mermaid—with barely concealed contempt. I was honest with him after I first found you clinging to the inside of the wreck with legs so newly sprouted they were pink and raw, still printed in the diamond pattern of your lost scales. It was only after I heard that familiar downturn in his voice, I realized my mistake.

This madness happens to women who come out to the coast sometimes, Cal says. Delicate constitutions and all. Nothing we can help. The salt air invades like venom, fogs thinking, makes us see what isn't there. As if I am the one lost in fantasy, unable to face reality without the firm support of liquor in my veins. I'd concede to the absurdity of the whole thing if I felt more favourably toward him. But he hasn't earned such generosity.

He telephoned the house the other day, again. He wants Mother to send me back to him in Iffley where he can lock me away in my room and prey upon my wealth in peace. He's started working over the rest of the family too, trying to convince them I'm not lovesick, only homesick. That this is all further evidence of the deep gloom he'd hoped time with my family would cure.

God, how I loathe him.

If I hadn't met you, I'm sure I could have gone on happily miserable with Cal for the rest of my days, content as a child who expects no more from love than a closed fist. I would have been a good wife. Patient. Obedient. Kind. A quiet, appreciable lamp.

How could you do it? Bring me up from the depths, push air into my lungs, and then let go of my hand?

It's not just Cal in denial. Everyone's starting to forget you here too, Mother and all the cousins. Even the servants you befriended look sideways at me. It's like you were never here.

Did you know that would happen? When you returned to the sea?

I've tried helping them remember, like a castaway stacking wood for a signal fire even though the ship has passed. I talk about the shoreline rescue who stayed with us for a time, how you slept in Aunt Cathy's room with the casement flung open and the way you took salt with your tea that one time, or how you never quite figured out sleeves, adjusting and readjusting the unwanted skin of your dresses—safe and charming queerness.

Never have I breathed a word of how you kissed me that first time on the landing after everyone else had retired for the night, hands pressed to both sides of my face, mouth open in hot, unfrightened hunger. I thought you would devour me.

I wanted you to.

I'm sorry I didn't tell you that sooner.

My daily visitations over the last few weeks have not gone unnoticed. No doubt at Cal's request, Mother has assigned servants to surveil me on my trips. She thinks I don't know but how could I not? The naked vacancy of the shoreline makes people stand out with our bold, unwelcome silhouettes. We don't belong here.

Is that why you didn't ask me to come with you? Because you knew I wouldn't fit in?

No—that's not it. I've gone over our fight dozens, hundreds of times now. The beach hasn't changed and neither has my memory of that night.

Cal had just telephoned again. He was drunk. Blustering. Someone—probably Mother—had reported our goings-on to him and he was threatening to come down here himself and sort me out. Those were his words. Sort me out. But I am not a puzzle, something to be pinched and positioned and made to order.

After I got off the phone, I was crying. You took my tears onto your fingers, your lips.

You said, "I love you."

You said, "I'll do anything for you."

So, I told you what I wanted and how I planned to make it happen. I would walk Cal down to the beach, to the wreck where we met, and you would take care of the rest. Everyone would think it was an accident.

Please understand, my love. I didn't realize what it meant to ask this of you. My only desire was to be rid of my husband so that we could be together without his meddling and interference. Without the threat of him looming over our happiness like a cloud's shadow that will not pass.

The request dropped between us like an anchor. My heartbeat pulsed in my throat.

"I can't."

You paused before answering. That tiny hesitation, like a foot holding open a door, gave me the wrong impression. I believed I could persuade you. If only I'd heard the warning in that first sample of your silence.

But I grabbed your face, both hands, like that time on the stairs, like I would kiss you.

I forced you to look at me. "People drown all the time."

Your eyes dimmed, and I didn't see how I was breaking your heart, not even when you told me you weren't a killer or when I replied—oh, God—that your kind had done it before.

I said, "I thought you loved me."

I said, "I thought you'd do anything for me."

I'll never forget the look on your face as you tried to pull away. Or that little choked sound, like the sickening press of a knife through fish scale and flesh, when I wouldn't let you go.

Cal didn't come in the end, the bastard. Not that week, or the next. He couldn't be bothered, or maybe he just forgot after sleeping off the liquor.

I came up with breakfast the next morning—a peace offering— but you were already gone: room empty, bed made, every wrinkle in the sheets smoothed out as though you'd never slept in it. I dropped my tray so suddenly the eggs surfed off their dish and onto the floor. The powdered sugar for the hotcakes spilled underfoot, tracking everywhere I went searching for you.

I raced down to the beach and there you were—sunbathing on a rock like something out of an old mariner's tale: lean, finned, covered in the wet shine of daylight. Strange. Magnificent. My heart crowded into my throat, and I shucked my shoes, hefted my skirts, and ran, one hand raised in greeting, though it might well as have been farewell.

It turned out to be a grey seal.

A seal, can you imagine?

The animal turned its head and looked at me with big, sad eyes, as if I were the dumber creature, before dragging its blubbery body off the rocky mantle and slipping effortlessly beneath the waves.

It probably goes without saying, but I wasn't thinking of you when I asked you to kill Cal.

I wasn't even thinking of him.

I was thinking of the hours we'd spent tangled in Aunt Cathy's childhood bed, disappearing into each other beneath dark kelp-coloured sheets, or the time I taught you to waltz on the sand: your hand in mine, my fingers in the small of your back, easing us back and forth in a slow gentle rhythm. I was greedy for more of these sunny moments, desperate to stay awake after sleeping through the first half of my life.

It's still no excuse. I just thought you deserved to know why I did it. Said those horrible things. I'd take them back if I could. I believe it isn't too late for us.

In a funny twist, I finally understand how Cal feels halfway into his nightcap. I'm still drunk on the hope you poured into me, my steady horizon unfixed, everything in triplicate—my hopes, my fears.

For better or worse, everything seems possible now.

℮◞

The ocean was still today, the sun laying a road of solid white down its middle like a path forward; no gulls crying overhead. Something drew me back to the wreck. I know not what, but I followed the instinct like you would have, and for the first time since finding you all those weeks ago, I climbed on board.

And do you know what I found?

The shaker you used to salt your tea.

A pair of long gloves you liked to wear because the pressure of the heavy silk reminded you of your absent scales.

One of Aunt Cathy's deep blue gowns she loaned you, with all the frills and buttons. The same gown you were wearing the first time we kissed.

This cherished collection, displayed with great care on a shelf of stacked driftwood, the dark mark of high tide just below. You kept them, these relics of our time together, preserved in this special in-between place, this hidden closet between land and sea. You kept them. I could barely breathe, so great was my wonder.

I let myself pick up each item, hold it in my hands. I rolled my thumb over the silk gloves, remembering your pulse jumping beneath. I pressed the gown against my nose. The fabric was stiff from the salt air but it smelled like you, or like the sea, which I understand now are very much the same thing. You cannot isolate the part that longs for the deep any more than you can separate the heart from the body and expect to go on living.

In the end, I left each item where I found it, resisting the temptation to take them with me.

Maybe you'll come back for them one day, and for me. Maybe you won't. I know now that I must be content with either outcome. I asked for signs—here they are. Signs we happened. Signs that companionship can take other shapes than cold apathy and violence, that it should.

Standing there, I suddenly knew what I needed to do, what I should have done when you were still here.

I slipped my wedding band off my finger.

I could've set the bit of silver down amidst the other artifacts where it could later be retrieved if I changed my mind. But instead, I clambered from the wreck, the empty pledge tucked tightly in my fist. I stood on the beach, our footprints long gone from the sand, and faced the sea.

Then I cranked my arm back, and let the band fly.

Tomorrow when I come down to the shore, maybe you will be here waiting, my message finally received.

I will take you into my arms, press kisses to your mouth, make apologies in every language my body knows how to. We will leave, not back to Iffley but to anywhere else in the world you want to go. I will show you Amsterdam and Paris. We will laugh together about all the things that don't make sense about the human world, all the silly beliefs people just accept as law, not bothering to question what else can be.

Or maybe when I come to the shore tomorrow, you will still be gone.

I will continue alone, sloshing about half full until I find another whose currents move in the same direction as mine. A lonely stranger who even now is lying asleep at the bottom of a vast ocean, waiting to be pulled up. Waiting to breathe free.

How wonderful not knowing which it will be.

FORTUNE FAVOURS
THE BRAVE

V.F. LESANN

Annie swam, fighting the cold Atlantic waves for every breath and cursing the day she'd first laid eyes on Tom Delaney.

The tail dragged heavy in her arms, a monstrosity of wire and cloth that looked elegant in the kerosene lamp-light of their little den, but presently felt like it was trying to drown her with a personal vengeance. She cursed the damned tail, and Tom, and Mack, and especially herself for saying yes to this madness.

Annie, my flower, Tom'd said, with that grin like she was the only woman in the world. Like she was Venus popping out of her clamshell, pretty enough to be worshipped. *How'd you fancy becoming a mermaid for me?*

She took a face full of saltwater like a slap, hacking and gagging, her eyes already burning like they'd swell shut. Something cold and sinewy slithered across her legs and her stomach cramped with fear, hoping it was only seaweed. Annie kicked furiously, pretending her anger and fear was heat enough to keep the ice out of her bones a little longer.

For a moment, she toyed with the idea of praying. But if nobody answered when she was a little girl with a shiny clean soul, she didn't imagine they were likely to start now.

And so Annie swam, hating bloody *everything*.

"Annie, my flower," Tom said, with his smile that was the bellwether for trouble or money or both, "how'd you fancy becoming a mermaid for me?"

Half-cut and happy, Annie cackled. "Do you think I look like a mermaid? You charmer!"

Mack levered his thick head off the kitchen table and peered at her, slit-eyed. "More like a mermaid than a fortune teller, if you ask me."

"Nobody did," she snapped. She'd been layering ink and soot in her hair for bloody years now to cover the red, perfecting a sultry nowhere-in-particular accent and the art of guessing what folks wanted you to tell them. Or what they most feared. They'd pay just as much for that. "I'll send Tasbem after you in your sleep, prick-for-brains."

Mack guffawed and refilled his mug from the bottle. "You ain't a witch and he ain't a real demon."

Tom, as drunk as any of them, was up from his seat and pacing. "Stow it and listen, the pair of you. Barnum's been all up and down the coast with his Fiji Mermaid, right?"

"Nasty little thing." Annie shuddered.

"Fish-end stitched up to a monkey-front," Mack added sagely. "He's got them forking over thirty cents at the door to look at it. Big man's got the Midas touch."

Tom nodded. "He has indeed. But what's on the signs?" He rubbed his hands together, on a roll now, and produced a crumpled leaflet with the flourish of an aspiring magician. "*Sirens*. Beautiful women, singing sailors to their doom and all that. They're paying to see the specimen, sure, but what do they really want to see?"

"Fantastic tits," Annie concluded. Mack grunted his agreement, smoothing out the leaflet reverently.

"So, who are we to deprive them of their dream?" Tom made a coaxing gesture, from the paper to Annie and back again. "It'd be easy. Mack's the fisherman who first saw her. Adds credibility. I'm the talker, laying the tale, showing them where to watch. And you, sweetheart, will be the mermaid."

"I'm the mermaid," she echoed. She was just on the right side of drunk to think it was a fair idea. "Do I got to have my tits out? You'll get me taken in for indecency, Thomas Delaney."

Tom waved his hand. "Only if you like. We'll have you far

enough out they can't see clear. You and me'll fashion you a tail to flip around. Brush your hair, float around a bit for them, then disappear back down the shoreline. Mack and me'll take 'em down to Bearberry Cove and keep 'em from leaping into the water and following you. You'll have to go in up the beach and pop around past one of the headland juts into the bay. If we're lucky the fog'll be rollin' in at twilight; use it like your curtain call. It'll look like you headed out to sea instead of back to shore, and by the time the fog rolls through, the show's done."

She refilled their mugs. The bottle was getting dangerously light. "You really think folks are going to pay?"

"Thirty cents for a stinking monkey-fish," Mack pointed out.

"Sucker born every minute, the big man says," Tom said, and sent her a rakish wink. "We'll start them out at a nickel and see where it takes us. If it were me, I believe I'd pay a whole dollar a day just to watch you swim around, even if I knew the trick of it."

She laughed and toasted him for drawing a blush from her. "All right," she agreed, "Let's make us a mermaid."

☙

Sunset chased her back to the shore. The thought of struggling through the nighttime sea with a mile of inky darkness and unseen creatures under her legs lit a fire in her muscles, and Annie dragged herself out of the water just as the last of the daylight was staining breaking waves the colour of blood. She dragged the waterlogged tail out of the surf with one-two-three lurches and flung it onto the rocks, taking a moment on her hands and knees to steady her heart. She was shivering so hard she could barely breathe and her limbs were cramping viciously. Her hair hung lank around her face, a muddy mess of red and trailing grey as the last of her fortune teller's disguise was scoured away by the saltwater.

A fine turn out tonight, from what she'd seen between swells. Plenty of bodies crowded around Tom on the shore, pointing and shouting and opening their wallets. Tom's mermaid would be another triumph for their little band, sure enough. The boys would already be home, counting the coin, drinking, and celebrating. Warm and toasty around the hearth. There might be a bit of cold stew left for her, if they remembered to set some aside for the star of the bloody show.

Hauling her cache of supplies out from the hollow log where she'd tucked them before her swim, she flung a blanket around herself and fumbled together a bundle of kindling with corpse-numb fingers. It took four tries to get a flame to catch. She hunched as close to her little fire as she could without setting herself alight, shutting her eyes and tallying up how much she thought they'd pulled in this time.

God above, that water had been cold though. Maybe she could spend her cut on a warmer coat for the winter.

Winter.

She opened her eyes with a sigh, licking dried salt from her lips. They wouldn't be able to keep this game up for much longer. Best to make their money while they could. The sun set like it had tripped over the horizon, turning the pines to dark spectres towering around her, rustling and hissing in the autumn wind. Icy water from her hair trickled down her spine.

From somewhere in the shadows behind her, a dry branch broke. Not falling from a tree, but as though it had been lying on the ground and someone trod on it.

Annie froze, her eyes darting to the tail in all its soggy glory. But no further sounds came from the trees.

She wouldn't press her luck. Muttering curses, she pushed herself painfully to her feet and stamped out the measly fire, throwing burlap around the tail before setting out for the long trudge home.

❦

"I think I must still have water in my ears, Tom Delaney," Annie said. "You didn't just say that to me."

Tom was at her knee like he was courting her all over again, his pretty eyes sparkling with cunning. "Just till All Hallows, my darling. It's not so far away as all that. Think of the crowd and coin we'll draw!"

She flung his hand off her leg and shoved herself to her feet, rounding the room to put the table between them so she didn't put her boot into his teeth. "A month and a half? You daft prick. You said we'd be done this by now."

"No, I *said* we'd see how the crowds went . . ."

"I suppose you'll be the one to swim out and save me when I freeze and go under?"

"You've got to start going further out anyway," Mack muttered into his drink, slouched at the table, insensible to the fight brewing overtop of him. "Damned punters started bringing specs and such for a better look at you. One old bird brought her opera glasses."

Annie stared at Tom over Mack's bald head. "You're not serious."

He studied her, frowning like she was a lock he couldn't pick, chewing his thumbnail. "We'll be bringing in money hand over fist. Living like kings before the snow flies, my pet."

"Oh, pet, *pet* . . ." She raked her nails toward him like she'd claw his eyes. "I'm not going to be your bloody mermaid a minute longer. Do it yourself. Or Mack can do it, his tits are big enough!"

Mack swallowed the last of his drink, set his mug down, and got to his feet, turning to face her. He didn't say a word, just *looked* at her. Ice crawled through her stomach. Her eyes went to Tom, who was watching her with mute disappointment. The air in the little house was thick with a sudden sense of threat, like Annie'd walked into a trap a long time ago but hadn't noticed until this minute.

"Just a little while longer, sweetheart," Tom told her quietly.

It wasn't a question.

She spent the next swim half-sobbing with fury, wrenching the damned tail free from tangling seaweed blooms, not caring if it ripped. Only half-caring if she went under. She almost wanted to drown out of spite, just to serve them right.

If she screamed, would Tom come out for her?

She didn't trust the answer enough to dwell on the question for long. When all you did was build pretty lies to earn your bread, it turned out there was precious little you could trust.

Annie was so lost in her own thoughts that when she dragged herself cold and aching onto the shore as night fell, it took her too long to realize that there was someone sitting on the log where her cache was hidden. Her heart bolted into her throat. The incriminating tail was already out of the water, sloshing in the surf like a dying seal.

"Hello," said the woman, who offered a warm smile.

Annie scrambled for the knife at her belt before remembering it was hidden within the log where the woman was sat. They'd had punters catch on to their games before, but Mack or Tom had always taken care of them once Annie pointed them out.

"What d'you want?" Annie said, her stomach twisting itself in knots.

The woman stood, gesturing at the log. "Here, you must be freezing. Get your things and don't mind me. I just wanted to . . . I don't know. Meet you, I suppose."

Annie darted for her things, tearing through the bundle for her flick-blade.

"I was out for berries the first time I saw you," the woman continued cheerfully, "I thought you were a real mermaid at first. I nearly wept, you were so pretty out there. And then when I saw you weren't my imagination I thought 'I've never seen anyone braver than her!' and I wanted to say hello. I won't go into the water over my knees, not for anything, even when it's warm. Anyway, I'm Eleanor Fitzsimmond. Ellie, if you like."

Annie's breath was stuck in short drowning gasps and the knife was almost warm in her freezing hand. She threw the blanket around herself and stood, the blade hidden against her belly. Eleanor Fitzsimmond was still smiling, the damned fool, the only anxiety about her perhaps a pinch of shyness. Her accent sounded like home, reminding Annie of bedtime stories about leprechauns and fairy-burrows.

"Right," Annie said, "but what do you *want*?"

Eleanor faltered. "What do you mean? I . . . Well, I only thought maybe I could bring you some tea or soup to warm up next time you came up here. I don't live but ten minutes away so it'd be no trouble."

Annie stared at her. "What's your game? You want hush money? A cut? What?"

The woman's eyes went wide, vividly green even in the falling shadows. "Oh! No, no, I've no intention to blackmail."

"Like hell," Annie snarled. "Tell me your game." Before her resolve could falter, she brandished the knife, quick-stepping towards the woman. "Tell me or piss off."

Alarm played over the woman's face, and she took a step back, her hands up. "I'll go. I'm sorry. I didn't mean to scare you."

A blade at her face and this impossible woman was sorry for scaring *her*. She even offered a nervous smile before slipping into the surrounding woods, her skirts bundled in her hands with the efficiency of someone who spent a lot of time in the scrub.

"Fuck's sake," Annie breathed. She should have felt nothing but relief at her being gone but as she put away her flick-blade with trembling hands, she felt a prickling sense of loss.

⌒⌒

Annie wasn't sure why she didn't tell the boys about Eleanor. Maybe it was because they were laughing and scheming together when she got home, but hushed up all cagey when she came in. Maybe it was just the accent. Or maybe she hoped the con would fall apart and she could go back to fortune-telling at the pier.

It would explain why she didn't change her place on the shoreline the next swim.

There was a basket waiting for her on her log, with warm soup and two fresh biscuits tucked snug under a fold of gingham. It reminded her of how her mum had told her to make friends with fairies, when she believed in such things. Just leave them something of good faith and they wouldn't do you mischief.

"Bollocks," she muttered.

It was delicious and warmed her up faster than the fire. She ate every crumb.

⌒⌒

The next offering came with a grey knit shawl over the basket. Then a packet of cookies. And finally, when the frost had begun to form on the shoreline, painting the reeds and wet rocks with pale crystals, the woman was there herself with her tidy dress and her nervous smile, holding the basket.

"Eleanor Fitzsimmond," Annie said. She would've been able to put more menace into it if her teeth weren't chattering fit to crack.

"Miss Mermaid," Eleanor said. "I've been worried about you. It's getting wretched cold in the evening and there's a killing frost coming. I can always tell. My legs pitch a terrible fit."

She stepped out of Annie's way as she went for her blankets and bag. Annie left her knife where it was this time, her stomach already rumbling at the scent of fresh biscuits.

"You're not going to keep this up much longer, I hope," Eleanor fussed. "Look at the state of you! Your lips are blue, and your poor hands . . ."

Annie flung the blanket around herself, wrapping the grey shawl over her sopping hair. With resignation, she gestured at the space next to her. "It's Annie. Not Miss Mermaid. You're a damn good cook."

Eleanor's smile was quick and earnest enough to send a shock through her. She was a pretty thing, with the sort of raven-dark hair Annie'd always been trying for when she dyed her own.

"Well, it's nice being able to make food for someone else again." She handed over the basket of treasures, which Annie tore through with shameless fervour. "It's just been me since my husband passed. I get on well enough, but life was certainly nicer with someone around."

The particular loneliness of a young widow, Annie decided, would explain Eleanor's desire to make social calls upon the woman who'd previously held a knife on her.

"Sorry," Annie said instinctively.

Eleanor smiled peacefully. "Oh, it's enough years gone by not to sting like it used to."

Don't tell me you're a woman alone, Annie silently begged her. *Don't make yourself a damn target for people like me.* "You do all right by yourself though?"

Eleanor nodded immediately. "I do! I stay plenty busy with the house, and I make enough at the market to get by. I sell things from the garden and preserves and a painting or two." Her smile turned shy. "I think I've been doing a bit of accidental advertising for you. I've been painting mermaids lately. Sitting on the rocks under the pines. They've got red hair though, and freckles if you look close."

Annie muttered a curse of disbelief against her spoon. "Lord Jesus, Eleanor. You can't be that thick." She gestured at the counterfeit tail with her now-empty bowl. "It's a con, yeah? Keep that up and you can paint a nice picture of me at the gallows."

Eleanor's ever-changing smile took a rueful turn. "I'm a widow who likes walking through the woods and leaves bread out for the fair folk, Annie. The day a soul takes me serious, I'll die a happy woman. Your hair's dripping down your back, that's got to feel wretched. Here, drink your tea, I'll help you."

She got to her feet and stood behind Annie, gathering her sopping hair and gently untangling it to work it into plaits. Annie froze for a moment. She didn't let people at her back—not strangers, not Tom, and certainly not Mack. But Eleanor had started to sing under her breath, a song Annie'd forgotten the words to but her heart still remembered, and the steam from the tea was making her eyes prickle.

Eleanor was there after the next swim, waiting with blankets and fresh biscuits and sweet blackberry preserves. Annie admitted, though only to herself, that she would've been disappointed had the shoreline been empty.

"The trees started changing," Eleanor pointed out, twirling a maple leaf the size of a flapjack between her fingers. She held it up to Annie appraisingly before tossing it into the surf, letting the waves sweep it out into the bay. "You'll stop before they're coming down the colour of your hair, won't you?"

Annie snorted, breaking a biscuit into pieces to savour it longer. "It's not just me," she said. The words were already out before she truly realized she was breaking one of their cardinal rules. You get caught, you don't snitch on the others, not ever. "The boys on the shore are bringing in the p . . . the audience, so they get a say too. And they figure we ought to keep going a while longer."

Eleanor made a noise of matronly disapproval. "That may be the case, but they're not the ones in the cold water, are they? Your say should count for double theirs."

It made Annie laugh. "I could kiss you . . . How'd you turn into the light of my rotten life, Eleanor Fitzsimmond?"

Her spirits were buoyed enough she didn't do anything more than roll her eyes when she got home that night and some tarted-up girl was scuttling out the front door, shooting her a guilty look. Mack's entertainment for the evening, or maybe Tom's. As long as the bird hadn't eaten her share of dinner, Annie couldn't care enough to spit.

She *did* care when the boys startled at her entrance, sending coins tumbling across the kitchen table. Far more coins than she thought there would be. She gave a low whistle. "Did you just rob that girl or did a prince come to watch my show tonight?"

There was a funny, thinking silence between the boys. She paused in hanging up her damp cloak, glancing at them.

"Well now, this is a couple nights' worth we're getting sorted," Tom said. Mack nodded, shooting Tom a look of barely-veiled approval.

The back of her neck prickled like someone was sneaking up on her. "Right. I'll take mine now then."

Tom tossed her a pouch of coin, already bagged. "For our lady of the fins."

She weighed it in her hand, her heart kicking into her throat, heat rising into her face. "Same as last week. Same as the week before." She bounced the bag in her palm again, wondering if Tom's quicksilver smile would be ruined permanently if she flung it into his face. "How exactly is it that the pair of you do nothing but brag about how many punters we're bringing in now, and the table's overflowin' with coin, and I'm getting the *same bloody amount* as last week?"

Mack, the bastard, sat down like he didn't have a care in the world and started stacking the coins again. She could've strangled the prick if her hands would've fit around his thick neck. Tom came over to her, his hands out placatingly like he could read her coin-hurling thoughts.

"Listen, flower . . . this is about Mack's girl, isn't it?"

She yelped a laugh. "Come off it! I don't care who either of you're fucking, so long as you're not fucking me over, Tom Delaney."

His eyes narrowed, making him look more dangerous than handsome. "Don't think that I don't see you coming in later and later. Roses in your bloody cheeks and all, Miss Donaghue."

Mack snorted. "So long as she keeps flapping that pretty tail for us, I don't care who she lets up her skirts. And neither should you, Tommy."

Ripping open the pouch she'd been tossed, Annie strode to the table and snatched a heavy handful of coin, jamming it in with her share. Mack got to his feet then, fast enough his chair legs squealed across the floor, and Annie glared up at him, teeth bared like a rabid thing, heart pounding fit to burst. "All I want is my proper goddamn cut, you pair of wilted pricks!"

Re-telling the tale to Eleanor the next night, Ellie gave a shriek of horrified laughter at that. "You didn't!"

"Just like that, I did! Would've said more too if I could think of anything good. Also, Tom thinks I'm screwing around now."

Ellie dissolved into giggles, leaning against her side, wet clothing be damned. "I'd be flattered. You two married then? I didn't see a ring."

"Nothing so permanent as that," Annie scoffed, rolling her eyes. "He's a fair time when he's not smitten with his own clever self."

"Damned faint praise if I ever heard it," Ellie said, wrinkling her nose.

Annie snorted. "Faint praise is enough, and all he deserves. Every girl ought to have someone to warm their bed, doesn't have to be a perfect tale." Belatedly remembering that she was speaking to a widow—it was hard to remember sometimes, what with Ellie as young as she was—she grimaced an apology. "Sorry, love. Suppose it gets proper lonely."

"I didn't think a dalliance would do much to warm a bed," Ellie said, resting her head against Annie's shoulder. "I've only had my Theo and loved him before we ever shared a bed. My memories are enough to keep the house warm. And getting to spend time with you warms me plenty."

"You're the one doing all the warming," Annie said. Ellie lifted her head and looked at her for a long, considering moment. Her lips parted like she was going to say something, or come closer, this woman who knew what love was and hadn't stooped to settling for less, even after losing it. The same thing Annie'd only ever played at, believing love was reserved for the rich.

Annie opened her mouth and stamped out the spark before it could catch. "What with the blankets and all," she said. "Nice and toasty, I am."

Ellie coloured faintly and drew her boots up onto the log, wrapping her arms around her knees. "From what you've said of him, I can't believe Mack let you out of there in one piece after you took the money."

"I told him I'd hex his codger off if he raised a hand to me. The whiskey already makes him soft as a gelding, and he wasn't about to risk his pride and joy."

Ellie studied her like she was a rare flower she'd never seen before. "Are you a witch then, Annie?"

"Nah," she said, "But you can't doubt the magic of a truly pissed off woman."

"That's true enough. But why do you keep with them?" Ellie

asked. "Really. They couldn't do this without you, but you could do it without them."

"What, the mermaid sells tickets to her own show? Or did we not think that part through, ducky?"

"You wouldn't have to be a mermaid anymore," Ellie said, her eyes glimmering with prospects. "You could be a fortune teller again, summoning Tasbem and calling on ghosts like you used to. You said that worked well enough, and you wouldn't have to freeze yourself half-dead doing it either."

Annie sighed and twisted her mouth into a smile, shaking her head. It was too difficult to explain that everything always came back to Tom. He'd told her he loved her as much as he could love anything, and Annie'd never met anyone who could match his clever mind. Even her "demon" was his: Tom had told her across a sweat-creased pillow that "there's a sucker born every minute", and she shortened the adage to Tasbem in his honour, she was that smitten back then, never assuming the sucker might be her.

But sitting here, cocooned against the cold ocean spray under a shawl next to Ellie, she couldn't find the words to explain all that.

Or maybe she just wasn't sure she believed it anymore.

For such a clever man, Tom's means of making nice with her was downright wretched. He bought her a fascinator, a pretty bit of fluff and feather she could perch in her hair doing precisely nothing. The uselessness of it almost made her laugh. She wasn't sure if he'd used his cut or hers to buy it either, and she didn't ask.

"You're trying to butter me up," she said. A month ago, she would've been flirting. Now she found the words coming out dull with defeat. "What do you want?"

"A man can't dress his lady up with a little French finery anymore?" he said, still trying to play the game.

"A man who's not Tom Delaney perhaps," she said, tired.

Mack had drawn into the room, noisily setting to work counting coin at the table, steady as clockwork. Slide and click, slide and click.

"All right, maybe so," Tom said, "but I've been listening to you. I know you're not happy with things the way they are, flower. So,

I've got a new idea."

Her heartbeat tripped into a trot. Over at the table, the sound of counting had slowed as Mack listened in.

"You've got my ear," she told him.

Tom grinned. "You hate floating around getting cold, right? So, let's liven it up. A hunt. We'll get the punters into a boat with Mack, let them think they've got a hope of catching you but when the fog rolls in we lose you behind the curtain . . ."

The last hope she'd been holding onto slipped from her, falling away into darkness.

She'd told them that it was snow. Tom and Mack said it was too early for snow, so it had to be rain, and then—after she'd thrust a handful of the stuff in their stubborn faces—hedged it back to sleet. Whatever it was, Annie was swimming through it, the cold burning her skin. The couldn't-possibly-be-snow turned to slush on the surface of the water, hissing like shaved ice with each swell. It hurt to breathe, let alone to swim. And didn't it just feel like she'd been stuck between two unpalatable choices just about forever now? Drown or freeze. Starve or thieve. Hang or leave her country forever.

The force of the waves thrashed her miserably about, and through the crystals forming on her eyelashes, she could just make out the shoreline through the haze of snow. Which meant they could only just make out her, if see her at all. "Go further out," they said. "Don't let them see you too clear." If they'd bloody listened when she said it was snowing, they'd know the punters could no more see her than she could see them, daft fools.

"Fuck this for a lark," she muttered, spitting saltwater. She pushed her aching arms into action, turning back towards her safe place on the shoreline. It felt like rowing with two oak clubs for all the feeling she had left, and pushing the tail along in front of her made her feel like she was going backwards. The shivering having stopped wasn't new, but the sudden thick sense of exhaustion driving her towards sleep was a problem. If she died out here, the waves would wash her body in eventually. And the boys would make a few more dollars selling her corpse, she was sure.

Growling through her teeth in a very un-mermaid-like

fashion, she thrashed on towards the jagged darkness of the pines. There wasn't a space in her mind for doubt that Eleanor would be there, waiting for her on the dark rocks where the waves broke, warm dry blankets clutched in her arms, eyes straining through the snow to catch a glimpse of her.

The tail snagged on something so horribly it almost wrenched her under as the swells came up behind her. Her numb fingers couldn't find purchase on the material and the scarce clothing she had on was catching and tangling in the wire. She was spending too much fight on getting it free, which she realized when she ran out of breath for cursing. Past the sound of her own heartbeat pounding in her ears, a voice seemed to reach her over the water: *leave it, get yourself to land.*

It sounded a little bit like rushing water and a little bit like Eleanor. She opened her frozen fists with effort and let the ocean tear the tail away from her. To her horror, it was scarce easier to swim even without it now, grey speckles creeping in at the edges of her vision. The shoreline had turned into a dark mass, a thousand miles away if it were a hundred feet. And there, shining impossibly among the thick trees, she thought she could see Ellie's tidy dress and pale, worried face. An icy wave closed over Annie from behind, blinding and deafening her for a moment, and when she emerged again, there was nothing but a dark horizon, unreachably far away.

But she was Annie bloody Donaghue, her own wretched mother's disaster of a daughter, and she wasn't about to go peacefully into the cold arms of the reaper.

With a sobbing snarl, she forced her burning limbs into action, clawing towards shore. The snow was coming down thicker now; if she got turned about, she'd be swimming out to her doom.

Her vision was down to a greying circle, but through the blizzard and crashing water, she could see a figure standing in the surf, skirts bundled with the efficiency of practice. *Never goes in past her knees* . . . What a thing it would be to make Ellie watch her die like this, disappearing not more than a hundred feet out. But another wave swallowed Annie and her block-numb legs were tangled in something that felt like clawing hands in her delirium. She was too sluggish to kick free, her hands too senseless to feel where she was caught, and the frozen air burned her lungs, each gasp shorter and more painful than the last. More water than air.

Suddenly, hands were on her, pulling her through the water with impossible speed. Her body was dead weight, dragging like a corpse as she slid in and out of wakefulness. And then there was something coarse and painful against her cheek and something weighing her down, keeping her arms and legs from moving. With renewed fervour, she struggled against it.

"Gently, Miss Mermaid. You're safe, I've got you."

The dampening weight resolved itself into a thick blanket, the harshness at her cheek the wet grainy rock of the shore. Annie gave a weak sob of relief, blinking hard, coughing water from her lungs. Annie's vision blurred into focus seeing Ellie, smiling at her as always, pretty green eyes sharp with worry.

"I'll live," Annie rasped. "Don't fuss. You won't lose me that easy."

Something was wrong though, something that hadn't quite found its way into her frozen brain. Because Ellie was lying on her belly over her, petting the wet hair out of Annie's face, but her body was still in the water. And she'd brought the tail with her somehow, only it was beautiful now, all iridescent and shimmery in the frothy surf, and it moved when Ellie shifted, twisting in agitation. Ellie's hair was down from its usual coif, hanging in long silken tangles across bare arms and shoulders and . . .

"Oh," Annie said, and the heat of shock felt damn near pleasant running through her. "Fantastic tits."

Ellie gave a yelp of surprise and stifled a laugh with curiously webbed fingers, a blush staining her cheeks. "You're not so bad yourself. I'm sorry, Annie. I never wanted to tell you . . . at least not like this."

Annie found a smile, pushing herself upright with a hiss of pain, pins and needles running all through her. She pulled the blanket tight around herself clumsily. "Can you . . ." She offered a vague gesture at Ellie's tail. "Can you change back? I'll share my blanket."

The sorrow bloomed in Ellie's eyes and she shook her head. "The ocean doesn't give 'happily ever after' for free, Annie. Not even for one of her own. And I loved my life on the land, my Theo, I really did. But it was always this or that. Sea or land, not both. One change, one lifetime. Once you return to the sea," she said, gesturing to her tail, her skin, "you stay in the sea."

"Never in past your knees," Annie finished. "Jesus, Ellie, I'm sorry. I just figured you for a shit swimmer, was all."

Ellie gave a little laugh, pulling herself a bit closer, moving in with a wave. She closed her webbed hand over Annie's knee, and it was as warm as ever. "It was worth it."

A thrill went through her. It had been a long bloody time since Annie had calculated her worth in anything other than dollars and cents, whiskey in the bottle and meat in the pot. She'd offered this strange woman nothing more than a couple indecent stories and a listening ear, and somehow that was worth an entire human life. Somehow, to Ellie, she was worth everything. She wiped her face on the half-soaked blanket, sand scraping her cheek in the process.

The wave pushed again, bringing Ellie close enough that Annie felt her breath warm against her chilled skin, then receded, threatening to take the mermaid with it.

Ellie looked from Annie to the shore, and back into the snow-blind horizon. "If those fellas come looking for you and find me like this . . ."

"They won't, the bastards," Annie said, stifling tears, not willing to let Ellie go. They'd not come looking after her since they started the ruse, but what if Tom or Mack did see her go under and came round the corner and saw Ellie? They'd do worse to her than Barnum'd done to his creature.

Annie gripped Ellie's hand tighter. "Could someone like me make a deal?" she asked.

Ellie tilted her head, resting her cheek on Annie's knee. "Depends what you want, I'd imagine. She can provide, but does so in her own way. The ocean always listens, she doesn't always answer."

With a hesitant hand, still tingling as the blood returned to her fingers, she brushed Ellie's shining hair back from her face. It was as soft as wet silk.

"What if I wanted a happily ever after of my own. To spend what miserable life I have with a woman named Eleanor, whether it be by sea or land?"

By now Annie'd seen many of Ellie's smiles, but this one was something new, undisguised surprise blown into delight.

"Well," she said, "they say a mermaid's kiss will do."

GLASS, PAPER, SALT

(CATHERINE MACLEOD)

There's a story about sea glass: when a sailor drowns at sea, the mermaids weep, and their tears turn to glass as they wash ashore.

It's the first story I can ever remember hearing. I thought it was nice of the mermaids to cry for someone they didn't even know. I was three, and probably a strange child, but I always liked that it was a story about compassion.

I've thought about it often since then—when I filled jars with mermaid tears from the beach at my parents' cottage, when my college boyfriend emptied them to make me a stained-glass window, when I admire the hundreds of them covering the windowsills of the High Crest Hotel.

And when I touch the red tear I wear on a cord around my neck, a present from a man who said I should learn to see what's right in front of me.

Tonight, it was a zombie in the middle of the road. Hard to miss, even for me.

Trace folded his hands on the steering wheel. "Its eyes are gone."

"Yes."

"You see how they follow you anyway?"

I did. I grabbed my crowbar, dropped out of the truck, and made sure they'd never follow anyone else. Trace plowed the remains into the ditch, then reached over to open my door.

"Nice job," he said.

"Thanks."

"We'll be home soon, now."

Soon, now. Like always, I smiled at the everyday Maritime expression that makes tourists think we have no sense of time.

Wrong. But even if we didn't have one before, we damn sure do now.

Trace's daughter, Lucy, came out to help unpack the supplies. We'd taken one last trip to Meesonville before the snow came, on the off chance we'd missed any survivors, but all we'd found was more food it would've been foolish to leave.

Lucy drove the truck out of sight while Trace and I carried the last bags of canned goods into the kitchen. He asked, "How are you feeling?"

"Tired. But it was a pretty good day."

"Good." He kissed me then, for the first and only time. We'd always known we were never going to be more than friends, but that soft breath of comfort was still sweet. We both knew what we weren't saying.

Lucy cleared her throat behind us. "I was going to ask if you needed any more help in here. Guess not, huh?"

Trace said, "No, thanks, we're fine."

"I can see that," she snapped, and slammed the door she hadn't needed to close at all.

I asked, "Should you go after her?"

"It's none of her business. She's just mad because there's something going on she didn't know about." I mentally applauded his attitude. It meant Lucy wouldn't get away with hers for much longer.

I said, "Goodnight, Trace."

"Goodnight, Ren."

I heard him talking to Clyde as I climbed the stairs to the top floor.

I like my room. One of these days it'll be too cold to sleep in, but that's okay. The bed is comfortable. The bureau is small, but I didn't bring much with me. A few clothes and my toiletries are tucked away on top of the gun I stole from the owner.

My agent, Emmett, once said, "Every book you've ever given me has a stolen handgun in it. Do you have a fetish or something?" He was probably joking. Maybe.

I said, "No, I just have an appreciation for possibilities."

Tonight, like always, I stop at the front window. You can see the ocean through the gaps between the boards. I love the silver look of it in winter. In a world where most things can change in a heartbeat, it's nice to know this won't.

Everyone who stands here runs their fingers through the glass pebbles like prayer beads—cobalt blue, rare amber, jade green, beer-bottle brown. A few clear drops filled with tiny bubbles, probably from something hand-blown. We know they're just pieces of bottles and jars thrown in the ocean years ago, smoothed by waves and sand. We know they're just beautiful trash.

But we still call them mermaid tears. Maritimers are raised on tales of pirate ghosts and sea monsters, so believing in mermaids isn't too hard. And zombies? Just one more damn thing.

I pour glass through my fingers and think, *Soon, now.*

As people do when they're not doing much else, we share our stories, tossing them out between watching for zombies and sleeping in shifts.

Clyde, whose fishing boat is our emergency exit, says most of the eels in the world come from the waters around Sable Island.

Sadia, who once ran a daycare centre, says the job taught her to be hyper-vigilant.

Paul, a retired math professor, can't find a formula to explain the rising of the dead.

Heather, whose five-year-old tackled the bad man scaring his mommy, mostly just cries.

Not wanting to frighten the others more, I've kept my story to myself.

Trace knows it, of course. I'd just been shown to my hospital room when he knocked on the door and asked, "Are you decent?"

"Yes."

"Should I come back later?"

It was a lame joke, but I needed to laugh. "Thanks for coming."

"No problem. I had rounds this morning anyway."

Then he dodged out the door as someone in the hall screamed. He reached back and grabbed my hand, leading me away from the dead bodies shambling up the hall, some of them naked and freshly autopsied.

He hurried me along, as shocked as I was, but on home turf. He led me down stairwells and through shortcuts only the staff would know. The dead were in every corridor, the screams unending. He got us out to his car. One of the dead was lunching on the parking lot attendant and didn't look up as we rolled by.

I closed my eyes tight, and didn't open them again until Trace said, "Renee? Ren? We're home."

We sat in the underground garage for a stare-y moment, looking for movement in the shadows, before getting out of the car. We had to pass the laundry room to get to the back entrance of the lobby. Some oblivious soul's clothes were going through the rinse cycle.

Trace muttered, "Good times."

We'd met in there. I would've bet real money a writer of dark suspense and a pediatrician wouldn't have much to talk about, but we did. I said I was looking for a new publisher. He told me about his brother's hotel. I said I was thinking of moving out of the city for a while. He told me about his recent divorce.

He didn't offer details and I didn't ask, but I got the impression it hadn't been civil. He'd moved into my building because it was close to his daughter's new school. She kept complaining about living with him, he said—the school was going to be stupid, and she wouldn't like her classes.

I said, "Let me guess, she's fourteen?"

"She'll be fifteen soon, now."

"I saw her in the hall once."

"Did she speak to you?"

"It was more of a polite grunt."

He shrugged. "At least she acknowledged your presence."

He never mentioned her mother. He didn't mention visits or birthday cards. I thought being fourteen might not be Lucy's only reason for being angry.

But I also thought it wouldn't have killed her to do her own laundry.

Lucy takes sentry duty most days now, moving window to window. Last night's zombie was closer to the hotel than I like. The cold weather will probably slow them down, but the dead are coming. We all have different theories about why, though.

Trace thinks they follow the roads because it's the easiest way. I think they just have the urge to keep moving, like sharks or tuna.

Or like Paul, who's started pacing when he's not sleeping or eating. I know it's just a nervous habit, but I leave the room when he starts. It reminds me too much of the dead man staggering circles outside Trace's apartment.

Trace told me what happened later. I don't remember smashing the emergency glass and bashing its head with the fire extinguisher, or Lucy yanking the door open, crying too hard to speak. The first thing I recall after that is hearing a TV announcer say, "Police are urging people to stay inside their homes," just as Trace said, "We're going to The High Crest."

There's a story about zombies: it's not really our brains they're after; they want the salt in our blood to preserve themselves.

I don't know who thought of that. All I ever got from *Night of the Living Dead* was "Aim for the head" and "Don't waste time arguing when the world's ending."

When I told Trace, he said, "It's still good advice."

He took the back streets, avoiding the bridges and most of the dead. There was more traffic than usual, but no gridlock yet. The car radio played occasional announcements with bursts of static in-between. The phenomenon was occurring worldwide. No one knew why.

We got to the hotel.

You can see for miles up here. When I commented on the view, Trace said, "It's the second biggest attraction. First is the isolation. People come here to get away from it all."

And they'd arrived before us.

I hefted my crowbar as the front door opened. In horror movies, the survivors usually have guns. We were a little more makeshift—on our way out of the apartment building, we'd armed ourselves from the janitor's closet.

The woman who came out carried a shotgun. The man behind her carried a bigger one. He said, "Oh. Hi, there."

Trace introduced me to Sadia, the hotel manager, and her husband, Clyde. Lucy asked, "Where's Uncle Frank?"

Sadia said, "He went down to the village this morning. I'm sure he'll be back soon, now."

He wasn't. Three days later we all gathered in the dining room, the five of us and six guests who'd been there before the uprise. What little news we'd heard on the radio hadn't been encouraging.

Clyde said, "Does anyone know of any place we'd be safe?" No one answered. "Does anybody *want* to go somewhere else?" No one did. "The pantry is full, but we don't know how many people we might have to feed. We need to stock up while the travelling is still good."

Nobody thought the snowplows would be out this winter.

Trace wouldn't let Lucy draw straws with the rest of us. She was still sulking when Clyde, Trace, and I left.

Meesonville is a pretty crossroad village with an official population of 3500 people, only 800 of them living right in the village. I thought that was way too many to take on if they were all dead until Sadia showed us a hidden closet in Frank's office. He'd never told Trace he was a gun collector.

"He probably thought I'd disapprove," Trace said. "He was right." There were a dozen rifles and a couple of handguns. He said, "I don't know how to handle one of these."

I said, "I do," and laughed at his expression. "What? I wasn't always a city girl. If I can find an upstairs window, I can do some damage."

I found one. *Meesonville Gifts* was unlocked. Clyde dispatched what was left of the owner and went upstairs ahead of me. It was mostly storage space. He made sure it was unoccupied, then looked out the window and said, "I see ten of them already. They heard the truck, I guess."

"I'll be okay."

"I'll come get you when we're done." He gave me a box of bullets. Around these parts, we call them shells—we just can't help ourselves. I poured them on the windowsill and ran my fingers through them.

I dropped the first zombie and targeted the second, thinking I should feel something at the thought of shooting ex-people besides satisfaction that my aim was still good. I decided to think about it later, then decided it didn't matter.

Playing sniper wasn't my only reason for being there. The noise would draw the dead away from the others. I was the tethered goat. No one could guarantee my safety. But going up there had been my idea.

Trace couldn't look me in the eye when he agreed.

Every so often I glimpsed him scuttling through the shadows

with boxes and bags and scared-looking people. I was the only one shooting. Clyde said he'd fire on the dead only if necessary.

After seeing him whaling on one with a shovel, I didn't think necessity would be a problem.

When I didn't see any more dead coming, I sat back and stretched. And saw a boy waving from the pharmacy across the street. I mimed *You see any others?* He shook his head and vanished from the window.

Clyde would be back soon, and no doubt more dead were on their way. I started opening boxes to see if there was anything useful.

There was.

Clyde and the kid from the pharmacy each carried out a box. One was full of books on edible wild plants and herbal medicine, probably for tourists who dreamed of going back to the land. But you never know when information might come in handy.

The kid said, "I'm Zack. Nice shooting."

"I'm Ren. Thanks." I followed him to his hatchback.

He said, "You want to drive?"

"No, I'm terrible at reading signs. I'd probably get lost."

He shrugged and pulled out behind Clyde's truck and four other cars. Back at the hotel, I met five more survivors with an impressive load of supplies. I was too tired to help carry them in and just dragged myself upstairs.

Trace found me at the front window. He ran his fingers through the sea glass, then linked them with mine. I said, "Did you find your brother?"

He said, "Yeah."

⌒⊚

There's a story about stories: we all have our own, and given a chance, most of us will write them down.

The second box I'd packed at the gift shop was full of new journals. I took one for myself and left the rest in the lobby. They were all gone by suppertime.

I've always kept a journal. My old one is in my suitcase back at the hospital. This one is well-thumbed—suddenly I have opinions about things I'd never thought about before. I don't know what the others are writing. Does Trace reminisce about his brother? Does Paul fill his with the elegance of algebra? What

Zack writes is anyone's guess.

Mourning his parents, he kept himself busy. Most days he went out scavenging with Clyde and Billy Menzie. He knew where there were things worth having if their owners didn't need them anymore. They raided pantries and drained oil barrels and gas tanks. They emptied medicine chests, nightstands, and some of the more common hiding places. Even before we scavenged the village pharmacy, Trace had a fair stock of drugs, some of which weren't even vaguely legal.

Zack helped board the windows and all but two doors on the first floor. He boarded the windows at the front of the second floor in case the dead found a way to get on the verandah roof. Lucy trailed after him, handing him nails.

"She has a crush on him," I told Trace.

"Does he know?"

"He's oblivious."

"Not to you, he isn't."

"Excuse me?"

"He calls you hard-core."

He obviously hadn't heard me screaming the morning Billy died of an aneurysm in the bathroom and came shuffling into the kitchen with his pants down. But I didn't argue—for an eighteen-year-old, *hard-core* was kind of sweet.

Sometimes he asked if I wanted to go down to the shore with him. We all go when we can, but never alone. This morning I washed my hands in the water and rubbed them over my lips, relishing the cold salt. I used to love swimming. I loved the ripples like almost-voices. I loved the wind blowing through the long hair I'd had cut months ago.

Zack pulled a glass jar from his jacket pocket and folded a note inside. It flew a good long way before it splashed.

I asked, "Who do you think will find that?"

"Other survivors, I hope."

"You think there are others?"

"Sure. They're probably holed up like we are. Houses, barns, maybe lighthouses. Just trying to hold out. None of the zombies can last long, right? I mean, they're dead, they're going to disintegrate eventually."

I envied his certainty. "Zack, tell me, what would you be doing now if the dead hadn't risen?"

"Right after I graduated high school in June, I applied for a job here at the hotel. What about you?"

"I was going to buy some ocean-front property."

We both cracked up. "Be careful what you wish for," he sputtered and gave me a one-armed hug. Even laughing, commonplace paranoia made us look everywhere but at each other. Which was how I noticed Lucy glaring at us from the porch.

She still has issues. I'm sure I understand some of them, including her crush paying too much attention to me. But I keep thinking she'd better grow up while she can.

Zack and I both turn around as the sound of the waves changes.

He says, "The tide will be going out soon, now."

There are bookcases in the lobby, the dining room, and tucked away in the halls. Frank was an avid reader who didn't mind sharing. Three of my novels were shelved on the second floor until I mentioned them to Zack. Now they're in his room. Apparently, he also has a thing for crazy women with stolen handguns.

It's nice to see someone wrapped up in one of my stories again. Writing them wasn't the worst thing I could have done with my time. The first few sold well. The ones after that . . . well, they sold. And then they didn't.

One of the last things Emmett said to me was, "You've lost your sense of direction."

There'd been signs my career was backsliding, but I hadn't seen them at the time. Emmett wasn't quite as happy to talk to me as he'd once been. Sales of my most recent novel had declined. An overseas publisher had dropped me. None of those things would have been too drastic by themselves.

But then Emmett refused my new novel, saying it needed too much work. Finally, he stopped taking my calls. He wasn't making much money off me anymore, and he hadn't agreed to be my agent out of the goodness of his heart. I had to crash his office and scare his secretary to see him.

Emmett had a ritual for writers at risk of dropping off his list. First, he did *The Spiel,* then he gave *The Present.* He said, "Ren, your work just isn't ambitious enough anymore. I want a *big* story, rich characters, deep conflict."

I was angry for a moment. I knew what I was supposed to do. Who did he think he was talking to?

Shit, I thought. He was talking to a writer who hadn't been doing it. I didn't want to admit to myself I'd been coasting for a while, but there it was. All the things I hadn't wanted to see merged into the big picture. I dropped my head in my hands, and he asked, "Are you okay?"

I said, "You've got a hell of a nerve being right."

"The problems here are obvious to everyone but you, Ren. You should learn to see what's right in front of you."

And I knew *The Present* was coming. Not everyone wanted to talk about it, but I'd heard stories. Some said it was the equivalent of a gold watch and a pat on the back. Others said theirs had inspired them to come back with a new book. Apparently, it was a crap shoot.

Emmett kept an old wooden trunk in his office, stocked with flea market treasures. I'd heard about a wooden puzzle box, a hand-painted teapot, and a glass paperweight containing a scorpion. He'd choose something and say, "Here, write me a story about this."

He rummaged in the trunk and pulled out a red mermaid tear on a black cord.

Red is the rarest colour of sea glass, and my favourite. Red tears are called riptide rubies. I said, "Do you know what that is?"

"Sea glass, isn't it? Why, you want something else?"

"No, it's beautiful, Emmett. Thank you."

"Write me a story about it."

He opened the door for me. I slid through before he could pat my back. I thought we might both be surprised—I knew a *lot* of stories about sea glass. By the time I got to the street I was wondering how I could connect them. Something that felt like hope tingled in my chest on the way home.

Lucy asks, "How long has this thing with you and my dad been going on?"

"There's no *thing,* Lucy."

"It sure looked like one to me." She's spoiling for a fight. I so don't care. "Then why was he bringing you home with him the day we left?"

"I lived across the hall from you, remember? He was in my hospital room when the dead rose. He saved my life."

She huffs softly. She's not going to let it go. "What were you doing in the hospital, anyway?"

"I was supposed to have a mastectomy."

☙

A month after my meeting with Emmett, when I had three stories written and a fourth half-done, I went to a dinner party I couldn't find an excuse to skip. After some good cannelloni and too much wine, I left with the guest of honour.

He found the lump.

I hadn't seen those signs, either.

☙

There's a story about breast cancer: that pain is the last symptom.

My oncologist said it's just an old wives' tale.

You'd expect it to be the last thing you feel when you're being eaten alive, but all I feel is a deep, constant weariness.

Soon, now, I think. Silly expression: we're constantly reminded of the passing of days. The ocean keeps perfect time.

It's going out in half-an-hour and taking whatever's on the beach with it. I'm sorry that will probably include the handgun, but I'm not waiting around to become another Billy Menzie, and I'm not making a mess for Sadia to clean up. I *am* leaving this journal for Trace, and my red tear for Zack. It's too bad he has to lose another mother figure, but it's better than him having to bludgeon me in self-defence.

It's checkout time.

I wonder what happened to Emmett. I'm sorry I won't have the chance to finish writing *Riptide Ruby*. I hadn't been that excited about a story in a long time.

Wouldn't I love to know how this one ends?

Glass, paper, salt, I think. It was a pretty good life.

And even if I'm not a sailor, maybe the mermaids will spare me a few tears anyway.

Soon, I think.

Now.

THE OYSTER WIDOW

JENNIFER R. DONOHUE

When the harbourmaster tells me my husband's ship is lost, I both knew it was inevitable and feel as though it is impossible. He had charms, protections, both that he wore and that were on the ship, in the very bones of the ship. Charms tattooed in his flesh, as some of us do.

I'd inked his last charm myself, that he would always find his way home, and I feel a fishhook-twist in my belly when the harbourmaster stands there on my doorstep, ledger of the ship's roster in his hands.

My husband was the captain and my grief is not my own. I have responsibilities. I take the ledger from the harbourmaster's hands, shut my door behind me, and we go to the first mate's house to tell her wife that she is lost.

My charms made me prideful. His ship returned home so many times. I ought to have had a special dress ready for today, of an entire trailing white sail, that I might cut away the hem, house by house, name by name to soothe the tears of the survivors on shore. Instead, I can offer them nothing but the reality that there is nothing that soothes. Nothing will ever suffice.

It was the cabin boy's first journey.

It was a net-maker's sixtieth year.

The cook had a new daughter waiting, born after the voyage went to sea, and whose face he will now never know, nor she his. Will she follow him to sea, I wonder, or go to the mountains, or call her mother's next husband "father," if there is a next husband.

The list goes on. I know all their faces, have known all their faces since I came here from my own little town by the sea, at another port. We have all had faces taken from us by the sea, and there will always be more.

When we are done, and the harbourmaster leaves me at my home, we don't say anything to each other, for what is there left to say? There was a storm. Another ship saw them founder in the waves. The next morning there was nothing. Their ship repaired their broken rigging and returned to port with their tale.

My grief is its own vessel, though I don't release my own sea of tears until we have gone to every house and said every name, and I am again in my house that is now half empty.

I stay in my house for days uncounted. Nobody comes to me in that time, for a charm or to offer me comfort, and I might be insulted but am instead glad to be left alone. I spend time with our things, trinkets from my travels and my husband's, and I still feel him. Not in the next room, not next to me, but I feel him, and I take that feeling and I look through my inks and my supplies, pulling the ones that impulse guides me to, and when I have enough, I sit at my table with my needle and, wrong-handed, tattoo an oyster knife on the inside of my wrist, channelling the feeling of him there, of knowing he's there, of seeking, of finding.

When I'm done, I sit and look at what I've done. I allow myself that, just a few moments. Then I put everything away, and dress, and comb my hair, and go out into the town.

Oysters, when they are very small, don't yet have shells. They swim about before they become so armoured and stationary. Do I think of my husband now as a baby oyster, inverted? Free of his shell?

Though I am a captain's wife, now widow, and an inker of charms, I have never before been a captain. I haven't the means for a ship of my own, and to tell people that I want to ship out to find my dead husband is not sure to be met with success. Support. A ship.

Even so, I cannot compel myself to lie. I will not risk an unknowing crew for my folly, for I am aware that however I find my husband, he will no longer be in a form one can expect. And I know he will not be returned to our life, though he is still my husband.

I meditate on this as I shuck oysters. I never had the taste for them, before. Now that I have left my house, going past my neighbours and down the cobbles to the first fish stand I come upon, I can stomach almost nothing else.

I will go to the docks. I will look at the ships there. If it is to be, then I will know the right ship, and everything will follow after that.

There is no place here that the salt air doesn't touch, but it is still strongest, most powerful, right at the water, on the sea-sanded boards. It is as if the sea is saying yes, I know you and you know me. You are wed to another and yet we will always be together, as we have always been together.

In my younger years, fresh from home and not yet wed, I did ship out, braiding rope and tattooing charms, and kissing cabin boys and girls. I thought I might never marry and just be footloose where the tide took me, and maybe the sea thought that too and was jealous when, on one of these voyages, I met my husband.

He ranked higher than a cabin boy but lower than a captain or mates, and he found excuses to come to me, for ropes, for charms, to give me a pearl from an oyster he'd shucked that morning, to share an evening rum. He was strong and lithe, and I kissed no more cabin boys, or girls, once I kissed him. The captain married us one day when both the sun and the moon were in the sky, and he gave me a hagstone for my wedding ring. I gave him a charm to protect his heart, a green rope tattooed around his finger. The whole crew danced together and had extra rum rations that day, the drink sweet on our salty lips.

He wanted a child, as so many do, and I wanted him. I did not prevent myself from quickening, and yet I didn't. He was not so rich, and storied, as to warrant having a drowned heir. And so he has left only me, and life goes on.

I think of this, as the sea air pats my face with familiar hands, pushes my hair against my neck, and I look at ships. I think that I still don't have that sailcloth dress, trailing a train for tears, but here, I could just add my salt to the sea's and who would be any the wiser?

But none of these ships are for me, and I leave the dockside again, though I do not yet go home. I wander this little town, mine by marriage. I have no family, here or otherwise. My sister went to the mountains and that was the last anybody knows of her. My parents were not young when I was; by all accounts, I was a surprise. Welcomed, loved, but a surprise. When I left home the last time, they knew it would be the last time, and first my mother took her final voyage and my father as well, within the year.

Not every vessel that leaves this port is a ship, I think. There are smaller boats, for pleasure, for fishing just for your family. I have had no need for one until now, indeed, never thought of it. Then I find the boat builder's house on the edge of the town that evening, warm yellow lantern light from her open workshop spilling down to the cobbled street. She is sanding the keel of a boat made of wood made golden by her lantern, and she raises her eyes to me as I approach, though I thought I'd been quiet.

We regard each other across the small distance; we aren't strangers, but we do not know each other. She knows, of course, what I've lost. Everybody knows what I've lost. Everybody feels their own losses, strewn through the town.

"I need a boat," I say, plainly, obviously, foolishly.

She sets her tool down and wipes her hands on her pants. I can see the fuzz of sawdust caught on her arms and neck. She rests a hand lightly on the wood in front of her. "This one is too big just for you," she says. "And is spoken for. I can make the next one for you."

"Thank you." I'm disappointed, but it's to be expected. "How soon?"

"I have one framed," she says slowly, and I can see the calculations running through her thoughts. She has to understand what this is about. "The next full moon?"

"Thank you," I say again. So long, but so close as well. "Can I help?" I ask after a too-long pause, after a too-long internal struggle. It is lowering myself, to ask this. It is admitting my desperation, my tearing grief, my invisible wound.

She hesitates; she knows I tattoo charms, she might know I once had a knack for ropes. She might even know of my renewed taste for oysters, as word travels fast on the sea air. "You can keep me company," she says carefully, finally.

"Good enough. Thank you." She nods, and picks up her tool, resumes sanding. I withdraw into the night, back to my half-empty home.

How long should I wait, before I return to keep her company? I turn around in my home like a fish in a too small bowl, even though there is all that space just for me. I visit the next oyster-seller down the line. I do not eat my oysters on the dock, there under the colourful awnings, at the tables left for just that purpose, dotted with bowls of bright citrus and shakers of spice.

I carry my dripping netting bags home and rinse them at my pump. I sit at my lonesome table and shuck them one by one, shells in this bowl, pearls in this cup, tears streaming like sweat to soak into the neckline of my dress, corners of my mouth puckering at all of the brine.

My oyster knife charm has a seeking energy to it, making my fingertips tingle as I go about my broken semblance of everyday life. Shucking oysters isn't *wrong,* but going to look at boats was more right. I keep myself away for one day, two days, then return to the boat builder's house on the third morning, carrying a bag of oysters.

I again approach the open workshop, and the first boat is gone, replaced with a boat skeleton that I immediately reach out and touch, before even bidding the boat builder good morning. Yes, my charm is thrumming, a second heartbeat . . . a third?

She seems to understand, smiling when I look up, squinting in the sunrise. "You're early," she says.

"This is more than a frame," I say.

"We've all of us lost somebody," she says, which is one of the most true statements one could utter.

"I think . . ." I trail off. What I want to say will make me sound as though I've taken leave of my senses. "Do you have a pump?" I ask instead, holding up the bag. Not every house does, and I am unfamiliar with this part of the town.

"Just through the back," she says, nodding. I go through the workshop, aware of her gaze, which is not suspicious but is curious. She must wonder what I hope to find, in this boat she will finish for me. Or wonder what finality I might seek. That is not my goal. I don't think that is my goal.

We share the oysters at a table she has near the pump and under a bower of flowering trees that we all seem to have, jewelled birds flitting in and out, piping to one another. "We haven't discussed payment," I say, which is rude but I need her to know that I'm not taking advantage of my station and grief. I'm willing to give her anything. Everything. Because I need this boat to find my husband. Without him, I am no longer what I was once, and can no longer become what I otherwise would have.

"We haven't," she agrees, shucking her next oyster. I can't help but be drawn to the opening of each shell, but I know now, this is not my answer. Not here. Not now.

"And you won't allow me to aid in its building."

"I won't," she agrees, dropping the empty shells in the bowl between us and meeting my gaze. There is a thing she will not ask, in my state, and that I cannot give. Not now.

"When I come back," I say, though the conversation has not progressed.

"When you come back." She drops her last shells in the bowl and stands up.

"I can give you a charm now, if you'd like." She hesitates. We are both too old for this sort of foolishness, I think. I am half out of my mind, if not fully, I think.

"I would like that," she says. "Tomorrow, when I stop for the day." She takes the bowl of oyster shells and tosses them into the corner of her garden, in a space between the trees.

When I leave her house, I again go to the docks, and buy more oysters that I take home to eat, my cup of pearls gaining several more.

I think about what sort of charm I'm going to tattoo for the boat builder; she may give me specifics, tomorrow. I can't anticipate, I can only bring what my heart tells me to. Mussel shells ground into blue-black ink. Salt from the mountains, that's so pale a pink that at a glance, it's hard to tell the difference from sea salt, but that will lend both protection and iridescence to the charm. A brighter blue, from the berries that bramble around some people's wells and pumps. Actual white, from a part of the whale that seems made only for this, and that helps prevent death by drowning. Seeking out what charm to create is not what my oyster knife charm is meant to seek, but it is doing so, to serve its greater purpose.

I do wonder what form my oyster knife will take, should I ever find what I seek. Just be a banal tattoo, with no more glimmer of charm left in my skin? Fade away entirely? I hope that I find out. I hope that this story does not end with me still sailing.

The boat builder demurs when I offer her oysters the next day, and I eat them alone at her table, trying to clear my thoughts, trying to still my roiling emotions and let my senses fix upon what her charm should be. Perhaps that sort of preparation is for nothing, and she will tell me what it is that she wants. Best to have a notion, if she doesn't.

I again sit and watch her work. It's curious that she had a boat already, so close to completion, but maybe it is a project she worked on between projects, so that her workshop was never seen to be empty.

Each time she stops, I think she is finished, but I keep my peace until I am sure. She hums a little as she works and doesn't look at me often. She seems completely at ease, and I understand now the kindness that she has given me, allowing me to sit here while she works. She doesn't require anybody's company.

She does eventually set her tools down, wipe her hands off, pick up some water to drink. "About your charm," I say. In a way, it's like coming out of a dream, speaking after all those hours. Night insects scree in the trees around her house, and the horizon is still just slightly glowing with the set sun, like when you walk to the waves and rub your hands over the wet sand to see the phosphorescence there.

"I hoped maybe you'd add to something I already have," she says, interrupting but almost shyly. "Come inside and I'll show you."

"I'll look at it," I say. Most people who tattoo, without even bringing charms into it, won't want to touch another's work. It depends on circumstance, though.

The first inside room is her kitchen, and she nods for me to close the door, then turns her back to me and unbuttons her shirt. I set my tools on the table as she lets the shirt fall; on her left shoulder blade is a seabird wing, poised at that moment before being spread for flight, driftwood grey and black-edged, with some white speckles. On her right shoulder blade is the outline of the wing's match, but it isn't filled in. It's good work. I look at it from where I stand, and then come in close to trace the linework with my fingertips. A few years old, long healed. Not charmed.

"She shipped out," the boat builder says quietly, matter-of-fact as everything else she's said to me. "And there was a sickness on her ship. Bad food. She didn't come home."

That there is so much magic in this world, and yet people can still die from something like bad food, twists my heart. "I can finish it," I say, quiet as she'd been. I didn't know. But I think I now know why the boat builder had a nearly complete boat already, and I'm thankful that I never asked. I'm thankful that she's willing to give it to me, after keeping it here for I don't know how long, waiting, dreaming.

"She had me lay on the table," the boat builder says over her shoulder. We are still very close and I step back from her.

"That would be best," I say. "I can finish tonight, I think. It will be hours, but . . ."

"I don't mind," she says.

"You should eat something first." We've been many an hour in her workshop.

"So should you." She turns to me then, as she picks up her shirt, and she smiles.

"After, then." I leave my things on the table. She cannot stand more oysters, and I cannot stand anything but.

They must talk about me, at the docks. Amongst the oyster-sellers. How could they not? But they are not unkind to me, and the timbre of their kindness tells me that they know who I am, of course, and they know how grief drives a person. We all do, here, I would say. We gain from the ocean, and also the ocean takes, always takes.

I eat my oysters and watch the waves and the birds diving in them, and as the sun sinks beneath the waves, my hands know the lines that the charm should take, and I go back to the boat builder. She's still in her kitchen, or in her kitchen again, I hope. Not that she stayed there, transfixed, awaiting my return. We all spend so much time here, awaiting returns. And sometimes we are left still waiting.

She lies on the table and I lay out my tools. I wonder what she is thinking, but that's a foolish thing to wonder; of course, she's thinking of her lost love, and of the first half of this tattoo. Was it planned, I wonder, or was it on impulse? Perhaps after a day of boat building, or when her wife returned to her from a successful voyage, and they had a celebratory dinner with the nice red wine, and afterwards when everything felt soft and comfortable and right, the tattoo was started.

I don't try to match the first wing exactly; the boat builder's wife didn't put a charm into the completed wing, I don't know if she had that talent, but I can tell her love from the inked lines, the shading, the detail. I've seen her work elsewhere in town, I think, her style is recognizable. But this tattoo, this unfinished letter, is a work of such love that none of the rest approach it.

I also don't give her a charm to ease heartache; I think that would be overstepping. In a way, I let my own charms guide me, laying in my intention for comfort and for safety. The left wing is mostly dark, speckled white, and the right wing is its ghostly twin, pale like the clouds at a sunset when both the sun and the moon are in the sky, dark bellied but pink threaded. I give her ease of sleep, protection of her rest. And yes, a little bit of protection from drowning, for we can all of us benefit from that, even if the only fear of drowning is in sorrows rather than water.

The boat builder is a good tattoo subject; she doesn't flinch beneath my needles, nor fidget, nor sigh. I wonder if she's gone to sleep, but there's a tense energy about her. I lean over for a cloth at one point and chance to see the shiny trail of a tear down her cheek. I don't say anything about it, since she and I are similarly adrift, after all.

Though my oyster knife charm is made for seeking, it is pleased with this work, and I feel a pleasant hum in my wrist and arm, confirmation that what I am doing is correct, in alignment, helpful to my path. I don't know how much time has passed when I am finally done, when I pat her skin off for the last time, gently, but feeling her muscle. Feeling the little magic of the charm. I have done all I can, there is no more to add.

"I don't know if you'll be able to see," I say, and it feels as though I'm interrupting a conversation that we weren't having.

"There are mirrors," she says vaguely, sitting up. I haven't been elsewhere in her house, just the workshop and the kitchen here. "In the bedroom." She slides off the table and walks off, and after a moment's hesitation, I follow.

There are no lamps lit, but the moon floods like daylight through the windows, and we go down a hall and into a room at the front of the house, where the ocean and the docks are visible, down the hill. There is a mirror in a stand, nearly as tall as a person, and she picks up a smaller mirror, wood-framed. These are her wife's, I think. The boat builder does not strike me as a person who troubles herself overmuch with mirrors.

She stands with her back to the large mirror, and moves the smaller one this way and that, so that she can see her newly-inked wing. I don't know her well enough to read her face, to tell if she's pleased or disappointed or just heartbroken, as we both are. I wait, and she looks, calm-faced but wet-eyed, and I become aware that we are standing next to her marital bed, that she is looking at her tattoos in her dead wife's mirrors, that she is bared from the waist up, and that were both our hurts not so raw, both our losses not quite so complete, there would be a certain progression of events, like knotting pearls into a necklace.

"Is it all right?" I ask in the tide of our silences, the waves of our breaths. I want it to be. It felt right. But I can't read her face.

She takes a deep breath, lets it out slowly. She lowers the smaller mirror and looks at me. "It's perfect," she says. She blinks, and a tear chases down her cheek. "I couldn't have hoped for this."

"I'm glad," I say. The distance still between us. I've earned the boat, I suppose. I can't bring myself to speak again, remembering the last charm I tattooed on my husband, a frivolous thing, a glimmer of luck for him to do well at a game he and his first mate would play; he suspected the mate had a similar charm. We drank wine and laughed together as I did it, just in our back garden under the trees, as the day slid into night. He shipped out the next morning. The next I heard of him was when the harbourmaster knocked at my door to tell me that his ship was lost.

The boat builder reaches out and brushes a tear from my cheek, her touch gentle but her skin rough. "I'll be finished tomorrow," she says.

"Thank you," I say. I can't reach back. Not yet. I don't want to go back to my empty home. I don't want to stay in the boat builder's house. Whatever task that I've charmed myself to do, I've left myself caught between what my life has been and what it will next become.

I pack up my tools and I leave the boat builder's house, because I do not want to trouble her, even though I think she will understand. I think nearly anybody here would understand, or that nobody else in the world would understand, and I think that, ultimately, is the nature of grief. It is exactly the same and entirely different, for each person.

I go back to my house, my empty home, not because I want to be alone there for a moment longer but because I left my cup of pearls there and want it with me on my voyage. It seems important, as if my actions themselves are working a charm, or maybe even a larger magic. I run my fingers through the pearls, feel them roll against each other and the sides of the cup, listen to the soft clacking clatter. All of these pearls who are not me, who are not my husband. But they're necessary. They're important.

I don't sleep, or if I sleep, I forget.

I cannot explain where I need the boat to take me, but my oyster-knife charm knows. The boat builder and I stumble in tandem through the sand in the cove where the children go to swim, the boat heavy between us, but yearning for the water through its timbers. It's been waiting for so long, I can feel that as we get towards the wet, dark, firm sand that the ebbing tide left for us, ghost crabs skittering disapprovingly from our path.

"I could come with you," she says finally, roughly, when we right the boat and set it down, as she raises the little mast and hangs the tablecloth sail. Was this the sail her wife would have used? I cannot ask. It makes me think of the sailcloth dress that exists only in my thoughts, sewn there as the harbourmaster and I carried our dark news from house to house.

"I have to go alone," I say, and she nods, checking the paddles where they are stowed, touching my anchor rope with her fingertips. It has been ever so long since I made a rope, and yet it came to me as easily as though it was last week.

"I'll be here," she says, and I catch one of her rough, strong hands in mine. There is so much unsaid, between us.

"I will come back," I say.

"Everybody who has left the land thinks that." But she doesn't pull her hand away until I let it go. I see something in her eyes, maybe a kiss, maybe an embrace, but we do neither.

"I know," I say, and we push the boat into the waves and I get into it as it begins to float. I bob there a minute, and she gives it another firm push, and then the sail takes a handful of wind and puffs out. It's too early to tell if it's the right heading, but I would feel it if it was the wrong one.

I sail into the day, eating when the sun is high above. Dolphins dance near me, leaping close with curiosity, even though I am not so large a vessel as to give them a wake to play in. A good omen, as everything has a weight.

I sail into the night, and the moon is not quite full, which is a relief. She'll keep her business in the sky, that way. The sky reflects a starry road onto the water, and my little boat travels it.

I don't sleep, but I don't get tired. I'm not entirely sure I'm in a part of the world anymore.

With the dawn, a reef, a tiny island, some smudge of land with a stray handful of trees that I can see. That my boat can see, I feel, and so we go there. I should have named the boat, I think, but what name could I give it but that which we saved for a child? Names mean different things, when used, when not used, when kept hidden away in your heart.

The land is not land. It was once a ship, and trees have grown from the living wood even as the vessel itself is dead, black-thorned and with red leaves. My little boat bumps up alongside it, and carefully I unwind a mooring rope, tie to a greened-over cleat. Will it bear my weight? I will know when I know.

I place my feet carefully, trying to avoid the thorns. I did not wear boots for my voyage, even though I've become my own captain and crew. I barely feel the first cut, a sting through my calloused foot, though the second gives me pause, my calf scratched deeply. My third is across the palm of my hand, as I reach out to steady myself, but this thorny ship island bears my weight, yes. Welcomes it.

My husband is here, though I cannot see him. Was this his ship? It seems impossible for me to not know. Maybe, below the water, more than one ship has amassed here, made this place. I walk the length, slowly, gathering more cuts. I return to the centre where my boat is moored, listening to the timbers groan and the branches rustle, and the splashing water.

I think for a moment that more dolphins have come to investigate me, but then a mermaid's shaved head breaks the surface, and she regards me with her gold-ringed eyes. "I'm looking for my husband," I say, before I lose my nerve. It's nonsensical, to come all this way in a too-small boat, to be standing on an island made of ships and trees, and to suddenly now be confronted with fear of failure. I've come so far, and do not know what success looks like.

The mermaid blinks at me, considering, reaches up to grip the edge of the ship island, lever herself up. By human estimation, she is naked to the waist, and then scales from hips to tailfins, but what use are clothes, to a mermaid? She is muscle, and scar, and tattoos, and barnacles of varying size stud her ears and skull, either by patience or design. My husband told me that far to the north, and the south, the mermaids there are more blubber than bone, more adorned with jewellery of their making, as there is less to get caught up in than in warmer waters. But still, they all shave their heads.

"There is no man here," she says after a while, her throat working awkwardly. I do not know how mermaids speak to each other, and how they speak to us; too little is known of them, and has been written of them.

"Not living," I say, choking a little on the last word. I hold out my hand, wrist, with the oyster-knife charm, as though that will make sense to anybody not privy to my thoughts. The charm is shouting to me, strongly, *yes, here*, and feels as though I could pluck it from my flesh and it would be as any other oyster knife I have ever seen or used.

She looks at it, though, and touches the hot blade on the bone of my wrist with her cold fingers; her nails are hard and hooked, almost the entire first joint of each finger. Then she closes my hand on its bleeding cut.

"Keep that out of the water," she says. "Blood calls."

I feel foolish, like a child. Of course, it does. But then I think, blood isn't the only thing that calls, and reach, stretch, into my boat for the cup of pearls. She watches me without moving, interested, wary; I don't doubt she could end my life with the slightest of gestures. She may yet. "I brought these," I say, offering the cup.

She takes it from me gingerly, curiously, but I can't read her expression as she looks at the pearls, rolls the cup in her hand and listens to them click, clack, click. She looks at my charm. She looks at my boat. She looks at my face. "You came here for your husband?"

"Yes."

"He is gone," she says.

"Yes." The tears come unbidden, and I am weeping like bleeding, hot on my cheeks.

She reaches out and touches my wrist again, quirks her lips, and touches my wet cheek. Then she pulls the oyster-knife off of my skin and slips into the water within the ship, leaving the cup of pearls bobbing at the surface. I'm afraid to touch it, and I am afraid to let it go, and watch anxiously as it floats and spins in the mermaid's diving wake.

But none spill, and it doesn't sink, and though I look for her, I don't see the mermaid before she breaks the surface again, through the ship's timbers and the tree roots and branches. It's all just too much.

The oyster she hands me is larger than any I've seen before, its shell orange and green and black, wavy and crenelated and dotted with barnacles like the ones adorning her head. "The whole thing," she says, opening it with the knife and pushing it into my hands after she loosens the flesh. "Even if there are pearls."

I close my eyes and tip my head back before I can lose my nerve. What reason have I to trust this mermaid, other than that she is here? I should not have expected, demanded, her to know anything about my situation. How could she? But the oyster slides free from its shell, followed by pearls that rattle against my teeth as I gulp, breathing through my nose, still weeping, I think. Desperate to find meaning in this and despairing that it is no different from my unbroken days of oyster feasts on the docks. Finally, I am left with the last kiss of brine and, gasping, let the shell drop.

It spins in an invisible eddy on the surface, drifting into the cup of pearls. The mermaid watches me still, and now I feel . . . grateful? Embarrassed? The same, mostly. She takes my hand and presses the oyster knife back onto my wrist, and it again becomes the charm that I tattooed, and that is when I feel different.

"Go back to land," she says. "You have something like what you sought."

"Thank you," I say. "I shouldn't have assumed—"

"No." And then she is gone, with the pearls, leaving both halves of the tremendous oyster shell, and I manage to grab them before they sink, despite her warning about keeping my hand out of the water. The salt stings, but I couldn't have avoided it.

I get back into my little boat, untie it from the ship tree island, and push off. At first the sails don't fill, and I have to unstow the oars, row painfully on my cut hand, rubbing the salt in deeper, rubbing blood into the wood. Dripping blood into the water, which I don't think about until nearly nightfall, when something bumps the boat. The mermaid again, I think, with my heart in my throat, but the shadow in the water is bigger, much bigger. It circles, rises, bumps again, the tip of its fin breaking the surface. Shark or whale, it doesn't matter which. If it capsizes me, that will be that.

I hastily draw in my oars; it isn't as though I wasn't warned. My little boat rocks and I hold back a cry; it would only make the creature more curious, if it can hear me, and might encourage a hunter.

I fumble in the bottom of the boat, pick up the oyster shell. I hold my hand over it, squeezing and releasing like my heartbeat, digging my nails into the cut, until in the first glimmers of starlight, blood slicks the glossy inside of the shell. Then I fling it as far as I can away from my boat, back the way that I came. It makes a bigger splash than I thought it might, and the final nudge from the creature in the water is accompanied by a slight tail slap that pushes me further on my way. I hold my face in my hands, shaking, waiting for it to return stronger, faster, perhaps frustrated at having been tricked, but it doesn't. When I raise my head again, a slight breeze has come up, and I am under way again.

I did not think it possible, but I doze off in the darkness, rocked in my little boat by the open ocean waves. Another *thunk* jars me awake, and I think that the shark or whale has come back to eat me after all, but I never refixed the oars and one slid to the bottom. I take the time to fix them now. I should be ashamed of my seamanship, even with no witnesses.

There is a glow on the horizon, and I think it is the dawn but no, it is the lighthouse at the harbour. Were I in a proper seafaring vessel, I'd be worried about the shoals there, but my little boat rides so high in the water that even at the lowest tides I've seen, they would be navigable and not a threat.

The boat knows its own way, and I'm not convinced that any of this has happened in the waking world. It could all have been a dream and I could still be in my house, waiting for my husband to come home. It could all have been a dream and I could still be eating oysters all day and sleeping fitfully in the small hours.

The boat bumps into the shore, as it bumped against the ship that was an island, and I get out stiffly, stretch, bend to splash the cool water on my hot face. I drag the boat up onto land, but can bring it no further on my own. I stand there a moment, feeling my toes sink into the wet sand. Where do I go? What have I done, actually? My oyster-knife charm nudges me towards the boat builder once again.

I'm sure others must be awake, but I see not a single other soul as I walk through the town, salt tightening on my skin as everything dries. I feel as though I am still swaying on the waves, but that feeling will pass soon enough; I'd forgotten it was something that happened, and laugh a little at myself. To have forgotten the dance of the waves like that.

The boat builder's workshop has the start of another boat in it, a true skeleton, the wood purple and fragrant. I press my fingers against it for a moment like a kiss and go inside her house. She isn't in the kitchen, no, she must still be sleeping, and I go down the dark hall to that room. Is this right? Am I doing right?

She stirs as I cross the threshold, opens her eyes, and looks at me as if deciding whether I am a ghost or a dream or a real woman in her bedroom, and then she opens her arms to me. I hesitate, thinking of the salt-rimed state I'm in, and she reaches out and catches my hand in hers. "It doesn't matter," she says, and I sink into her embrace.

Later, when the dawn has filled her room with light, and she is stroking my tangled hair and I am listening to her heart beat, our bellies pressed together, I know what I've done. I know what my voyage accomplished. I draw away from the boat builder and go stand in front of her wife's mirror, naked, to look at the new curve to my body. The baby I am carrying, that my husband left me in the ocean.

The boat builder stands behind me, runs her hands down my sides, rests her chin on the top of my head. "Did you find what you needed?" she asks, softly, sure but wanting to make sure.

"Yes, I did," I say. Will he be a sailor, will she be a boat builder, I don't know what life will hold for my child, but it will be the best that I can give them.

CONTENT WARNINGS

The authors and I have compiled what content warnings we believe might be relevant to each of their stories. Unfortunately, there is no real way for us to ensure that we cover every possible trigger for every reader, so this list ought to be considered a guideline rather than an exhaustive list.

A Witch's Christmas contains mental illness, death by suicide, and genetic depression.

Portrait of a Mermaid as a Young Woman contains parental death and grief.

Skelf includes forced marriage, controlling parents, being held against one's will, homophobia, and magical paralysis/transformation.

Salt Breeze contains death of an intimate partner and (possibly?) death by suicide.

Salt in Our Blood, Salt in Our Tears contains deaths of family members and general death.

The Ghost of Violet Gray contains death of an intimate partner and death by suicide.

Rage Against the Sea contains death by suicide.

A View of Water contains child death, death by suicide, and murder.

Human, Still contains an attempted death by suicide, although it is ambiguous that is what's happening.

Sarah's Kitchen contains familial death, including the death of children, as well as ghosts.

Seaweed and Gossip does not contain any obviously challenging material.

On a Northern Shore contains death by suicide, allusions to light, period-typical homophobia, and allusions to and speculations of murder.

Daughter contains implied violence and death.

Sink Your Sorrows to the Sea contains mention of suicidal ideation, death of a spouse, miscarriage, and sexual assault (which is not depicted on the page).

The Deep End of Longing contains implied domestic abuse.

Fortune Favours the Brave contains drowning, intimate partner abuse and manipulation, threats of physical violence and intimidation, alcohol consumption, and the loss of an intimate partner.

Glass, Paper, Salt contains death by suicide, cancer, and zombies.

The Oyster Widow contains death of an intimate partner, grief, and grieving.

BIOGRAPHIES

Like a magpie, **Rhonda Parrish** is constantly distracted by shiny things. She's the editor of many anthologies and author of plenty of books, stories, and poems (some of which have even been nominated for awards!). She lives in Edmonton, Alberta, and she can often be found there playing Dungeons and Dragons, bingeing crime dramas, making blankets, or cheering on the Oilers.

Her website, updated regularly, is at http://www.rhondaparrish.com and her Patreon, updated even more regularly, is at https://www.patreon.com/RhondaParrish.

Her last Tyche Books anthology, *Water: Sirens, Selkies and Sea Monsters*, won the Douglas Barbour Award for Speculative Fiction. But no pressure, *Saltwater Sorrows*. No pressure at all . . .

E.E. King is an award-winning painter, performer, writer, and naturalist. She'll do anything that won't pay the bills, especially if it involves animals.

She's intrigued by gothic ghosts, loves the sea, and is a woman, so she had to be included in this collection.

Ray Bradbury called her stories, "marvelously inventive, wildly funny, and deeply thought-provoking."

She's been published in over 150 magazines and anthologies, including *Clarkesworld, Daily Science Fiction, Chicken Soup for the Soul, Short Edition*, and *Flametree*. Her novels include*, Dirk Quigby's Guide to the Afterlife: All you need to know to choose the right heaven* and several story collections.

Her stories are on *Tangent*'s 2019, 2020, and 2022 year's best stories. She's been nominated for a Rhysling and several Pushcart awards.

She's shown at paintings at LACMA, painted murals in LA,

Mexico, and Spain, and is currently painting a mural in leap lab (https://www.leaplab.org/) in San Paula, CA.

She also co-hosts *The Long Lost Friends Show* on Metastellar YouTube and spends her summers doing bird rescue and her winters planting coral in Bonaire. It's all about the sea and ocean with this woman. She's happiest under the water.

Check out paintings, writing, musings, and books at: www.elizabetheveking.com.

Natalie Cannon (she/her) is an author, editor, and indie game developer. A graduate of Scripps College and FDU's MFA program, her short fiction has been published by Ink & Locket Press, Serving House Books, JayHenge Publishing, and now by Rhonda Parrish. If you like sapphic werewolves, play her game *Moonrise*. If you'd like to keep up with Natalie, sign up for her newsletter at https://tinyletter.com/CannonNews.

Morgan Melhuish (he/him) is a queer writer and educator from West Sussex. May to October he swims in the sea twice a week, but is yet to find cursed driftwood. In 2023 his work will be published in anthologies by Timber Ghost Press and Wyldblood. You can find him on Twitter @mmorethanapage.

Paul A. Hamilton is a writer and engineer living with his wife and two children in Northern California, where they can regularly visit the seaside. His work has appeared in *Shock Totem* and *Leading Edge*, among others. In his spare time, he enjoys playing tabletop games, reading books, creating art, riding roller coasters, and listening to the waves.

Laura VanArendonk Baugh writes fantasy in a variety of flavours as well as non-fiction and a smattering of other genres. Because she is a nerd, when she learned how a whaling ship had set an entire island afire as an ecologically disastrous prank and had shortly after suffered their own tragic disaster at the hands of nature, she had to go read the story of the *Essex*. It stuck in her mind, and the women left behind in whaling towns seemed the right subject for a story which needed both sea and sorrow. Laura lives in Indianapolis with one husband, two dogs, a stash of fair-trade dark chocolate, and a stockpile of disused words needing new homes in fiction. Find more stories and downloads at LauraVAB.com.

Sarah Van Goethem is a Canadian author of short stories and novels. She lives in a century farmhouse where she feeds her soul in her very own dark forest, but she's equally as enticed with a misty shoreline.

Her novels have been in PitchWars, longlisted for The Bath Children's Novel Award, and shortlisted for CANSCAIP'S Writing for Children Competition.

Three of her short stories have been nominated for a Pushcart Prize, and one of these was a finalist for the CBC Nonfiction Prize. All can be found on her website at SarahVanGoethem.com.

Adria Laycraft is an author, freelance book editor, and wood carver living near Calgary. The moment she saw the call for this antho, she knew just the story for it, thanks to a haunted visit to Dunnottar Castle in Scotland. Her second novel *Jumpship Dissonance* launched last fall, with book three on the way in 2023. You can find her short work in *Neo-Opsis*, *On Spec*, *IGMS*, *Tesseracts Sixteen,* and many more. Follow FB Page "Book Editing Tips" or watch her carve, bark hunt, and interview wood carvers on her YouTube channel, Carving the Cottonwood. Learn more at adrialaycraft.com.

Dino Parenti is a writer of dark literary and speculative fiction. He is the winner of the first annual Lascaux Review flash fiction contest and is featured in the Anthony Award winning anthology *Blood on the Bayou*. His short-fiction collection, *Dead Reckoning and Other Stories*, is out with Crystal Lake Publishing. He lives in Los Angeles.

B. Zelkovich writes Speculative Fiction, anything from dragon hunting and space whales to demon-dealing and ghost tales. She likes to explore human emotions in inhuman situations. When she isn't escaping into her imagination, she escapes to winding trails with ocean views.

Find her fiction in *LOLcraft: A Compendium of Eldritch Humor*, Wyldblood Press, *Luna Station Quarterly*, and online at bzelkovich.com.

Lisa Carreiro has roots on the east coast, and visits there as often as possible. When not searching for mermaids and land sharks, she can be found wandering through old seaside cemeteries. Her short fiction has appeared in *On Spec*, *Tesseracts Eleven*, *Strange Horizons*, and the *Playground of Lost Toys* anthology, among other publications.

Lea Storry owns a writing, editing, and publishing business. She's also a published and indie published author. Lea grew up in Nova Scotia and has lived around the world and all over Canada. However, she currently lives in landlocked Edmonton, Alberta with her husband. The title of her story, "Seaweed and Gossip," had been crashing around in her head for twenty years after hearing a roommate in Sackville, New Brunswick, talk about her summers. The roommate said that when she went home to Havre Boucher, an oceanside community near Antigonish, Nova Scotia, she headed to the shore with her mom and friends for some "seaweed and gossip."

https://www.instagram.com/family_lines/
https://twitter.com/familylines
https://www.goodreads.com/author/show/14250642.Lea_Storry

Nikoline Kaiser (she/they) is an author and poet with a degree in Comparative Literature from Aarhus University. She has been published in both Danish and English, and her work focuses primarily on family, grief, and queer themes. All three are present in her story "On a Northern Shore", the bare bones of which was rummaging in her head for a long time. *Saltwater Sorrows* was the perfect opportunity to finally write it down.

When not writing, she works on a project communicating information about women authors around the world. Her bibliography and social media can be found here: https://nikolinekaiser.dk/.

Elin Olausson is a fan of the weird and the unsettling. She is the author of the short story collections *Growth* and *Elin Olausson's Shadow Paths*, and has had stories featured in many publications. "Daughter" is one of several stories she's written about post-apocalyptic worlds and the broken women inhabiting them.

Elin's rural childhood made her love and fear the woods, and she firmly believes that a cat is your best companion in life. She lives in Sweden.

Growing up, **Chandra Fisher** fancied herself a mermaid and spent her summers in a twelve-foot above-ground pool, only coming out to eat and sleep (and only under duress). As a teen she studied to become a lifeguard and worked at swimming pools and summer camps, swimming, canoeing, and even cliff diving. She is a mother of four babies, three of whom were born in the water. Now she spends her time writing stories, many of which have elements of water. You can find her at: www.chandrafisherwrites.com.

Hayley Stone is an award-winning author, poet, and narrative designer best known for her weird western, *Make Me No Grave*, and the sci-fi series, *Last Resistance*. Her short fiction has also appeared in *The Magazine of Fantasy & Science Fiction* and *Apex Magazine*, among others. She lives in Southern California with her partner, two cats, and a persistent longing for the sea. Hayley loves connecting with readers, writers, and merfolk at her website: www.hayleystone.com.

V.F. LeSann is the co-writing team of Leslie Van Zwol and Megan Fennell, united for greater power like Captain Planet, and sworn to tread the wobbly line between grit and whimsy. Despite leading landlocked lives, they're lovers of the ocean and wanted to dip their toes into this anthology. Oddly, this is their first mermaid tale which does not take place in outer space.

Catherine MacLeod's previous publications include work in *Nightmare*, *On Spec*, *Black Static*, Tor.com, and several anthologies, including *Fearful Symmetries* and *The Playground of Lost Toys*.

Raised on Nova Scotia's north shore, she grew up hearing stories of mermaid tears, brave sailors, and mysterious sea creatures. Zombies, not so much.

Jennifer R. Donohue grew up at the Jersey Shore and now lives in central New York with her husband and their Doberman. She has never eaten an oyster. She works at her local public library where she also facilitates a writing workshop. Her work has appeared in *Apex Magazine*, *Escape Pod*, *Fusion Fragment*, and elsewhere. "The Oyster Widow" takes place in the same secondary world as her novella *The Drowned Heir*, which is available in hardcover and ebook. She tweets @AuthorizedMusin.